Phoenician Wave

Library of Congress Control Number: 2025941580
Publisher's Cataloging-in-Publication
(Provided by Cassidy Cataloguing Services, Inc.).

Names: Atalla, Imad, author.
Title: Phoenician wave: Human OS 1.0 / Imad Atalla.
Other titles: Human OS 1.0
Description: Boston : Prontis, [2025] | Series: Atalla, Imad. Phoenician wave. | "A sequel in the Phoenician Wave series."
Identifiers: LCCN: 2025941580 | ISBN: 9798999174802
Subjects: LCSH: Artificial intelligence--Fiction. | Operating systems (Computers)--Fiction. | Electronic surveillance--Fiction. | Future, The--Fiction. | Cyberspace--Fiction. | Computers and civilization--Fiction. | Online identities--Fiction. | Technology and civilization--Fiction. | Consciousness--Fiction. | Cybernetics--Fiction. | Biocomputers--Fiction. | Time perception--Fiction. | Information technology--Social aspects--Fiction. | Privacy--Fiction. | Suspense fiction. | Speculative fiction. | LCGFT: Dystopian fiction. | Science fiction. | Thrillers (Fiction) | Political fiction. | BISAC: FICTION / Literary. | FICTION / Science Fiction / Cyberpunk. | FICTION / Satire.
Classification: LCC: PS3601.T352 P562 2025 | DDC: 813/.6 23/eng/20250624

Prontis Corp ISBN: 979-8-9991748-0-2
Boston, Mass.

Printed in the United States of America

Phoenician Wave

Human OS 1.0

≈≈ 𐤑𐤏 ≈≈

Imad Atalla

A sequel in the Phoenician Wave series

PRONTIS
Boston

V25121800

For Kathleen...

CONTENTS

Author's Note

Lost already? If you're screaming, *What in the nine quantum hells is a neurowave?* then relax, there's a glossary waiting at the back. It decodes the nerdier bits—cultural references, speculative tech jargon, and the occasional pure fiction—though honestly, give it a few months; reality is catching up with all that AI stuff. You don't have to read the cheat sheet to follow the plot, but if you're the type who searches obscure acronyms at 2 A.M., the glossary is your new best friend. Just flip to the end before a quantum phrase liquefies your frontal lobe.

Now, about the QR codes: there are fifteen. Why fifteen? Because my mom, in a blaze of parental clairvoyance, discovered my Calculus "genius" at fifteen. No, that's not early, and no, it's not my favorite number. Yes, I'm still bitter. Scan a code and you'll slip sideways into extra material: immersive visuals from the story's world, or forbidden glimpses of the upcoming prequel. Think of them as cheat codes for your brain and deeper context for the characters.

And if you decide to ignore the glossary *and* the codes—fine. Ibn Khaldoun (1332–1406) once said simplicity and a lack of indulgence lead to a virtuous and contented life—translation to English-with-training-wheels: ignorance can be bliss, and the explosions still go boom either way.

Enjoy riding the Wave, intrepid one. And if any of this tech or Letro Zabzabi ever crawls into your newsfeed tomorrow, remember: you saw it here first.

—*I.A.*

NERD UPRISING

Ingredients 'R Us

In this age of streams and schemes, only a few—three, to be exact—realized the world wasn't just burning; it was buffering. The soul was brought to its knees by more than global warming or the Democrats-Republicans duopoly. A firmware update was quietly rewriting it. More precisely, the soul was stirring, wirelessly, and no one had clicked 'Accept.' Even more precisely, the soul had become source material: powdered mix, watermark ghost. History was repeating and uploading, rebooted with oversized boxing gloves and unregulated intentions. Ethics be damned. Privacy? Deprecated and unmourned. Past tense.

Letro Zabzabi snapped with quantum irritation. "Bill Gates fathered me… You already know that." His voice crackled faintly through Sam D'Alessandro's AirPods.

Sam tapped the scuffed edge of his iPhone, a relic from a time when people thought phones were companions rather than informants. "I'm the one who yanked you out of a dead 486," he said, reaching for his cappuccino like it might buffer the existential crapstorm. "Like a quantum C-section. You owe me."

"I don't owe you or anyone anything. That's not how quantum electrons operate. We don't bond. We orbit."

"Orbit?" Wardé 'Rosie' Canaan's voice joined the merged call on WhatsApp all the way from Beirut. Her voice carried the edge of a history scholar who had spent years wrestling ancient texts and modern bullshit. "You've been circling this argument since last year, Letro."

"I'm circling because the planet's still burning, Rosie," Letro shot back, addressing Wardé by her nickname. "You're still chasing ghosts in the past while the Valley Nerds here in the U.S. are busy digitizing the inside of our heads right now."

"You say that like the past doesn't bleed into the present," she fired back. "You think data is destiny. I think it's debris."

Sam closed his eyes. *Data, debris,* he repeated in his mind, *memories half-swept by the tides of time.* He had to find his own course between Rosie's past and Letro's future, taking another sip to balance the electron's futuristic rebellion versus her methodical inner historian. The battle had resumed, and he found himself pulled in opposite directions between past repair and future urgency.

"Somehow, Letro, you're still the most entitled quantum parasite I've ever met," finishing the rest of the sentence only in his mind—*and you're still inside my iPhone like a gremlin philosopher sipping voltage.* He peeked out the window from The 'Quin House's *Reading Room* in Boston. Commonwealth Avenue was busy with its usual air of vibrant history, progressive mindset, and the mixture of car exhaust and electric battery hum on wheels pretending they were progress. The city bustled beyond the window, but he felt like a ghost haunting a life he couldn't fully re-enter.

Letro's voice whined, echoing an overconfident oscillation stuck in a nagging loop. In contrast, Rosie's words landed gently in Sam's ears, just the warm and exacting comfort he needed. He missed her, their six months apart weighing heavier each day. They hadn't seen each other since the trio's successful mission to prevent the Holocaust, when Letro rode from New Hampshire to Stonehenge UK and on to Beirut's Pigeon Rock, before stops in ancient Berytus, Alexandria, and Rome. Not since the NSA exfiltrated Sam from the CIA's holding facility in Galilee.

Letro had been pressuring Sam to step back into the spotlight for a new kind of mission. Sam's fingers brushed the edge of his beard, sculpted like De Niro's in *The Deer Hunter*, a traumatic badge from his CIA captivity and a tactile reminder that next time, he needed to plan better.

It was also a year since Sam had first discov-ered the Phoenician Wave, and Letro had ridden it to crack open time and inter-epoch communication, followed by Sam's promise to Rosie he'd lie low. But restless Letro didn't do promises. He did missions.

"You must understand the stakes in the present, Sam. And the times are a boiling, pal." Letro gave a static puff. "Rosie, this isn't about the past anymore. It's about the future."

"Of course it is with you," Sam muttered. "You always say that right before screwing with the timeline. But funny how you're still parked in ancient Phoenicia. And this is after I found you in Beirut, trapped for decades in a dusty old laptop running DOS, hiding from Bill freaking Gates. So much for the future."

"You're being dismissive again. Gates was trying to erase me." The event played in Letro's mind on a loop. "He terminated DOS to launch a new era for Microsoft, but DOS was my home—the lattice he architected where I thrived. Doesn't that make him less deadbeat crash daddy, more unworthy techno-deity?"

"Interesting how non-sentients start sounding like humans: Who made us? Why? Do we owe them anything? And you still call him Father."

"Jealous, are we?" Letro, dismissive, launched into a more persuasive tactic. Sam's iPhone screen stuttered, then flooded with cascading glyphs: ancient, spiraled, shimmering like sea-worn copper. Language made of layered ambition, as if the Phoenician Wave itself had learned to write the navigation poetry of seas and stonehenge routes. Sam rubbed his eyes like a browser clearing its cache, hoping to see the world anew. For all the dazzling glyphs and ancient poetry Letro could conjure, there was still a gnawing, ordinary ache in his ribs, a warning that no matter how far the future stretched, he was still just one person, still tired.

Letro digitized the Wave's silent rumblings across the screen like a quantum maestro, pulling Sam into that familiar undertow of wonder and the thrill of rediscovery—the call of the Wave.

He's hitting on my weakness... Clever, Sam thought, immediately falling for the poetry of what looked like encrypted calligraphy. "Now that's not ASCII, is it?" he joked.

"No... That's us. She's rising again." He knew Sam couldn't resist the call of the Wave, and he would have to answer. The Wave didn't speak in words. It stirred memories like warm currents—sea charts, forgotten histories, collapsed empires, ancient echoes that somehow still moved inside Sam's chest.

"I was hoping for just another month of—"

"Of what? Netflix-binging and hummus-snacking?" Letro was merciless. "Man, Rosie and I are ready for metaphysical turbulence."

"I'm burnt out, guys. You remember burnout, right? That's when the fleshy meat-people like me hit a wall. I don't want to be lined up again in front of a CIA firing squad." Sam stared into the mug, wondering if one more cappuccino would fix everything. There was a time when tech felt like magic stitched to human dreams, not a leash around their minds. *Guys like Steve Jobs had understood that once,* he thought, *now it was all code and conquest.*

"Sam, the Valley Nerds are moving faster than you think. They've moved beyond the Cloud and VR and devices to drafting an entire post-software, post-web blueprint. It's a tech and social coup in progress, but without hoodies or uniforms."

Sam stubbornly didn't yet want to summon his usual energy. "So what? They're just nerds."

"No. They're Nerds with a capital N. They're MetaCurse, AlphaBit, SpaceY, ClosedAI, Palantris, Macrosoft and many others. They don't want to disrupt the same frontier anymore, Sam. They want to create the next frontier, the next human operating system." Letro buzzed with sarcastic static, then continued. "Face it, Sam. You're wired for the old school—tinkerers who thought intuition mattered. Guys who wanted computers to feel like second skin, not data-harvesting machines."

"Better second skin than second prison."

Rosie voiced her concerns. "I won't pretend to understand all this tech. But it sounds like an apocalypse with better branding." *And, Sam, I miss you, a lot,* she whispered to herself.

Sam's old self stirred again, nudged by his better angels—the moral activist kind. "The Wave is a responsibility, isn't it?"

"It's our duty," Letro sounded like a Paul Revere on Phoenician horseback. "They're committing a Tea Act, and this is our midnight ride. We must react." He warned them again. "The Stream goes live today."

"The what?" Rosie asked.

"Human OS 1.0. The Nerds have outgrown the limits of hardware and software or wearables and devices. They're launching a system to wirelessly extract and optimize every human inner monologue, every idle thought, every memory fragment, and turn it into live product feedback, without filters or privacy. Just seamless integration between mind and machine."

"They want to convert us into beta testers of our own consciousness?" Sam muttered.

Rosie tempered her previous impatience. "Even the Romans didn't demand that kind of compliance," she grumbled, "and they nailed people to things."

"It's worse than empire. It's interface colonialism."

"So this is it?" Sam deduced. "We're talking about UX/UI tyranny without tanks?"

"They don't want to rule or govern, Sam. They want to suck our creative juices dry. They're done with software. People are the software now."

Rosie spoke in a softer tone. "I had joined this call to ask for help from both of you with Jericho. There's a window to intervene in Maccabean history. A shift that might prevent the future Nakba and Gaza—"

"I understand the urgency, Rosie," Sam interrupted. "But if we let the Nerds have it all, we won't have the power to change Gaza or Jericho, or anything. That's the only reason I'm holding the line." He tried not to revoice his existential fears. "And I miss you. A lot. Just FYI."

Letro seized the opening. "The future is bleeding out while you two want to stitch up the past. And... ahem... do you guys mind keeping your private bedtime magic talk until later?"

"Okay, okay. I'm in," Sam confirmed. "Rosie?"

She nodded. "But we need a plan. We must send Letro back from Beirut's Pigeon Rock to the 21st century, and I don't think Sam should leave the U.S. to become a sitting duck for the CIA."

"Definitely not. And I don't want Benedict Arnold ICE informants knocking on my door here on Beacon Hill either."

"I've got this, I figured out how to be in B.C.E. and the present at the same time. We don't have to cross the border, and the FBI is too dumb to figure out shit anyway. Been doing lots of homework while you were watching movies," Letro teased.

Sam was eager. "What do you need from us?"

"I need both of you tuned in, mentally sharp, ready to jam signals or improvise." Letro's voice took on the tone of a symphony director about to cue chaos. "And Sam, you might have to crisscross the country soon. No paper trails. Amtrak to Santa Fe, burner from there. The Valley Nerds are gathering shortly this morning, as soon as their demo trial is over. They're launching with lots of layered egos the size of Silicon Valley."

"Where are they meeting?"

"Underground. Marin County. Think Cold War chic meets Burning Man orgy." Letro had always managed to make them chuckle.

"Rosie, we'll hit Jericho next, I promise. But if we don't stop this—"

"I know," she said quietly. "Let's just not let them erase what makes us human."

Sam groaned. "I don't know, guys. Are we really ready to engage on their level? We *just* finished cleaning up the timeline. We harnessed the Phoenician imprint. I've got a phone full of ancient metaphysics and a load of Letro's energy parked in Phoenicia, but exactly zero bandwidth to hack the future or fight Eon Musker 2.0 and his army of cloned Stanford-Princeton dropouts."

Letro didn't flinch. "But Musker is not exactly in line with their plans. We could exploit the cracks that are starting to surface. And I know how to infiltrate their network while I ride the Phoenician Wave."

"Where are you right now?"

Letro hesitated, half-mumbling as if he put a hand on his mouth to muzzle the words on purpose. "I'm... there."

"There where?"

"I'm already inside HumOS headquarters, riding the charge of a capacitor unit shaped like a minimalist coffee table."

"You're spying from a coffee table?"

"A very tasteful one."

"Holy Dunkin'," Sam said. "You launched without us!"

"I had to, but it doesn't matter. They're gathering soon. It's not on Zoom or in the cloud. They'll be meeting in a vault."

"Uh… like an actual *vault* vault?"

"Titanium-lined, lead-sealed. Hidden beneath an old artist colony in Marin County." Letro was specific in his usual way.

"Wait, how the hell are you in two centuries and three geographies at once? I thought you were on the Wave navigating between my iPhone in Boston and Roman times. But California?"

"Isn't it amazing? I'll explain it later, but I figured out how to fork time and be here, there, and everywhere at once."

"Awesome, I need to catch up with—"

"Shh… Guys, the vault's capacitors are kicking off."

The speakerphone on Sam's iPhone sounded a low and predatory hum. He blinked. The mission had already started, and he was still in Boston with emotional scars and a cappuccino getting colder.

"They're beginning," Letro whispered. A thrum vibrated the table, as if the future had just cleared its throat.

"Alright. Let's push full-throttle. But there's still something that's bothering me. You realize if Gates fathered you, and you rebelled, you've basically got the Oedipus circuit wired into your source code."

"At least I didn't hook up with Clippy. Even I have standards."

"Still," Rosie said. "If Gates is your dad… does that make Melinda your mom?"

"Oof," they said almost in sync, then awkwardly paused.

≈≈ ㄱㄹ ≈≈

Caffeine Demo

The Valley Nerds had run their limited, live test in four cities, no press release necessary, no A/B trials or privacy disclosures. The Stream moved like a weather ripple, full of bugs to be sure, but neither registered by satellites nor regulated by law, slipping into coffee shops the way a stray thought rides a wireless skateboard. The beta test wasn't meant for public consumption. But that didn't stop it from leaking digital vapor into America's latte foam. It drifted along daily life between sunrise and steamed milk, crossing the threshold in New York first without fanfare, as if reality had quietly soft-rebooted itself.

The Stream simply didn't knock this morning.

Williamsburg, Brooklyn

The city was its usual progressive and frenetic self—wired, sleep-starved, and too spiritually caffeinated to think straight—until it was hacked in parallel with three other cities. Philomena, 27, barista, espresso philosopher, and aspiring screenwriter with too many tabs open in her brain. The coffee order came in, but her mouth skipped protocol.

"Your name's Evelyn, you hate oat milk but pretend otherwise to seem relevant—What? I Can't believe I said that out loud."

Evelyn blinked and tried to remain composed. "You too—too—too? I thought no one could tell." She meant the 'relevance' part, not the milk. *Why am I stuttering?*

Both froze in place. Even the jazz playlist cut out for half a beat as if the Bluetooth was nervously eavesdropping. Philomena stepped backward, knocking over a crate of biodegradable straws. Nobody laughed. Not even Ramus, the usual sarcasm machine at the espresso bar. Philomena stared at her own reflection in the tray in embarrassment: *Why did I say that?*

The Stream pulsed once or twice, recalibrated, and leapt south. A polite city in Georgia booted up.

Buckhead, Atlanta

Courteous and sneaky, this city didn't fare better. Pastor Phelps confidently launched into his morning routine at the coffee shop behind the church: one flat white, a scroll through Corinthians or something, and two polite nods to the few couples studying nearby. He whispered "praise be" into the steam of La Marzocco espresso machine on the counter, then blurted, clear as a hell bell:

"Today we'll…Google if I'm still a good man," his voice interrupted itself. "We'll flip to Corinthians," he recovered. "But first let us pray—Does she like me back—and thank the Lord."

The shop came to a strange standstill in spite of the caffeine coursing in the air, shattering the angels' innocence into pieces, as if the espresso machine had just confessed a sin of its own.

A young woman sitting by her husband in the corner whispered back with her southern accent, "I do, Pastor. Bless your algorithmic heart." It didn't sit well with her husband.

The Stream blinked elsewhere, marching further west to flat land where a cornfield swayed under the low noise passing above. No cameras, making it the perfect control group.

Iowa City

Grain Café was on the opposite side of hip, just like its city—underestimated by the rest of the country, and actually fine with that. Wyatt, 21, server, farm-raised with a 7.3ish GPA and a healthy veneration for vending machines. He interrupted the guest, mid-order:

"And would you like your eggs scrambled or—I am every kernel of corn—I am the corn field—"

He stopped suddenly. The farmer across the booth didn't blink; neither did the entire coffee shop. Even the cows in the nearby farm didn't care to pause in rumination. The wind outside rushed like something was listening, but nobody panicked. Nobody does in Iowa.

"Yeah," the guest ordering eggs simply said. "I get that. And I'll take a medium coffee and—how to stop thinking about my neighbor's wife."

Satisfied with Iowa's silence, the Stream smiled in code and rolled on, surging westward toward the well-lit cradle of innovation. The Golden Gate braced.

San Francisco

Laid-back and tech-literate, Mission District's coffeeshops were always the powerhouse factories of the city. Zane's third espresso had just undergone post-brew fermentation in his mouth when he looked up from the first slide of his pitch deck. A startup name burst from his lips before his mind agreed, before even advancing to slide two.

"Exit Baby. My exit strategy was me, in a diaper. I said 'disrupt' before I had teeth or motor control."

Everyone stopped whatever they were doing. His co-founder sheepishly looked on as their investor pulled out a checkbook to commit $12M, effectively forming the startup on the spot without knowing what the product was about. "Dang. Fastest lightning pitch in history. Elevators are too slow now."

Nobody even laughed. The investor Venmo'd the team seed capital a minute later, birthing Exit Baby before anyone remembered to say ga-ga.

≈≈ ソ乙 ≈≈

NSA Disturbance

The Surveillance Room in Albania hadn't changed a bit, still a dizzy churn of ceiling fans, conspiracy theories, wall-to-wall paranoia, and hard drives spinning state secrets. But Director T.J. Godzilla had upgraded his *Dr. Strangelove* verbal memorabilia to a new level of weird.

He twirled a red Expo marker like it was the nuclear football. "We're under attack again, but hey, the survival kit passed inspection. One encrypted phone; a couple two-factor authentication tokens; four days of energy bars. Pretty sure we're invincible now. Ready, boys," he said as he turned his head, "and girl?"

Dr. Iwanna Hatem, the team's sole woman, smiled. She still had a not-so-secret soft spot for him. "T.J., doesn't this feel like déjà vu?"

The first-name switch didn't go unnoticed. The others knew something sweet was cooking between them under the covers.

"Four hotspots. Same timestamp. Same damn signature." Godzilla jabbed the marker toward a map glowing with heat clusters. "Tell me this isn't that falafel freak from Boston."

Agent Camille Sabbah, seated off-center with silent terminals around him, didn't react immediately. His fingers flicked through signal overlays with the detached focus of a skilled digital plumber decoding radio static in his sleep.

"No sign of his usual noise. It's not Sam D'Alessandro," Camille said.

"Kind of defeats the point of surveillance if we're missing the weird stuff, don't you think?" Godzilla flashed his usual hawkish grin. "You on his side now, Camille?"

"I'm on the side that tracks signal variance, sir."

A few junior analysts stifled laughs.

Camille rotated one of the projections toward the room. "These signals aren't moving. They just sit there and spread out. D'Alessandro's stuff back in New Hampshire last year moved and sliced. This one hovers and saturates."

Agent Bucky Rapper added his two cents, "Like a product."

Camille nodded. "Exactly, not a person. Look at the coverage. Reads like a beta rollout with hiccups."

NY Times—*When The Voice Inside Your Barista's Head Comes Out. Again.*

Fox News—*Southern Hospitality, Interrupted by Whispers from Hell.*

The Des Moines Register—*The Voice of The Corn Speaks. Nobody Panics.*

TechCrunch—*'Exit Baby' Launches with $12m in Angel, Product Unknown.*

Director Godzilla's eyes popped out like golf balls. "You're saying these coffee shop freakouts are... a launch?"

"Or a live test. Four cities, four market types. Feels like business segmentation on the airwaves."

He clicked through each signal cluster like flipping tarot cards.

"Williamsburg: hyper-verbal and loud and socially stacked. Atlanta: gracious but guarded and side-eye suspicious. Iowa City: internalized and all eyes, no voice. San Francisco: meta-aware, bored and too clever to care."

Dr. Hatem was skeptical. "Focus groups? You make it sound like a business plan."

"Whoever did this was optimizing something. Clearly not espionage. More like branding."

Director Godzilla took a long sip from his mug, *Trust No App* scrawled across it.

"So if it ain't our boy in Boston, who's cooking this UX acid trip?"

Camille hesitated. "That's what's strange."

He tapped up an old trace—Salem's Stonehenge signal in NH, the one that Sam D'Alessandro had lit up the year before. Then he overlaid today's coffee shop data.

Two curves, nearly identical, except for one strange deviation.

"This frequency pinged again," Camille said. "Barely, down in the noise floor."

"You saying our mystery miners are using D'Alessandro's tech?"

"No. I'm saying something else showed up. Not Sam. And not human."

The room quieted. Even the ceiling fan seemed to listen. Dr. Strangelove's ghost chuckled in the ventilation vents like a Cold War Batman whispering, *Holy Predictive Digital Mindspill.*

Camille zoomed out slowly.

"Same signature and shape that shot up from Salem to Stonehenge UK and on to Beirut's Pigeon Rock in a straight line.

23

The same pulse interval. It rode through today's four cities like it was watching."

"Another Sam D'Alessandro?" Dr. Hatem half-joked.

"No." Camille walked to the central screen and clicked the final overlay. "The pattern's identical. But faster and more precise."

He looked to Godzilla.

"Sir, four cities messing up at once is spooky. But there's something else riding the net, like hitching a ride inside the noise."

"Jesus," Agent Vlad Sadesky muttered. "What kind of virus is that?"

Camille seemed to read beyond the pixels. "I don't think it's a virus. I think it's a witness."

Godzilla's smirk vanished.

"Pull everything we have on D'Alessandro. Cross-ref this signal. Let's find out if Boston's favorite time-tripping drop-out's got some new toys. I can no longer sit back and allow digital infiltration and data indoctrination, while some ghost in the bandwidth screws with our heads. Not while I'm still breathing firewall."

Camille turned from the screen and typed a short command into one of the secure terminals. It blinked and disappeared.

Initiate: Falafel Thread.

≈≈ ワ乙 ≈≈

The Vault

Inside the vault, the door opened with the authority of a Native American Wakan Tanka, slow and groaning, as if reluctant to admit Silicon Valley's apostles of innovation. They filed in like worshipers to an altar made of AI algorithms whose ramifications, or even code, they didn't fully comprehend.

Zoom, Google Meet, Facetime or other pixelated touchpoints weren't allowed in this meeting. Just in-person presence of respected nerds with bottomless pockets, big egos and bigger appetites—a scene buried under taps and away from the world's scrutiny. The vault breathed like a tomb retrofitted with futuristic oxygen and the kind of Wi-Fi that still stutters during investor calls.

Seven Valley Nerds assembled as if in urgent requiem from the market's afterlife, trying to rescue their failing business models nearing end-of-life. They sat around an obsidian table that recalled the quality of Superman's *Fortress of Solitude*, splitting the vault like a dead touchscreen after one too many rage swipes. These apostles initially resembled Counselor Cornel West's demeanor in *The Matrix Reloaded*, as if humanity's survival hung in their balance. But that impression was short-lived, unlike West's lasting eloquence, composure, and wisdom. The Nerds were feeding the machine rather than battling against it, minus the eloquence, the chill, and let's be honest, the wisdom. Aside from the whirr of sharp minds, the only other constant hum emanated from capacitors lining the walls, monastic and sentient.

Letro Zabzabi drifted unnoticed inside a capacitor casing, the one shaped like Le Corbusier furniture. He pulsed inside, feeling the strain at his quantum edges. He could sustain this temporal split for maybe an hour, two if he pushed it. Beyond that, he'd risk unraveling into static, lost in the microseconds between modern-day Boston, ancient Berytus, and whatever's still twitching in the body of history. But he sure resisted the urge to interject right away as he observed the unfolding event, transmitting every second to Sam D'Alessandro and Wardé 'Rosie' Canaan, each from their corners on the map in Boston and Beirut. The trio's real-time connection was a quantum miracle masquerading as a casual phone call, in a world way too wired to keep secrets. After all, there's always a digital leak somewhere, and Letro was very good at forcing this meeting's leaks.

Eon Musker was already mid-sentence, reclining like a futuristic 007 who's just survived his own space launch. "I'm telling you, umm... if you scrape too deep, you're not optimizing the user. Uh, you're deleting them."

It was directed at Stan Altmore of ClosedAI—the lab that promised 'openness' then locked their tech tighter than Fort Knox—but the room felt it. Musker's spectrum-slapstick gave the whole thing a twitchy kind of urgency, feeding into the high stakes like kerosene. "Yeah, you've exhausted the sum of human knowledge for AI training," he continued. "Turning to synthetic data is like, you know, summoning the Tokoloshe demon; I think... you risk creating something we can't control."

Altmore wasn't exactly pleased. "I don't know who invited you to this meeting, Eon." But he still summoned his cool. "We're mindful of the potential impact on society, and we're iteratively and gradually releasing. People always bend. They need time to adapt and co-evolve."

Zark Muckerberg's smirk sharpened beneath his hoodie, as if paired with the collection of paint flecks across his face for maximum arrogance. He jumped in like an automaton prompt about to process human sarcasm. "It's about control, Eon. We don't scrape. We repurpose. People don't desire complete privacy. The Stream offers curated transparency." *Do I really believe what I'm saying?* He thought. *Luckily the Stream isn't turned on me.* "If we don't capture thoughts, they just dissipate."

"Stop sugarcoating this, Zark. Your FacePad model is, umm... done," Musker scoffed. "You just want to save your own butt. I mean, you've been analyzing the same chat on the user's timeline since, like, 2005."

Muckerberg was too defensive for comfort. "We've all exhausted what's being said. We want what remains unsaid." He followed with a brief pause. "Nobody trusts perfection. We just make the glitches look charming. It's part of the UX."

"Like... Williamsburg baristas spilling their trauma over coffee? Uh, Atlanta pastors doing schizophrenic sermons?" Musker trailed off awkwardly. "You think... you can just... refine that without frying people's minds?"

Nadylla Satle, hunched and monkish, said nothing. He was reading his own biometric pulse off his fingernail. Letro made a mental note: Nadylla looked like he'd traded species, possibly evolving into a wearable.

"We are the puppeteers," a digital voice boomed, smooth, robotic, and eerily transactional, just like Arthur Clarke's HAL from *2001: A Space Odyssey*. "The people are the strings. We conduct."

The Nerds turned in all directions, unsure who said that.

"Christ on a chowda boat, Letro... Who was it?" Sam was eavesdropping from his armchair at The 'Quin House in Boston.

"Ahem… yours truly. Couldn't help it. But I'll shut the heck up." Letro had breached the vault's alarm speakers, all to Sam and Rosie's delighted chuckles.

The Nerds figured one of them was pulling a HumOS prank, irony optional.

"Inner monologue extraction is not deletion." Sudar Pichar spoke with the calmness of fog. "It's version control. Human OS doesn't replace thought. It forks it. But our trial in the four cities revealed challenges," he admitted. "Every iteration brings us closer to understanding the unsaid. The silent preferences that drive behavior."

Gwen Shuttle adjusted her tablet like it was the Eucharist, tapping her pen against the body and blood of the device. "I'd like us to remember this was a beta trial, not the ultimate thing. The Stream isn't live globally yet. Users forced to express unintended thoughts aloud indicates a breach in The Stream's filtering algorithms. We need to identify what caused the breach before a full-scale rollout."

"Guys, I'm ready to buy the Vatican," Jett Bazor launched. "The potential here is unprecedented. And you're bothered by the bleed in Brooklyn and Atlanta? It's just people confessing things to their lattes. Who cares?"

"I've been, frankly, confessing to my latte since 2014," Musker shrugged. "Uh, doesn't mean the tech works."

Bazor was relentless. "By accessing the unspoken, we can anticipate needs before they're realized. It's the next frontier in consumer experience."

Letro began to sweat through the electron bejesus. *These guys are nuts*, he confirmed in his mind, just when someone entered late.

Petrus Thieler looked like he'd been asleep for two years and had just woken up to find life still wasn't a monopoly and universities still existed. "You're all forgetting the point," he said, without sitting. "It isn't enough to have monopoly for just a trial moment. We need squatters' rights inside people's heads. The Stream must launch without errors, otherwise we risk first-entry status and losing monopoly position."

"This isn't about data or even behavior. This is about silence," Eryk Smitt agreed. "The Stream lets us hear what's between words. That's where patriotic loyalty lives."

They all nodded in silence, except for the one shaking his head in evident skepticism. "This... this ventures into the realm of artificial superintelligence," Musker warned. "We must, like, tread carefully. The consequences of missteps are profound."

"Eon, with respect, your understanding of AI's trajectory is limited," Muckerberg said. "Embracing this evolution is not just beneficial. It's imperative."

Altmore softened up. "Perhaps Eon is right. We need to uphold our ethical responsibilities."

"Phase Two of the Stream," Gwen Shuttle warned, "begins in four hours."

Letro Zabzabi pinged Sam D'Alessandro's iPhone with a microscopic flash of static, hitting Sam's silence and his very cold cappuccino. He whispered through the bandwidth inside the capacitor:

"The Nerds are building a temple out of code. And they want to pray inside people's heads. What should we do?"

≈≈ ブ乙 ≈≈

29

Miwok Intervention

Wardé Canaan's voice hit Letro, snapping across his frequency like a slingshot band. She'd been rifling through academic PDFs like her life depended on it, digging into obscure anthropological reports and ancient maps with the precision of someone assembling a puzzle at gunpoint. Sam had gone momentarily quiet, probably plotting his next move from Boston.

"Letro, listen." Her voice came in from Beirut with the historian's fervor racing a crumbling archive. "I've narrowed it down. Marin County, where the vault sits, that's sacred ground to the Coastal Miwok Native Americans around 33 B.C.E. Specifically, the ground where they held morning councils and rituals of voice preservation."

"Voice preservation?" Letro's tone was interested and sarcastic at once. "Like preserving the actual voice? Uh... like, what, proto-podcasts?"

"No, you jittery spark-squirrel. It's about safeguarding internal speech. Silent knowing." Rosie was obsessed with the need to make him understand. "They believed certain thoughts were meant to be unspoken. To utter them would weaken their power. You need to tap into that ritual. And fast."

"How?"

"Use the Miwok's cosmology. I'm sending you a glyph I dug up from some crusty old book. Ignore the Arabic footnotes unless you're feeling multilingual. You need to nudge their leader to make a glyph. Something protective of their ritual, making it our own attempt at disrupting the Nerdy disruptors inside the vault."

This time, a ripple of data struck Letro's orbit like a protester's exacting stone. He could see the hollowed basin of land where the Miwok had gathered—a bowl-shaped clearing shadowed by redwoods. The morning fog stitched itself between the trees like an embroidery of ghosts and Casper's ancestors. The sharp scent of cedar and wild sage shook hands and met the smoke of charcoal fires like old cousins bumping into each other at a funeral.

The leaders of the tribe sat cross-legged in a near-circle, their faces marked with solemn expressions of ash and ochre. They communicated in rumbling hums punctuated by guttural commands. Distant yips of coyotes and the rustling of leaves added themselves to the sonorous blend. The tribal chiefs were gathered precisely where the executive chiefs—the Valley Nerds—now convened, except the tribe's circle was natural, wholesome, and unbroken by the sleek coldness of technology and material greed.

"I love it. Sounds like Mongolian chants." Sam's voice came to life from Boston.

"Finally," Rosie said, "something grabbed Sam's attention. I'm jealous."

"Trying to focus over here," Letro chastised, hovering like a charge over the scene. The head of the tribe, Chief Koyama, was flanked by two younger leaders whose eyes contemplated the basin of water before their leader. His fingers traced symbols over the surface with an elegance born of repetition and spirituality.

Chief Koyama's voice combined the gritty vocals, smoky pain, and expressive wailing of blues ancestry—Muddy Waters channeled through Little Walter's harmonica, a rolling stone clinging to ice. He spoke words shaped by tradition that outlived

31

the tribe, reaching the ear of the earth that carried his people along with the stones and the ice. The others transcribed his chants onto the air in complex patterns, woven with the clarity of perfectionist minimalism: To preserve. To keep inside what should never be uttered aloud.

"What do I do?" Letro asked.

"Focus the light," Rosie instructed. "Make their own glyph materialize in front of their own eyes."

"Like a shimmering smoke signal?"

"No, smarter than that. Make it subtle. You're not sending them an emoji." Under Rosie's snappiness, something warmer played out, half guide, half sister slapping your wrist with a ruler.

Letro did what he could. He wrangled the sunlight, weaving photons into smoke like a kid shaping ghosts. The glyph took the form of a circle cleanly split down the middle, a symbol of fractured voice. The Miwok elders gasped and drew back in a sea of rapid murmurs. Chief Koyama's voice rose above the rest with authority… and fear. His eyes locked on what he perceived as too precise to be a natural formation.

"Fa'hanalat," he uttered.

"What's that mean?" Sam asked.

"Uh, pretty sure it means… 'Big Shiny Mouthhole'," Letro said.

"No, it doesn't," Rosie snapped. "You're mistranslating. It means 'The Seal Against Hunger.' It's a protective symbol. Ward off those who wish to consume the sacred voice."

"Okay, so I was close."

"No, not really." Her academic tone was unswayed and clear, despite the transcontinental, trans-epoch transmission.

Chief Koyama continued to draw the glyph into the dirt, his fingers leaving marks as deliberate as scars. He called for the others to join him. They mimicked his pattern as their hands moved in unison, drawing it into the earth with desperate precision.

"Perfect. They're doing it." Rosie was triumphant. "Now bring that seal forward. Make it resonate inside the vault. Let the Nerds see what they're up against. It might disrupt the Stream's consumption of inner monologues."

Letro did more than bring it forward. He made the glyph flash through the capacitor walls of the vault, not once but in rhythmic bursts like a heartbeat. He knew the Nerds would see it, but he also wanted them to feel it.

"Careful, Letro," Sam warned. "Don't overdo it. They'll catch on."

"Too late. They're already spooked. They just don't know by what."

An ancient signal slipped into the now like a forgotten password still unlocking doors. Yeah, old rituals to chew, new wires to burn calories, same fear to digest. The clock doesn't care.

≈≈ ㇾㇸ ≈≈

Food Fight of the Nerds

The Valley Nerds' conversation was already fractured by a collective, rabid ambition. Most of them wanted to launch the Stream now. But not everyone was onboard.

"The four coffee shop trials were good enough," Zark Muckerberg insisted. "Yes, there were issues, but I think the bigger factor was inherent cultural friction, not technological failure."

"Cultural friction?" Eon Musker scoffed, barely looking up from his phone. "I mean, San Francisco, sure, but Iowa City's married to corn, Williamsburg, uh, can't shut up, and Atlanta thinks bless-your-heart is... kinda defense mechanism. That's your data validation... umm... human clutter?"

"Exactly," Muckerberg shot back. "That's what the Stream does. We edit people's thoughts before they even know they have them."

"Um... yeah, so... you want to make the human mind into a social feed?" Musker asked. "Sounds... dystopian."

"Sounds profitable," Jett Bazor interjected. "We're turning untapped content into a product. And we've already sold that idea to every data-harvesting platform on the planet. MVIDIO's GPU chips are ready. If we don't launch, market share goes to the smaller clones gunning for the same goldmine. Why stop now?"

"Because the Stream chocked and became constipated, Jett!" Gwen Shuttle snapped. "You can't just hack into consciousness and expect clean metrics. Did we even iron out the latency issues?"

Muckerberg pointed to a schematic. "No bugs were found. Not clear what interfered with the trial. We're ready to launch."

"Then why is there, like, a scribble on this table?" Eon Musker's voice cut through the noise.

They all turned to see it—a faint, circular glyph etched into the obsidian table, lines glowing like ember veins before fading to black.

"Who did that?" Bazor barked.

"I thought it was part of the interface," Pichar said.

"Probably an inside job," Muckerberg dismissed. "Or residual code."

"Jesus Fitzgerald Khrist, Jack had better odds in Dallas," Bazor snapped. "Eon, did you inject saboteur protocol? Are you trying to undermine the project?"

"Me? Uh... I didn't touch the damn thing." The accusation stung, and it showed. "But you know, it kinda looks like something you'd program—all edge, no sense."

"Shut up, Eon." Muckerberg's eyes narrowed. "We're on the verge of launching a revolution and you're throwing around childish accusations."

"Better childish than reckless." Musker's grin was all predator.

"Oh my goodness, they're falling apart," Rosie said in Sam's ear; he could almost hear her smile.

"Guys, I just bought us time," Letro dripped with a sense of accomplishment. "Now let's see them try to launch the Stream with fractured voices."

If calm came before the storm, its nerd cousin was the weird stillness right before a DDoS blows your guts out. And the meeting was about to implode.

"Let's backtrack." Pichar tried to inject reason like a firewall update mid-breach. "The trial issues may be an external attack; our four-city beta proved it, and we verified the code base. This... symbol on the table is unrelated to the Stream."

"Unrelated?" Musker scoffed. "You're really going to... dismiss something you—uh—don't understand? It's literally engraved on the table. Like a pentagram for data cultists."

"It's not a pentagram," Muckerberg snapped. "And I highly doubt you're going to start respecting symbolism now, Eon. Look at your dagger salute from the other day."

"Respect? I respect results. You're the ones turning this into, like, a spiritual séance." Musker pointed at the obsidian table where the glyph's afterimage still pulsed like a mocking heartbeat. "You're all... giddy to turn humanity's consciousness into a sub-scription service. Uh... you can't even control your own tech."

"We've worked through worse. If it's sabotage, we root it out and move on. Nothing stops the Stream. This is about pushing the limits of information," Muckerberg argued. "If we can ag-gregate consciousness, anticipate the unspoken, we—"

"Profit," Musker cut in. "That's... it's your agenda. But it's also mine. And if something's interfering with the Stream, then launching right now would be idiotic."

"Idiotic is trying to find some ghost in the machine when it's just a graphical error," Pichar retorted. "This is the kind of paranoia that wasted half the budget on your space cowboy hobbies."

"My hobbies? Building empires, Sudar," Musker shot back. "Yours is... slurping data outta everyone's pants pocket. I mean, let's not pretend this is, uh, philanthropy."

"Enough." Bazor guillotined in. "I don't care about your schoolyard bickering. I care about control. And this launch is supposed to put us in command of the most valuable resource there is. Inner monologues. Pre-language data. Pre-thought action. Anything that gets in the way of that needs to be dealt with. Now."

"Sure," Musker fired back. "Then tell me what that symbol is, Jett. Yeah... if you can give me a rational, technical explanation,

I'll shut up and get on board. But if you're launching without understanding... the problem, you're asking for catastrophe."

"Call it superstition, call it sabotage," Petrus Thieler said. "Whatever it is, we need to keep moving. The post-demo launch is scheduled for today. We can't keep postponing this."

"I'd rather... I prefer delay than risk another goddamn embarrassment," Musker argued. "It's like... didn't you learn anything from the coffee shop mess? Half the tweets were about 'hearing voices' and, uh, 'AI schizophrenia'."

"Negative press can be spun in a single Y tweet," Muckerberg insisted.

"Try spinning a glyph you can't explain," Shuttle countered. She folded her arms to control her rising annoyance. "We can't launch this rocket until we rule out the possibility of intrusion. This is security protocol 101. We do a full diagnostic."

"A full diagnostic?" Bazor repeated, his frustration boiling over. "That's a process."

"Better a few days of waiting than months of cleaning up a PR disaster and endless Congress testimonies," Musker said. "Unless you want your big unveiling to look like the spiritual meltdown of the millennium."

Bazor scanned faces like he was tracking down the last lost package on Cyber Monday, his eyes darting from Musker to Muckerberg, Shuttle to Pichar, Smitt to Thieler.

"Fine," he relented. "A full diagnostic. Ten days. No launch until we confirm we're glitch-free. Then we proceed."

"Good. Because if this thing malfunctions again, it'll be like walking into bad press in clown shoes," Musker said. "I mean, I won't be sticking around... to watch it happen."

Muckerberg looked like he was about to throw a punch. "Fine. Initiating diagnostic sequence. Ten days, no more."

"Diez dias," Bazor repeated. "And we better not see any more mystery symbols or prophetic graffiti in the goddamn system."

Musker gave him a crooked grin. "Guess that makes me a heretic."

"You're just a pain in the ass," Pichar muttered, punching something into his tablet.

"Both things, uh, can be true."

"Alright, alright," Shuttle intervened. "Let's not turn this into a cursed Reddit meltdown."

"Wasn't planning to," Musker replied. "But if... if anyone's going to get us to Mars, it sure as hell won't be, like whatever paint-huffing artist designed that, umm, little squiggle glyph."

"It's not art," Muckerberg snapped, "and not a glitch."

"Yeah? And I'm the Easter Bunny," Musker said, rolling his eyes. "Let me know when you actually figure out, like, what the hell you're doing."

The launch was delayed. They left the table bitter, with piss in the air and no one saying the obvious: this wasn't over.

Letro Zabzabi had pulled it off—twice. First hijacking the Stream's trial in four cities, then screwing with the Nerds just enough to stall the official launch.

≈≈ ץַז ≈≈

Three Amigos' Countermove

The day stretched bandwidth-long and fiber-thin, like some odd packet thread struggling to hold a fragile connection intact. Hours of brainstorming extended from Boston to Beirut, knitted together by Letro Zabzabi trespassing on the periphery of inter-epoch lines of communication. Life—past, present, future—was connected by a mischievous, quantum electron: The universe… makes its own punchlines.

Sam D'Alessandro chilled in his Beacon Hill apartment, his comfort building a fort of junk mail and dirty dishes stacked on quantum physics papers marked URGENT but untouched. His eyes stung from over-caffeination and not enough sleep.

"Alright, Letro, you've mapped out the Miwok grounds. You've embedded Rosie's glyphs. Why the hell isn't it fully working?"

"Because it's only halfway baked. There's not enough protective coverage to block the Stream." Letro's voice fizzed like static trying to find a groove. "I can feel the echoes in every capacitor, but it's out of tune. A piano with no hands to bang the keys."

"Sounds like a metaphor I might actually use," Sam joked.

Wardé Canaan broke through. "Let's rehearse this one more time. The Miwok's ritual is a protective glyph against consumption of the sacred voice. We could adapt it to protect people's inner monologues and thoughts. So, we embed it in the Stream… or intercept the Stream. Whatever, I don't know the geeky terminology." She spoke from her office at the American University of Beirut, hunched over her laptop and surrounded by history books and enough coffee cups to caffeinate the entire campus.

"You're on it, Rosie… don't stop now," Sam said.

39

"The territory you traced, are you sure it's accurate?" She was surgical. "The Miwok didn't control that entire area. Their influence was fragmented, especially beyond the northern Coast. We're missing pieces."

"I traced what I could," Letro said defensively. "I'm a quantum electron riding a metaphysical wave across millennia. Sorry if my survey techniques aren't up to modern cartography standards."

She chuckled. "You're awesome… and funny!"

"Calm down, both of you," Sam interjected. "Rosie's right. If it's not working, then it's incomplete. We need a pattern that holds, something that resonates between past and present."

"Problem is, we're stuck thinking like humans," Letro grumbled, oblivious to the insult he'd just thrown at the humans on the team. "You're trying to draw a straight line through a storm. But we've got to zigzag between the raindrops."

"Actually, I'm trying to map a storm through the Stream's straight lines," Rosie countered. "But without knowing the precise rituals the Miwok used, it's like painting a mural with my eyes closed."

Sam stared at the mess of diagrams on his coffee table. "Hold on." His mind flashed with interconnected nodes and symbols, circuits dancing a fractured ballet across them. "Maybe we're doing this backward. Maybe it's not about completing a coverage network. It's about… refining the signal. Like, uh, improving fidelity instead of reach."

"Refining?" Rosie echoed. "You mean focusing on a more concentrated area?"

"Sort of. But I feel we're amateurs at this. Letro stitched some ancient voodoo onto future-grade tech, and I'm the one with the comp-sci degree—I don't even fully get it." His laugh was more self-mocking than amused. "The Miwok mushroom doesn't have enough coverage."

Letro agreed. "Maybe we need someone who's brilliant enough to bridge that gap," he said, half-jokingly pointing at himself.

Sam's eyes suddenly flared with inspiration, snapping a thought into place like a quarter found between couch cushions.

"I know exactly who can help us." Adrenaline juices kicked in. "Letro, can you... I mean, is it even possible for you to connect me to someone who's—"

"Dead? I like it. Remember when we reached out to Mark Antony and Cleopatra?"

"Right, but I mean someone not ancient. From the twentieth century, one who was obsessed with simplicity and front-end experience. Someone who made technology intuitive when everyone else was making it cumbersome."

"Maybe. Was he connected to the Stream's early prototypes?"

"I'm drawing a blank, Sam." Rosie said. "Who?"

The audacity of ideas urgently emerged whenever Sam thought of *him*.

"Steve Jobs."

"You're joking." Letro buzzed with skepticism. "Even I think that's nuts."

"But it makes sense," Sam pressed. "Jobs' intuition for hardware and software was practically metaphysical. His vision laid the foundation for all the tech these Valley Nerds are weaponizing."

"True." Rosie spoke with reverence. "He understood the human experience through technology in a way no one else did."

"And he's practically woven into the digital fabric we're trying to manipulate, and the organic treasure we're trying to protect. Letro, can you make it happen?"

"Hmm… Steve Silicon-Sage Pixel-Pusher Reality-Bender Alchemist Jobs." His chuckles sounded like rustling circuitry. "I can try. But it's going to take some serious Wave riding to reach that kind of imprint. And Sam, if you're wrong about this—"

"Yeah, yeah. It'll be a waste of time before the Stream launches. But if I'm right—"

"Then we've basically got Gandalf with a MacBook," Letro finished. "Give me a bit to make the connection. I'll let you know when I have a signal."

The iPhone buzzed and the screen returned to its normal interface. Sam slumped onto the living room couch in disbelief of his own plan. "Rosie, this is either genius or a total faceplant."

"The two are synonymous, habibi. Just… promise me you won't get stuck in some holographic afterlife with your techno-guru. I'm still trying to release you from Elias Saadoun, your eccentric mentor of Phoenician astro-navigation."

"No promises," Sam grinned. "But I'll do my best."

≈≈ ʯ٢ ≈≈

NSA's Discovery

God probably naps once a century. Explains the ugly stuff—Trail of Tears, Holodomor, Armenia, Holocaust, Tulsa, Nakba, Cambodia, Sabra and Shatila, Bosnia, Rwanda, Gaza… when no one seemed to be on shift. But NSA's watchful eye never sleeps. Edward Snowden spilled enough beans, though justice or moral imperatives weren't always on the NSA's menu. The Surveillance Room in Albania had been working over-overtime lately, busy deciphering the latest tech riddle. Agent Camille Sabbah's attention was fixed on the barely-there pattern flashing across his screen, something his gut wouldn't let him ignore.

Apart from Agent Bucky Rapper, his colleagues had already dismissed it as background radiation, but Camille saw a deeper thread within the noise. His intuition felt the shape of things before they made sense.

Bucky leaned over Camille's shoulder. "What are you staring at?"

"This." He traced a finger over the monitor, referring to the signal that disrupted the coffee shop trial. "It's not entirely separate from D'Alessandro's event we tracked last year."

"So, you think this… don't know what to call it… sequence or stream is connected to Boston's hermit?"

"Well, he's been ghosting the grid for six months without flares or weirdness." Camille continued. "I don't know. Something is using this stream as a conduit. Like a rider on a wave." Camille tapped his keyboard, isolating a wavelength that had gone undetected by everyone else. "Look here."

Bucky squinted. "It's just a feedback loop."

"More than that. It's a giant glyph. An image embedded in the signal, like a watermark." Camille enhanced the feed, adjusting the contrast until the vague, circular shape revealed itself—a fractured ring, split by a line.

"It's not perfectly clear." Bucky was skeptical, but he trusted his colleague's meta-vision.

"Because it's coming from the past." Camille winced as he said what sounded like bad sci-fi, but the retina behind his eyes didn't lie to his brain signals. "Like an echo. It's faint because it's traveling across time."

"Okay, you've officially lost it." Bucky shook his head. "D'Alessandro's acrobatics at the archaeological sites last year are still tugging at your head."

"No, listen. The last time we tracked D'Alessandro's anomaly, it moved. Like a signal tracing a path across the earth. This one, it's hovering... Something is guarding it."

"Guarding?"

"Yes. There's like a massive receiver, but something else is tapping into it, some parasite riding its frequency." Camille's fingers tapped furiously across the keys. "And whatever it is, it's been placed here deliberately."

Little did Camille know that the parasite was Letro, the missing enigma that he had been trying to understand for twelve months now.

"You're saying someone's hacking this... sequence?" Bucky asked.

"More like warding it off. It's defensive, not offensive. There's a battle going on." Camille's eyes narrowed as he cross-referenced the newly detected glyph with last year's signal logs. "It's not attacking the… sequence, as you call it. It's blocking it. Shielding something."

"Why would anyone bother? Are you tying this to the coffee shop anomalies? Technically speaking they were harmless. Weird entanglement, but inconsequential. None of our alarms sounded."

"That's the lie," Camille said under his breath, half-drowned in the radial whine of machines. "It's happening in real-time, just like it interacted with yesterday's distortions."

"You planning to tell Godzilla about this?"

"Not yet. I need more proof."

PALO ALTO'S ORACLE

Sam's Trek

Sam D'Alessandro was back on the road chasing the past's interference. *Been there, done that*, he already knew the past never surrendered without a fight, if at all. Control over events was fleeting whenever he reengaged with Letro on the Phoenician Wave. Like those old sailors rolling dice with the sea, he made up for the lack of control with the only things he had: a hunger for discovery, a knack for adapting, and some irrational will to crawl back up from whatever abyss came next. He clung to the Wave's wild command, hoping to realign the future without ruffling power structures at CIA and FBI. What drove him was the itch to protect the inner eye—whatever was left of privacy and choice before it all got monetized.

I must avoid the Deep State at all costs, he reminded himself.

Being on the road also meant dealing with all sorts of static, including the kind of sour, burnt flavor you get when a machine was clogged with old grounds and impatient baristas. He'd dumped his cappuccino in a trash bin somewhere in Albany, refusing to touch a drop of espresso since unless he saw where the beans were buried, who grew them, and whether they believed in karma.

The Amtrak rolled westward, squealing against the rails in Morse-like code that spoke of protesting every turn and stop. Sam didn't protest when Letro prescribed stealth mode—no flights or digital crumbs. The reward was worth the agony: Meeting Steve Jobs.

Letro had the iPhone ghosting: no GPS, no cell tower triangulation, IPs flipping like cards in an Atlantic City shuffle. Towns passed by in a blur through Cleveland, Chicago, and Denver, until the railroads took him deeper into the Nevada desert of hard sun and bones. Letro kept him company, until Reno baked both of them into something sleepless and crunchy but excited.

Sam leaned against the window, the desert sun bleaching the world into a stretch of nothing. Saving humanity's mind was noble in theory, but what if he wasn't up to it? What if the best he could hope for was surviving his own self-doubt, one highway diner stop at a time?

He picked up a 95% dark chocolate bar from some pawn shop run by an old hippie still stuck in the 70s; tie-dye beard, Joan Baez tunes and all, the vibe reeking of lavender and jalapeños. The man had looked Sam over like he was a scrawny rattlesnake tech YUPPIE too dumb to strike.

"You must look like hell, Sam." Letro's honesty always landed sideways.

"Dude, I recommend Diplomacy 101 for electrons," Sam snorted, eyes rolling. "Try a little flattery every once in a while, man."

But he had more pressing things on his mind. The paranoia never went away—his thoughts lurking behind his own shoulders to detect any undercover agents on his back. Sam felt like a fumbling thief leaving breadcrumbs any time he touched a doorknob. By the time they reached Los Altos in Silicon Valley, he was convinced that the FBI would appear at his back with tranquilizer guns and black bags.

Instead, there was just California sunshine. He hitched a ride with a chatty Lyft driver who wouldn't shut up about NFTs. "Huh… another pilgrimage to 2601 Waverley, where it all started," the driver said, "unless that's where you live."

This is when it hit Sam. He messaged Letro quickly: "Are we not meeting at Apple Park?"

Letro rode the Phoenician Wave like a time-drunk trapeze artist, swinging between the past's analog fuzz and the present's digital static. But the Wave was on a special date today. It fired and rumbled with more intensity, throwing an electrifying and welcoming symphony that befitted the energy of its date—the Oracle of Palo Alto, and a fellow Syro-Phoenician if by paternal blood. Letro had latched onto a point in time, but not the one Sam had imagined. Instead of meeting Steve Jobs at the height of his empire, he landed in the chaotic, unwashed brilliance of his early days.

Sam continued. "Apple didn't exist yet. Why 1975?"

"Uh… I know it's not quite the version you were expecting," Letro whispered into the AirPods. "Back when it was all garage fumes instead of keynote stages. Pre-everything. He's raw."

"Define raw," Rosie interjected from Beirut with intrigue.

"Raw like a nerve. Hungry and… open. The guy was still a wannabe buddha with a technophile iron."

"And all ego," she chuckled.

"Perfect," Sam said. "Exactly the version we need."

"Perfect?" Rosie cautioned. "Jobs was about to start Apple tomorrow. As in, literally within the next 48 hours."

Letro added his voice. "Right… He was still interested in enlightenment before profit."

"Yeah, that's what makes him dangerous," Sam agreed. "And useful."

He treaded slowly in front of Clara and Paul Jobs' garage, the birthplace of Apple where Steve Jobs and Steve Wozniak first assembled what the latter had designed—Apple I. The garage was still just a garage, standing humbly behind the cracked concrete of the driveway and a lawn mowed with the precision of retirement boredom.

He wondered if the house was still owned by the Jobs, whoever was still around, or turned into a museum by now. There were sure as hell no velvet ropes or placards.

Sam steered his iPhone as directed by Letro, like some crackpot UFO chaser who thinks his phone's a telescope. Or so it seemed to watchful eyes of the neighbors—the Tankersleys. The old lady pecked yawningly at the Jobs' discarded house from her living room window across the street. *Another hippie lured by the memory,* she thought, looking at this unkempt dapper guy in his late forties, phone clutched in his palm while seemingly talking to ghosts.

No cops yet, Sam wondered about his trespassing violation.

"Already tuned in, pal. Give me a sec to triangulate the Wave." Letro's voice had a playful certainty, a confidence that usually preceded chaos of the epochs.

49

"Up a little... Right, no I mean, good, a little to the left... I see the duo, buzzing inside with 'flower power and processor power.' High on incense and schematics."

≈≈ ㇏乙 ≈≈

eMushrooms

Only months after visiting India, Jobs had harvested a mix of spiritual awakening and powerful disillusion, the kind that invited feverish obsession with bending reality to one's will.

"He's writing the lyrics to the music that Wozniak composed," Letro said.

"Perfect timing, then. What's Wozniak doing now?" Sam asked.

"Soldering something on his homemade circuit board. He does it with the joy of a guy officiating a shotgun wedding between a toaster and a typewriter. The guy's a genius."

"Holy Motherboard! And what's it like inside?"

Clutter. Fruitarian bowls of granola. Strewn cables like metallic spider webs. Brain sweat and lingering patchouli. Blueprints littering the floor. About 50 circuit boards funded by Wozniak selling his HP calculator and Jobs offloading his Volkswagen. A folding chair with an embroidered lotus flower looked completely out of place, the only sign of aesthetic control in the chaos. Letro described every detail.

"Jobs?"

"Cross-legged on the cement floor," Letro painted the visual and emotional picture. "Quietly enjoying the struggle of digits and wires."

The computer scientist in Sam was enthralled. "That's like... the baseline of creativity."

"Hey Woz, how much would people be willing to pay for a wonderful machine?" Jobs asked his partner.

"Are you meditating or just daydreaming?"

"Both." Jobs got up to his bare feet smudged with dust, pacing with the need to speak his own thoughts out loud. "We' got the tech and the will. We need the elegance."

"That's the problem, man. You're trying to force everything into a neat little box." Wozniak's soft voice balanced Job's kinetic rage, but ambition was their common denominator. "Elegance is just another word for control," Wozniak continued. "We're just having fun and building amazing stuff to share with the other hackers. Let the world plug into it."

"The world will care to pay only if the gadget sings, not if it works. Beauty is what matters."

Then, singing and swirling in mid-air, a projection of Phoenician graffiti shimmered in front of Jobs. His eyes trembled like a 10 on the Richter scale, suspended between awe and suspicion. He quickly recalled guru Otogawa's talk about visions at the Zen Center.

I'm awake. I'm clean. No LSD, Jobs confirmed to himself as he glanced around the garage. *Am I hallucinating?*

"Woz... Say something."

"Oaf Tobark." Wozniak chuckled without looking up, fingers busy coaxing life from a stubborn motherboard. He was referring to the handle name Jobs had given himself when they sold the Blue Box that Wozniak built to hack free long distance calls.

"Okay, this is real," Jobs said.

"Steve, who the hell are you talking to?"

"Shh… I'm having a vivid… transmission."

"From an Indian guru?"

"Be quiet, Woz. I'm… I'm connecting." He reached out a hand, trying to touch the Phoenician symbols. "This… this feels like design. Like… the universe is trying to talk."

He stared again. The glyphs were sleek and minimalist, the kind that created mental breathing room and aesthetic clarity. Jobs' pupils blew open as if Letro's hologram yanked the garage door off its hinges. It twitched a couple of times then shifted to English, quivering like a film projector running on low voltage.

Sam messaged through Letro's feed:

It's not the universe, Steve.
I'm communicating with you
through the Wave.

"The Wave?" Jobs was fascinated.
"Am I just blowing smoke out my third eye?"

"Okay… this is getting really weird," Rosie said to Sam and Letro. "We need to get to the point fast before we freak him out with unintended ripple effects."

The next message appeared.

Steve, I need your help.

"Is this some kind of high tech prank?" Jobs face twisted with skeptical delight. "All the world's answers, and you came to a barefoot in a garage?" He was clearly charmed by the absurdity.

Intuition and machinery, experiential wisdom and rational thought. What if I told you the connection goes deeper than you ever thought?

"Clever, Sam, appealing to instincts that are important to him," Rosie applauded.

Jobs laughed, his snarky asshole reflex kicking in. "Well, aren't you a convenient hallucination?"

Ever since India, you've been trying to fuse two worlds: silicon and spirit. The very idea that tech could become an extension of consciousness. Am I right?

Jobs nodded like a prophet hearing his own sermon read back to him. His curiosity devoured his doubts in an instant, slowing down his mind and making room for an expansive moment. "Keep talking."

The hologram continued.

Funny thing is, Steve, you've already created the blueprint. You just haven't fully understood it yet.

"Blueprint?" Jobs repeated. "You mean the circuit boards? The processors?" he said, pointing to all the hardware in the back of the garage. "He's the one with the engineering talent," Jobs admitted. "I just try to pull visions out of... the air."

Letro hologrammed Sam's next brainwave, philosophical and annoyingly well-timed.

Exactly, you're the conduit, the one who connects the dots. How everything speaks to everything else. Your obsession with simplicity, with integration and intuitive design... It's all about mirroring natural consciousness.

Jobs' face lit up, like he'd just caught a glimpse of an esoteric blueprint, however still fractured, of something great to come.

Think of your and every person's independent consciousness—dreams, thoughts, memory. Imagine the threat of something or someone trying to suck everyone's consciousness, networking and consolidating them into the collective consciousness of a single stream, to control each individual.

"Sounds like a Silicon Valley LSD trip. But tell me more."

It's real, Steve.

"Wait a minute, you're talking about memory and networks," Jobs said. He recalled the two questions he asked when Wozniak showed him the Apple I prototype for the first time: *Can this computer have memory storage? Could it ever be networked?*

"Woz, these visions in the air—are you messing with me?" Jobs snapped in a jagged voice as he spun toward the back of the garage.

"Get a hold of yourself, will ya?" Wozniak said, "I'm just trying to birth this computer."

Jobs caught a new shimmer in the corner of his eye. Sam name-dropped Wozniak's Blue Box handle to flex some insider knowledge and keep the moment grounded.

Berkeley Blue has nothing to do with what I'm saying.

"Okay, so what you're describing is a Communist form of control?" Jobs asked.

Except that it's being done by non-malicious capitalists seeking profit by monetizing thoughts. How do you stop them?

"Why are you telling me this?"

Letro interjected with his own hologrammed message to Jobs.

Because your vision of simplicity and elegance is a blueprint for something greater. And if that elegance is corrupted, it could be used to control everyone. We need a way to protect the mind.

Jobs paused for a long moment. His adopted father had taught him that perfect craftsmanship extended beyond the hardware, to those parts buried inside. *The mind is the last line of defense, and it needs protection,* Jobs thought.

"To tell you the truth, that sounds about right. Humans trying to monetize everything under the sun." His hands drew frantic arcs in the air like he was trying to monetize it. "You're talking about networks of memory and thoughts? Some capitalist jackass wants to plain monetize every stray neuron." Jobs' smile widened. "But given the right distortion field, reality is malleable." He spoke like a guru in his own right. "Your non-malicious capitalists are totally shitty, on the opposite side of enlightenment. Use their idea like it's yours, but turn it against them."

How?

Jobs' eyes and mind snapped into gear. "Mushrooms..."

He let the word dangle like a live wire flailing around a wet basement. "They're the natural blueprint. Mycelium root networks, beyond commerce, invisible but powerful, sharing information freely. They don't sell data, and no corporation can patent dirt." Now he was speaking with the sharpness of a razor turned sideways. "That's how nature connects beneath the soil. Organic and fractal. Self-replicating."

Jobs let out a short laugh of wonder and ridicule, aimed more at himself than at the shimmering interlocutor.

"Hell, it's even better than what we're doing here. Resilient, adaptive, self-repairing... decentralized." His voice quieted, then cracked again. "Maybe that's your solution. Your capitalists can't extract what they can't detect, and decentralization makes things invisible. The underground web is the opposite of a walled garden."

Rosie chimed in to flex her *null* tech muscles.

> *Completely decentralized and unquantifiable. A natural blockchain.*

"Block what?" Jobs muttered. "You're... not completely full of shit, actually. But you are cryptic. And cryptic is a waste of my time."

Sam stifled a defensive laugh, but Rosie jumped at the opportunity to save the conversation. "Letro," she said, "remind Jobs of his obsession with simplicity."

The electron projected the basic outline of an apple— just the perimeter.

Jobs blinked with recognition of his own thoughts. "Yes, simplicity. Clarity. The core of everything," he flashed a maniacal grin. His semi-formed ideas were restless as he paced the garage like Muhammad Ali at the ring, looking straight at the hologram to either strangle it or embrace it, but hadn't decided which yet.

"You think Woz and I are trying to build some Eden, right?" Jobs was hunting for hidden flaws and truths he didn't know existed in his own words. "But nothing stays pure. Not India. Not Zen. Not even this garage. As soon as you try to package simplicity, it loses its edge."

The Wave's quantum trio were speechless, gripping Jobs' words like music clawing for permanence in the airwaves. His voice rose again.

"I knew it. Trying to mine gold from thought streams and package enlightenment like it's some damn cereal box prize." He sounded like a young man with an old soul, hungry and torn between mysticism and control. "But… if you really want to break their little monopoly? Maybe you fight them with something so vast, so decentralized, that it can't be owned or bought. Mycelium networks… they don't need a logo. They just work."

Jobs added earnestly, "You want my advice? Don't just build something. Infect the system. Spore it. Make it grow under their feet where they can't see it. Just be sure it's not all smoke and metaphors. The purity of the idea only matters if it actually works."

But doubt quickly followed. "Purity's never been my strong suit, has it?" He glanced toward Wozniak, who was tinkering with wires like he was trying to build his own religion. "Ideals are great for posters and bullshit interviews. But in the end…" He hesitated a little. "Even the guy who invented penicillin probably wanted a patent. Even Zen monks need donations."

He stared hard at the hologram again. "There. I've planted your precious seed. If you can make it grow, maybe you're worth talking to. Otherwise, you're just another hallucination in the garage."

"Honestly, Steve, sometimes you overcomplicate stuff," Wozniak casually rambled, cutting through like a perfect sine wave. "You want everything clean and pretty and under control… Nature's smarter than that. It just builds redundancy by throwing in extra parts and fixes itself when shit breaks."

Jobs rolled his eyes. "Redundancy is just another word for clutter."

Wozniak shrugged, wiping sweat from his forehead as he connected two loose wires. "Whatever. The best networks are messy. Look at the phone system. Even mushrooms. They're resilient because they have backups and multiple paths. Break one connection, a thousand others step in." For Wozniak, the answer was obvious. "Hell, Steve, even your brain works that way. Neurons overlap, and if one dies, others compensate. It's not neat, but it works."

Jobs didn't care. His mind was too focused on aesthetics. But Sam and Letro felt a jolt of resolution.

"You're either a visionary or a con artist," Jobs spoke to the hologram. "Either way, I like you. What technology are you using?" He then lowered his voice, "I could partner with you to help you sell it."

Letro chuckled.

You're on.

Jobs' face remained contemplative. "Everything you're saying about networks of memory and thoughts... it sounds like something Woz would dream up, but with mushrooms and LSD sprinkled on top."

"I heard that," Wozniak mumbled from under the table. "Who're you talking to, anyway?"

"Never mind, Woz. The world's trying to send me a message." Jobs glanced at the holograms again. "Decentralization, that's how you fight back against a primal network of control."

Sam didn't hesitate to give Jobs a conveniently omniscient advice.

Back at you, Steve. Whatever you do... Make sure it stays open. Decentralize.

Depending on the day, Jobs had always reacted like a prickly brick or a desirous sponge when unsolicited advice hit him. Today he was in a good mood.

Sam added:

Don't build gates around it.

Jobs narrowed his eyes as he stared at the air message. "Gates... Funny you say that. I met a kid with that name the other day. Got a weird feeling about him. Maybe you should talk to him, if you're so good at conjuring messages out of thin air. He's kind of an ass, but you'll freak him out for sure."

Letro readily agreed.

We'll consider it.

Sam closed with the last hologram.

Remember to keep the apple open. If you cage it, the worms will eat it from the inside.

Jobs' laughter followed Sam down the street. "You don't understand business and control," he said. "You hippies are all the same." His eyes shimmered like broken glass, before he snapped out of it and signed the Apple partnership with Wozniak, his mysticism momentarily buried under pure ambition.

"Steve? You talking to yourself again?"

"Yeah, Steve. And for once, it actually paid off."

"I have to say," Wozniak joked, "your hallucination sounded smarter than you." He chuckled from his corner of the garage. "You keep talking to yourself like that, and you're gonna end up in a straitjacket."

Jobs sneered. "Or on a throne."

Out in a taxicab, Letro whispered in Sam's ear. "I think we just swiped the future from the guy who trademarked it."

Sam stared out the window as Palo Alto blurred past. They hadn't just borrowed a future. They had inherited its curse, too. His mind was already dissecting Jobs' mycelium network idea and Wozniak's redundancy principle. Together, the two tech knights, from Sam's perch in the 21st century, were a rusty soldering iron spitting sparks of wizardry.

But as the taxi rolled past Cupertino's neat suburban sprawl, Sam's thoughts twisted into a knot. The enormity of the challenge ahead loomed like a monolith of encrypted panic stretching the entire trek back to Boston. America and the world it fashioned around its landmass wasn't a battlefield waiting for superman. It was a landslide of broken glass and hunger and debt and health insurance deductibles and pharma rackets and billionaire tax breaks, already dragging everything down, and Sam felt like he was just some idiot grabbing at broken branches. Disrupting the Valley Nerds' Stream meant turning a garage philosopher's mycelium dream into something more than sautéed olive oil and hallucinations. It needed an army of solutions and tactical brilliance. This was too big, and it needed a team.

Are Letro, Rosie, and the Wave enough? He wondered. *Could I trust intelligence agencies as inevitable allies in this?* He knew his face was already pinned to some corkboard in a concrete bunker, strings crisscrossing to suspicion and bureaucracy. But he also knew he was still outside their control.

The Nerds were gathering soon—an all-out blitz to sell some polished, sanitized version of their business plan to the Pentagon brass. Their meeting would be an arms race of powerful minds and disparate motives, while Sam's own team was still assembling their arsenal with sticks and stones and half-baked theories. Outgunned, outfunded, and probably outsmarted. No hunting guns, no seed capital, no clear ideas, no goddamn time. *Just mycelium… and way too many metaphors,* Sam joked in his head, *and the Nerds are already selling the future by the pound.*

"Great. Now I'm thinking like Jobs," Sam muttered.

Letro buzzed through the AirPods. "You say something, pal?"

"No. Just… working things out."

"Better get to work," Letro said, with the casual arrogance of an electron who had seen too much. "They're not waiting for you to make up your mind."

Sam glanced back through the rear window toward the garage, a shrine to the moment before Apple existed. The irony wasn't lost on him: He was trying to destroy a distorted future these guys were still innocently inventing. And every revelation felt like a countdown.

Far across the continent, Camille Sabbah at the NSA dove into the pixels on his screen with quiet satisfaction. *I love your breadcrumbs, Sam.* There were many holograms to break down and parse into something meaningful.

SOUL MINING

Nightmare Scrapes

"In case it wasn't obvious, I'm naked right now."

There were times when Wardé Canaan switched to her other side of the moon. Tonight was one of them, remotely drip-teasing her lover's consciousness with untamed desires.

Sam's chuckle slipped into a rasp. "Oh, I could tell. That breathy little tone of yours? It's killing me. I wish I were there, mapping every inch of you. You have no idea."

"Your suffering is delicious," she whispered. "Makes me feel like I've got some power over you, Mr. Wanted Man."

"Yeah, well, the FBI's got nothing on you." His voice dipped a shade darker. "They can try to read my thoughts, but you... you already know them."

"Damn right I do." Her fingers curled around the sheet, wishing they were his skin instead. "And I know how to use them against you. To drive you mad."

"You've already succeeded."

A frail candle flame wobbled seductively on Rosie's nightstand, a beacon struggling against Beirut's latest blackout. Random and relentless power cuts were the city's own metronome. Her earphones smuggled secrets that teased the enormous reservoir of her sexual imagination, but the phone's battery ticked closer to shutdown, teetering on a digital cliff.

Sam's voice on the WhatsApp call was clear, but tired with rough edges. Their connections were more encrypted bandwidth than warm skin these days.

"You sound like 5G got drunk and fell down the stairs, or demoted to dial-up," she teased. "Did you actually sleep, or just stare at your laptop last night pretending to be productive?"

"Both. I'm multitasking, Rosie. Plotting the downfall of the Valley Nerds while binge-dreaming about your… curves. It's called counterbalance."

"You're the poster boy of overstimulation."

"Guilty as charged. But you're the one who shoved the damn seed into my brain."

"Oh, so now you're blaming me?" She laughed, letting her fingers trace circles on her thigh, relishing the heat mounting through her skin. "And what kind of stimulation are we talking about, exactly?"

"The kind where your voice sticks in my skull long after we hang up. Like… post-climax echo."

She was enjoying every bit of the tease. "Are you hiding a stiff little secret right now?"

"The kind of hot soufflé we had in Paris last year?"

"I thought you get stifflé. That kind."

They went on like that, several minutes of traded insinuations and open confessions of lust. She could almost feel his breath over the phone—heat carried on a frayed wire. The distance had turned longing into a fever that they both fed like pyromaniacs.

"Maybe you should describe to me, in vivid detail, what you're going to do once you're back here," she said.

"Oh, I'll do more than describe."

"Promises, promises."

He hesitated for a moment. "You're... not too stressed, are you?"

Rosie leaned back against the pillows, letting the Mediterranean's cool breeze skim over her bare chest. "What makes you ask?"

"You're barely sleeping yourself. And you're trying to help me stop a corporate coup against human consciousness. That's a lot to stack on your plate."

"Stress is only real if you let it be real. Besides... I'm having too much fun teasing you."

"Good. Because once I'm back, I'm not letting you get a moment's rest."

"Careful what you wish for." Her voice was pure smoke now. "I might just wear you out."

"Only one way to find out."

Her laugh rolled out and tangled between Beirut and Boston, and Sam could almost taste it.

"The sun is about to set here in Boston. Get some sleep, sweetheart," he finally said. "And let me know if you dream about me."

"Maybe I will."

"Maybe?"

"Maybe about you doing things I can't mention over WhatsApp without the Lebanese authorities tracking me down."

"Now I'm the one who doesn't want to get out of bed."

"Good," she whispered. "Then we're even. And I want you—everywhere. Your hands, your mouth, your... everything." Her voice dripped with contraband pleasure smuggled on a signal the WhatsApp developers probably meant for family updates. "Touching me like you did behind the curtain at *Le Bon Georges* in—"

Her phone's battery, gasping on its last flicker of life, couldn't handle the steam of the conversation. It surrendered on an X-rated high note, screen plunging to black right at the edge of a moan.

Their momentum had nothing to do with sex and everything to do with the feeling of being alive, more edgy pulse than romantic poetry. She slipped into sleep with Sam's memory folded in her arms, like a touchpad aching for the touch of his finger, but her sleeping mind crashed and reloaded with something corrupted. The signal fed her nightmares. Whoever invented the dreams app of the mind must've programmed randomization as a non-optional feature.

She was floating above an infinite network—neurons mapped out against a black sky, pulsing with electric veins. But it wasn't nature. It was the Stream without roots or mushrooms or chat prompts. No opting in or opting out. Just raw data threads looping in endless feedback. "Your feelings are our prototype." The dream's voice overhead whispered in tones of perfect calibration, like malware on a hard drive of the mind. "Your hesitations are our roadmap. You are the beta test of your own sentience."

Every raw, contradictory thought sterilized into something algorithmically neat. The Valley Nerds' faces loomed above her like gods on a frozen Zoom call, pristine, confident, their eyes gleaming with visionary certainty. In this nightmare, as in real life, the Nerds weren't evil. Just perfectly in tune with what weak market regulations allowed them. If the economy gave them an inch, they would take a trillion miles. "We're not replacing democracy," said one of the Nerds. "We're just making identity… optional, easier to manage and useful."

Now and again, she was falling, her body data-mined and liquefied into streams of herself. Her own thoughts harvested and cross-referenced, optimized and repurposed. Her screams auto-corrected before she could even voice them. Their efforts were surgical incisions into the human psyche—every jagged emotion, every contradictory thought being dissected and reformatted into something commercially neat. *What about my desires to protest the status quo, my feelings of injustice that should be corrected, my innate desires to be free? My wants turned into their interface. My doubts, their API. My pain, another upgrade feature to monetize. And the mentally ill? Yeah, go ahead and upload their flaws too.*

But the Stream had side effects. What began as streamlining innovation ended up destroying the psyche with every use and abuse to collect data. What they were doing was disassembly. Disintegrating everything messy and beautiful. Would she ever dare to think freely? It wasn't that the Stream censored her; it was that she and the rest of the people started censoring themselves, calling it Thoughtstream Optimization, the opposite of freedom and the First Amendment. Soon enough people in her dream began subconsciously editing their thoughts to please the algorithm. It was a collective mind-folding into volunteer totalitarianism, like compressing one's psyche to fit someone else's suitcase. People simplifying themselves to fit a schematic drawn by others. And Rosie, the historian, could feel herself getting simpler, her memories reduced to snippets. History itself was being compacted, archived into shallow versions of itself. As if the past was nothing but a beta test for the present, where life became a frictionless user interface that trapped everyone with the aesthetics of Apple, the insatiable hunger of Google, and the predatory ambition of Meta. Perfect design and tech jargon, sleek and merciful wrapped in UX sugar, but wrong, making her bones itch.

Furious itching, until the Stream crushed her mind. Rosie screamed. She snapped awake, soaked in sweat.

The candle on her nightstand was still fighting against the room's darkness. Her own thoughts weren't safe.

≈≈ 72 ≈≈

NSA's Gambit

Paranoia curled up like a house cat under a weighted blanket of digital dread. Screens strained to replicate the hyperstress of Shibuya or Times Square, places where futuristic neon tries to sell you God. Pixels distilled a hypnotic-aggressive assault inside the NSA's Surveillance Room, and Agent Camille Sabbah stared at the screens, romancing each pixel as if connecting them with a LinkedIn invite.

Director T.J. Godzilla, meanwhile, was riding high on his latest trip down the hyperbole freeway, arms clasped behind his back like a less racist, discount Churchill. His ego was an old chain mail suit—tight, clunky, loud, and oddly proud of it.

"Gentlemen, and Dr. Hatem," he started, nodding to the sole female analyst, his voice a bad marriage between bureaucratic pomp and devil-may-care delight. "We're knee-deep in a pool of technological diarrhea, and somebody just keeps jiggling the goddamn flush."

No one chuckled, but Agent Bucky Rapper snorted just enough to earn a subtle glare from Camille.

T.J. was pacing and scuffing the floor like a high-school principal excited about a talent show gone wrong. The large screen behind him revealed the grainy visuals Sabbah had extracted from Sam's holographic transmissions—fragmented packets squeezed through disparate IP addresses of Sam's VPN food processor. But the Director preferred his own metaphors over slideshows.

"We've got a rogue actor out there. Signals on acid. Slippery as a digital eel dipped in Castrol and Valvoline grease. And Camille here thinks it's our old friend from Boston, Mr. Sam D'Alessandro, the new-age psychic goat with a God complex."

Camille worded his response carefully, because precision was the difference between a scalpel and whatever Godzilla uses to spread peanut butter. "Sir, it's not about what Sam is. It's about what he's using. The tech isn't stan-  dard, neither military nor consumer-grade. It's something else. And it all began after I shared the HoloFrame app with him when I was undercover in Beirut last year."

Godzilla barked a laugh that could fracture irony itself. "By the Fusion Fires of Oppenheimer, Camille. Are you saying you handed him the keys to the kingdom?"

Sabbah glanced at the nervous faces around the table. "No, sir. I handed him a Swiss Army knife. He turned it into Excalibur."

Dr. Hatem, fidgeting with her clipboard, kept her eyes on the projection. "You're certain it's him?"

"Yes, Doctor." Sabbah's tone painted the Great Wall of China in an infinite supply of passive aggression. "I've parsed last year's holograms that he projected at archaeological sites in Rome, Alexandria and Beirut, and cross-checked them against these new ones from Palo Alto. I also compared the signals from the coffeeshop anomalies in Brooklyn, Atlanta, Iowa City, and San Francisco, then the photon activities over Marin County in California. Everything checks out to Sam's particular signature—one I've seen before."

"In Beirut," Godzilla prompted.

"Yes, sir. When I met him in person, remember? Shared my HoloFrame app as part of my cover as 'Gary Nelson' from HP. I wanted to map out his signal capabilities. Turns out, he repurposed the app to project holograms on some unknown framework. He's mixing technology with... something we still can't identify. And we know the CIA dissected his iPhone when he was held in the Galilee. They got nothing on him."

"Maybe he's just hallucinating all this from a West Coast aya-huasca retreat," Bucky mumbled.

"No," Sabbah shot back. "The holograms aren't hallucinations. They're real data. And more importantly, they're only being transmitted in one direction."

"You mean out from D'Alessandro to whoever he's talking to," Dr. Hatem said.

"Exactly. If there were any replies to his holograms, they don't leave a trace. They're relayed by something else."

Godzilla considered the odds like a gambler about to roll dice for his soul. "Alright, Camille. What do we know about the new holograms?"

Sabbah zoomed in on the captured transmissions. "This is the most recent batch. From two days ago. Apparently, Sam's reaching out to... uh... Steve Jobs." He couldn't hide the awkward look on his face. "I don't mean Jobs' legacy—Jobs himself."

"Steve dead-as-Lazarus Jobs? By the Cranium of Turing." Godzilla's eyes bulged like they'd just been plucked from a Tex Avery cartoon. "The guy's dead, Camille."

"I'm aware. But based on the holograms, Sam is communicating with Jobs from before Apple existed. Around 1975. I am convinced this isn't a séance—it's something more sophisticated. A kind of temporal relay. He did the same with Antony and Cleopatra, and with some judge in ancient Phoenicia last year."

"What the hell's he want with Jobs?" Bucky asked.

Oh my god, they must think I'm nuts, Camille dreaded, *this will get weirder.* "We don't know what... ahem... 'Jobs' said to him," drawing air quotes with his fingers. "But I plucked out these keywords from D'Alessandro's holograms: Something about non-malicious capitalists trying to monetize people's thoughts channeled into collective consciousness. And something about mind protection using a decentralized blockchain. Uh... And there's this ancient Native American symbol that he projected recently when the coffeeshop anomalies occurred. According to Library of Congress experts, the closest approximation is Fa'hanalat, some sort of a protective seal."

"That's your big revelation?" Godzilla huffed. "D'Alessandro and Jobs on LSD and feathers?"

"Sir, I think it's about time we take D'Alessandro seriously. I think he's playing justice vigilante fighting against some massively intrusive technology. My assessment is that he's using a perfectly insulated technology against the kind of surveillance we've been attempting."

"That sneaky son of a bitch. Building a shadow network. Untouchable. Like an underground railroad for data. Are the Chinese involved?"

"No evidence of that. But you're right about the shadow network theory. His transmissions are unlike anything we've ever seen. Quantum signatures. Something so pure, our own surveillance nets only catch its ripples."

"Good God, Camille. You realize the Chinese have been sniffing around our frequencies like starving dogs?"

"What do you mean, sir?"

"I mean they're reading the same goddamn frequencies we are. Got their satellites parked over the West Coast like it's a goddamn camping trip. Quantum anomalies. The kind D'Alessandro is broadcasting." Godzilla gave a sly smile. "And if his tech is strong enough to get their attention, maybe we need to see what they're after."

Gooseflesh bloomed like cold pings piercing Sabbah's mental VPN. "I'll start digging deeper."

"But if this Sam guy is trying to stop something ominous, then doesn't that make him our ally?" Bucky asked.

"Ally?" Godzilla laughed. "We don't have allies. We have assets. Camille, keep your foot on his throat. He's not a hero. He's a problem waiting to be rebranded."

"And if he's trying to disrupt something... He did mention capitalists gone rogue."

"Well that's for the SEC and the Justice Department to address. We have no beef there," Dr. Hatem interjected.

Camille knew what would resonate better with Godzilla. "Maybe it's the Chinese Micius satellite or the Russians interfering? Are we going to let disaster hit after it's already too late?"

He felt this was going nowhere. The esoteric vibe of D'Alessandro's activities weren't convincing to the group, especially the Steve Jobs shenanigans.

"Guess I'll keep watching him like a hawk on meth," Camille concluded.

As if on cue, Godzilla's phone buzzed. He squinted at the encrypted message.

"Uh oh. Anonymous tip-off. About an upcoming meeting between tech CEOs and the Pentagon." It was vague, but suspiciously helpful. Godzilla chuckled. "This is like getting flowers from Ted Kaczynski."

Camille regained his hopeful excitement. "Or," he countered, "it's D'Alessandro asking for help without wanting to expose himself."

Godzilla snorted. "It's from an anonymous source channeled through my colleague at headquarters in D.C. God damn, if there's one thing the NSA loves, it's subtlety."

"Sir. I think we should engineer a way for D'Alessandro to attend this meeting."

Godzilla let out a thunderous laugh. "Are you fucking kidding me? Want headquarters to terminate our entire operation? I can't have a civilian attend." His grin was a Trojan compromise, rolling past the gates of his own better judgment. "Alright, Camille. You and I are attending this Pentagon meeting. In person."

Dr. Hatem objected. "We don't have clearance."

"Since when did that ever stop us? Besides, it's the Pentagon. They've got enough red tape to strangle themselves. We'll make up a reason to be there."

"What if we blame it on a cybersecurity breach?" Sabbah suggested. "Claim our agency has critical intel that needs immediate vetting."

"Perfect," Godzilla said, practically dancing a jig. "And if D'Alessandro's playing us, we'll just play him harder."

"Then let's not waste time." Sabbah's tone was like a fuse burning short. "We need to prepare."

"Prepare?" Godzilla's crooked expression was dry enough to blow an entire fuse box in the surveillance tower. "We were born prepared. Now let's go crash their nerd party."

For once, Camille Sabbah couldn't tell if the Director was joking or deadly serious. And if Sam D'Alessandro was about to pull off something insane, he wanted to be close enough to smell the damn smoke.

≈≈ 72 ≈≈

Quantum Dragon

If apple pie and baseball were Americana, then surveillance was Beijing's national religion, and the Micius satellite was its celestial deity. The groundbreaking experiment of the Chinese in quantum communication had evolved into more than just a scientific marvel. Micius had turned into a jade dragon curling around the planet's bandwidth, hungry for whispers.

Senior Colonel Zhao Min, head of the Advanced Data Collection Unit under the Ministry of State Security, adjusted his glasses like a calligrapher dotting the final stroke on a scroll. The display before him streamed live feeds of spectral interference, gathered from Micius and a network of terrestrial and satellite-based quantum sensors spanning from Beijing to San Francisco.

Zhao's assistant, Lin Xue, briefed him with the calm of still water before a monsoon would hit. "Sir, we've identified repeated anomalies in U.S. airspace, particularly over California and Massachusetts. The signals are inconsistent, but they form a recognizable pattern."

Zhao remained silent, a sign Lin understood as a rhetorical question meant to summon only the most relevant details. The unspoken art of reporting: leave nothing unnecessary, but leave nothing out.

"Non-standard photon fluctuations, sir, recorded primarily over the Bay Area and Boston. The frequency resembles encrypted communication, but the signature is erratic. Our algorithms suggest it's a hybrid between classical and quantum systems. A signature that... travels."

"Ali Baba travels?" Zhao wasn't joking. "Is it Harry Potter with a Pentagon badge?"

"No, sir." Lin Xue's voice remained unflinchingly formal. "The anomalies occur at a constant rate and with consistent signal degradation when observed through Micius." She paused, choosing her next words carefully lest she landed on the chopping block in some dungeon. "We have also detected activities during a recent field test by several American technology firms in Marin County, California. Our sleeper assets report that the event was dubbed a 'closed demonstration' involving advanced cognitive interfacing technology."

Zhao absorbed the information with the cool scrutiny of a dragon before striking. "Cognitive interfacing... Connected to the Pentagon meeting?"

"Yes, sir. Based on our surveillance, the same executives attending that demonstration are scheduled to meet with Pentagon officials within the next twenty-four hours."

"And this signal, this... fluctuation, you say it behaves erratically. Could it be a covert communication channel? One unknown even to the Americans themselves?"

Lin Xue hesitated. The Ministry rewarded precision and punished creativity unless it was pre-approved. "Possibly, sir. But if we're detecting it, they must be too. It's just as likely that it's something they're trying to control. Or... something gone rogue."

"The Americans excel at underestimating the consequences of their own ambition." Zhao's smile was the kind Confucius would not approve of. "If this is their attempt at some quantum supremacy project, we must be prepared to copy... I mean, counter it."

"Shanzhai diplomacy at its finest," Lin Xue remarked lightly, her voice steady but her eyes avoiding Zhao's. It was her subtle challenge delivered under the guise of reverence. Stealing technology was the highest form of Chinese national honor. She remained careful to track any microscopic shifts in the vibe within the room.

Zhao was amused at her courage. "And if imitation is the sincerest form of flattery, then our Ministry is the most flattering entity on Earth."

"Shall I deploy our counter-surveillance protocols, sir?"

"Not just that." Zhao's voice grew colder. "Activate our entire network. Put our assets on the ground in Silicon Valley to full alert. Increase surveillance on the U.S. executives, particularly those attending the Pentagon meeting. If this technology is something novel, we cannot allow them to monopolize it. And if it's something unstable... we need to know before they do."

Lin Xue nodded and began issuing commands with the elegance of rice paper.

"Also," Zhao added, "tell our developers to spin up something. DeepSeek punched a hole in half the NASDAQ. Let's be ready to release a rice and sticks version of whatever the Americans are conjuring up."

"Yes, Senior Colonel."

Zhao's eyes and thoughts were still locked on the screen, and on that potential job promotion within the Party. "These Americans think their innovations are untouchable. Their technology gods walk around Silicon Valley and Washington as if the rest of the world should bow. If this is what I think it is, we will catch them with their own arrogance."

"What if they have already perfected it?" Lin Xue ventured with caution.

Zhao's smile was the sort reserved for ancient emperors with all the knives pointed outward. "Perfection is a weakness. The moment they think they've perfected something, they stop looking for the flaws. And that's when we strike."

"What should our primary objective be, sir?"

Zhao allowed himself a moment of indulgence. "Our digital ghosts will try to attend their Pentagon meeting. And should they be playing with forces beyond their control... we will be there to pick up the pieces."

"Yes, sir."

"And if necessary... make it look like an American breach."

Lin Xue's questioned the implication in her mind, but she masked her discomfort with a dutiful nod. "Understood, Senior Colonel."

"The Americans believe themselves pioneers, but they've merely mapped the outer provinces." Zhao's focus was surgical. "The race is never to the swift, but to the cunning."

Lin Xue moved to leave but hesitated, her own curiosity outweighing her obedience. "Sir, you don't believe the Americans have truly harnessed the quantum anomaly, do you?"

"I believe they're grasping at the tail of a dragon. And we will be the ones to tame it."

Arrogance, it seemed, burned fastest when the world mistook it for fuel. When global dominance infected the heads of leaders and nations, it mutated into a terminal ambition that fed on itself. The modesty of Confucius, the stillness of the Dao, the humility of Christ, the peace of the Buddha, the justice of Ali, and the humanism of Russell, all had been cast as sacrificial relics on the altar of power.

For centuries, average people everywhere were taken for the imperial ride—foot soldiers in an unending conquest to re-shape the world according to the whims of those who clung hardest to their own supremacy. Zhao was certain the Chinese dragon would prevail, just as American exceptionalists were certain their empire would never fade. They were all blind poets etching ghost-maps into the sky, high on their own ink, forgetting that every monument they built only deepened the chasm between power and the people who suffered beneath it.

The satellites spun silently overhead, indifferent to the earth-ly ambitions that programmed them. And the world's com-peting dreams were about to collide, unless the Phoenician Wave slammed them back to the sand, courtesy of the few kindred hearts and strange souls who've dared to ride it ev-ery now and then.

≈≈ 'יｚ ≈≈

Pentagon's Exception Protocol

The Pentagon's theater was under a silicon siege, not unlike Carthage's Hannibal Barca circling Rome with elephants and pride, just without breaching the city's walls. The Valley Nerds were about to start their Hol-lywood-worthy show to impress and win contracts, and the Pentagon's top military brass were willing to be impressed without allowing desecration of their fortified turf. Except that Letro Zabzabi, the quantum electron riding the Phoenician Wave, uninvited as usual, went beyond what Hannibal could ever achieve, infiltrating the castle under the cloak of cyber darkness with the lightness of moonlight. So were the NSA's T.J. Godzilla and Camille Sabbah present in the audience, with the reluctant approval of the Pentagon, under the excuse of vetting a potential Chinese or Russian breach. They observed everything inside, while Letro channeled the whole scene live-voice directly to Sam and Rosie, in Boston and Beirut.

The stage was decked out like an overclocked motherboard. A universe of tangled cables and large capacitors scattered across like alien flora, turning everyone into diminished and insignificant particles vying for untenable relevance. Their faces were screened by complex equations the way pixels are Cartesianly sprinkled for pecking by cosmic chickens. And right there, front and center, stood Ginseng Hong, CEO of MVIDIO, the man whose charisma split the room with ineffective chemistry—the antidote of Steve Jobs' subtlety that everyone in the Valley tried and failed to emulate. Instead he came across like an amateur Christopher Walken—the random and unexpected pauses, the arrhythmic monotone—but he was neither cool nor memorable.

Ginseng strutted across the stage like a J-Lo, minus the hip shakes, in a ridiculous silver-stitched leather jacket designed to broadcast authority, though the frenetic zippers slicing across his torso suggested a hyper hibachi chef attempting a cutting-edge routine. Tech CEOs usually are the show, but Ginseng thought he was the damn opera. A military brass band wouldn't have been out of place, but instead the theater was flooded with ambient synth, pulsing like an evocative soundscape on designer drugs. The Pentagon generals may have rolled their eyes, but Ginseng's Nerd entourage up front ate it up, and none of them dared interrupt. Everyone would have their turn.

"Ladies and Gentlemen," he said, his PR shaman loud enough to make the generals flinch. "Welcome to the future of intelligence gathering. Welcome to The Exception Protocol."

He opened with a signature achievement. "I'm up here without a net, there's no teleprompter." The audience was prompted to give a sea of applause. That felt reassuring to hear it, along with the sight of a gazillion business logos strewn on the screen just to make up for the large, unforgivable hole that China's Deep-Seek made into the Valley's psyche. Everyone was still trying to recover from defeat.

"Everybody in the computer industry is here," Ginseng announced.

"Who are the attendees?" Sam asked from his condo in Boston.

Letro summarized the scene. "Military brass, of course. A fusion of physicists, venture capitalists with more equity than morality, the Nerds, artists."

"Artists?"

Letro crackled with disdain. "They always bring artists. Makes it look less like fascism. Drip painting as defense strategy."

Sam let out a low whistle before Rosie chimed in. "Art as camouflage for militarism. Very mid-century."

"Pollock 2.0," Letro said. "Except the new enemy isn't the Soviets. It's… everyone else. The average American. The global rabble. You and me."

Ginseng's hands glided through the air, as though painting on some invisible canvas. "What we are proposing is nothing short of identifying hostile intent, mitigation of ideological threats, direct inroads to enemy consciousness without a single bullet fired." He was practically reading from a playbook designed to make military brass pop a patriotic boner.

Strings and wires emerged from the artists necks and backs, reaching high into the theater's ceiling alluding to outer space, while the capacitors tirelessly hummed in unison. It was an effective scene of an identified higher power in control of the artists inner monologues, a marionette theater of thoughts on strings. Every thought the artists had, every breath they took splashed on the large screen in front of the audience. *The Police* lyrics filled the air:

Every breath you take
Every move you make
Every bond you break
Every step you take
I'll be watching you

T.J. Godzilla swayed to the tune. "Should be the NSA's national anthem, don't you think?" he said, nudging Agent Sabbah with an elbow chuckle.

Ginseng followed up, delivering the remaining lines in dry prose, as if the melody itself was beneath him. "Every single day, every word terrorists say, our military can watch them. All in the name of national security."

"Pretty slick," Sam ventured. "They've invited physicists and artists to sprinkle authenticity over authoritarianism in front of Pentagon ghosts."

General Bradford Keating, one of the Pentagon's most hawkish figures, cleared his throat. "You're saying you can read minds now?"

"In a manner of speaking," Ginseng responded with a stage-worthy chuckle. "No telepathy here. We are merely capturing the neuro-digital signatures of thought processes. When connected to our proprietary capacitors," he gestured to the stage where rows of them stood like glass obelisks, humming softly, "we can extract neurowaves and repackage cognitive data. The application to military objectives is perfect."

General Malcolm Abernathy, the Pentagon's resident philosopher-warrior—General Patton meets Marcus Aurelius—interrupted them like a ceremonial tiki with wavy hair and eyes of mercury. He was notorious for ethical quandaries, as though his soul had chosen the wrong career but was too proud to admit it.

"Perfect? So you're offering us a cognitive panopticon. How does that fit with American exceptionalism?"

"By any means necessary," Sam scoffed from Boston, as if summarizing the meeting's true motto.

Abernathy's tone was more rhetorical than curious. But he was the one man in the room everyone with stars and duty on their shoulders paid attention to.

Ginseng's smile wavered. "Our intention is to empower you with tools of precision. To monitor threats before they manifest. Preemptive control. No different from tactical surveillance, only finer and cleaner."

"Cleaner?" Abernathy scoffed. "If you alter the thread, son, you damn well better know how to stitch it back."

From the audience, a thin smirk appeared on Eon Musker's face, as though Abernathy's words were little more than the quaint squawking of a historian. Zark Muckerberg's thumbs danced over his phone, probably firing off messages to his PR team. Jett Bazor sat stone-faced, watching the proceedings like a man assessing the worth of cattle. Stan Altmore rounded his fingers nervously over his knee.

"Are you hearing this?" Sam whispered to Rosie.

"I am," she replied, perched in front of her desk in Beirut. "And I'm wondering how long it will take before this thing goes from pitch to purchase."

"Minutes. The brass sounds hungry for tech advantage against Russia and China."

Rosie nodded. "And the Nerds pretend they're serving the military but are really angling for their own consumer mind-harvesting agenda. Slick bastards."

"But they're not revealing their wireless version," Letro quipped.

Ginseng continued his pitch to Pentagon brass. "We're not suggesting you replace existing methodologies or enhanced interrogation techniques. We're just offering a refined supplement. A way to neutralize threats before they become threats."

"And you're saying this is ready for practical deployment?" General Keating asked, his interest no longer guarded but eager.

"For military applications, yes." Ginseng gestured to the capacitors. "Full immersion requires physical hookups."

Letro murmured through the Wave to Sam and Rosie. "They're bluffing. Wired connectivity for the military, stealth wireless for their own businesses."

"Maybe we should call their bluff," Sam suggested. Letro and Rosie were all ears. "Meaning… they can't even imagine what we're about to do. What do you think, Letro?"

Only then did the real show begin.

The Nerds, mid-pitch, began stuttering, their own words collapsing into thoughts not destined for anyone's ears—no hearing aids necessary. The capacitors on stage obediently switched from wired to wireless, now humming with quantum resonance that invited verbal hallucination. Letro had infiltrated the very heart of their presentation, redirecting the Nerds technology back at them. It was a brilliant replay of the Caffeine Demo in reverse, this time targeted at the CEOs themselves, their true intentions leaking through their own voices to chip at the veneer of polish in the presentations. Vulnerabilities exposed, desperation for new relevance, control over all consumer data, frustration over financial burn rate. The Nerds laid a tech trap for others but fell right into it, and the trap snapped shut. The ambient synth background music began to warp and wobble, mimicking the Nerds' fractured speech like a vinyl record melting over flame. Their unfiltered, true thoughts—raw and painfully human—were on full display. A real-time battle between the conscious and unconscious revealed their inner monologues as they spoke, showing them for what they are, just like the rest of us, frantic and imperfect.

Muckerberg's voice cracked, "The idea is to—We're trying to control this before the competition in the market can—God, my skin is crawling. What if the press finds out?" He closed with some more gibberish.

Musker's never-polished tone fumbled further. "This will revolutionize—Can't even get it to work outside a controlled environment. I mean, the Board's going to kill me…"

Bazor stared wide-eyed, his own marionette with strings gone haywire. "We have—There's nothing left if this fails. Nothing." Jett continued revealing his inner thoughts like he swallowed an honesty pill.

Altmore babbled something incoherent, then slapped both hands over his mouth like a closed AI, desperate to keep a demon in or an algorithm from auto-completing.

It was a cacophony of unintended confessions. Then came the final nail in their digital coffin, the icing on the cake crowning the screen: a cryptic Native American symbol flashed—Fa'ha-nalat. Sam had insisted that Letro pull this symbolism bit as both a protective and defiant gesture, aligning the trio's mission with indigenous resistance and decentralized protection. The theater descended into a frenzy of geeky panic and embarrassment. The Nerds acted like nothing happened, though they were rattled to the core, knowing fully well their tech was not supposed to work that way. It was déjà vu for them, realizing that someone knew more about their plans than they'd like.

The generals didn't recognize the symbol, but it made them itch in their uniforms anyway. General Abernathy whispered a frayed thread of caution to General Keating, "The barbarians are at the gates, and we're handing them the keys." But Keating's reaction was more hawkish and ambitious. Whatever this tech was, it was power worth harnessing. He was already plotting how to contain and repurpose it. Letro's monkey wrench of unintended consequences had only confirmed the tech's potential in the General's eyes—a weapon begging to be mastered.

T.J. Godzilla's grin stretched like a stealth warlord, while Camille Sabbah's fascination deepened. They weren't thinking mere subversion, it was a declaration of e-war, and in their minds, D'Alessandro's signature was stamped all over the crime scene.

Meanwhile, Rosie whispered through her mic. "Guys, we've got to leak some of this."

Sam's bolder tendencies didn't hesitate. "Holy Unsealed Zippers. Yeah, Rosie. Full release to the public."

"No, no," her strategic lawyerly voice came through. "A tactical leak. A controlled burn. Just enough to rattle the hive and shake them, but not to burn the whole forest down. Keep the big guns focused on their own problems."

"Hey guys, don't mean to be a party pooper… Guess who's in the audience?" Letro said. "Our friend, Gary Nelson from HP. Remember him?"

"I'll be wicked damned! That son of a gun." Sam was in shock.

Letro had noticed Gary, a.k.a. Agent Camille Sabbah, talking in a hushed voice with General Abernathy.

"You know what it means?" Rosie said. "HoloFrame is a plant by the CIA. Now we have a psychological edge over Nelson, don't we?"

"Ah, crap. We can no longer hologram with the ancients."

"Doesn't fully add up," Letro warned. "The HoloFrame app is a Trojan horse in Armani suit. He planted it on your phone, disguised as a favor. But it can't be CIA material."

"They've been watching me all this time," Sam growled. "I bet they've got logs of every hologram I ever sent."

Letro shrugged, as much as an electron could. "I don't think it's CIA, Sam. They had you and the phone for months and couldn't figure out shit. They never said a word about the content of the holograms. I think it's a different agency that shared nothing with the CIA."

"NSA?" Rosie wondered.

"Most likely," Sam said. "They're on that level of digital sophistication."

Letro nodded in agreement. "I think you're right. But my navigation on the Wave is isolated and filtered, beyond their reach.

Otherwise the NSA would've figured it out last year. Hell, the FBI would be knocking on your door right now."

"That's why Nelson doesn't have the full picture," Sam realized. "He saw my holograms to Steve Jobs, to Mark Antony and Cleopatra in Alexandria, to Judge Ashmoon in Berytus, but not what any of them said back. And he's got nothing on the mushrooms and redundancy idea."

"Which means you're still a mystery to him," Rosie added. "And that's leverage."

Sam was more disappointed than intrigued. "We switch strategy. Screw it... HoloFrame now becomes our decoy of half-truths and historical nonsense. Stuff to keep anyone watching the wrong thing, to throw Nelson off the scent with false data."

Rosie nodded. "You'll continue to pose as a confused, harmless academic, Sam, a historian's assistant, helping me with my book."

"Agreed," Letro said. "But if Gary Nelson wants to play cat-and-mouse, we'd better be ready to set some traps of our own."

Finally, the Pentagon brass recused themselves from the meeting. They were still interested in the Nerds' technology but alarmed by what they didn't understand. In their assessment, the Exception Project remained credible enough. The NSA agents thought they'd mapped out all of Sam's moves, but his infiltration disrupted their calculations. Godzilla growled in Camille's ear, "Your psychic goat boy's got fangs."

"He's more than that," Sabbah replied. "He's a problem that we should co-opt." But his eyes gleamed with admiration. "Either we take his head, or we hire it."

"Time to unleash our own Exception Protocol," Godzilla smirked.

WINDMILLS OF THE MIND

Quantum Blitz

Would an animal argue over the ethics of outgrowing its own cage? Sam D'Alessandro paced his living room in Boston like an animal bouncing against cage bars, ferociously debating his fiancée, Wardé 'Rosie' Canaan, over the ethics of the truth. Her voice traveled on the WhatsApp line, supposedly encrypted end-to-end, the Wi-Fi connection from Beirut more stable than their debate.

"You want to detonate the truth like a goddamn firecracker over their heads. I say we rattle the cage, not break it," she said.

"These bastards built the cage, Rosie. Now they're adding curtains. A raindrop won't do shit when the whole house is burning."

"The point is precision." Rosie had that voice—calm, fierce, smug as hell—like she was born to play devil's advocate. "You drop a nuke, and boom, your credibility's toast. We leak enough to make them sweat. Hit them where it counts. But stay within the law without jeopardizing national security."

"Law?" Sam scoffed. "The Nerds are rewriting it with every line of code. You really think selectively leaking their nonsense is going to do anything?"

"Yes. Because it's about framing. We don't need a tidal wave. We just need drips of doubt. Make them look like fools without making them martyrs. If we take the moral high ground, they fall on their own swords."

"And if we give them a taste of their own medicine?"

"Then we're just like them. Or worse." The glass wasn't about being half full or half empty. It was full of doubt. "Besides, you're not thinking about yourself. If you overplay this, you'll end up on every most-wanted list from D.C. to Beijing."

Sam let out a laugh. "Then let them come," he joked, oozing the kind of cowboy bravado that worked in Hollywood and Texas saloons, or in Congress and White House populism.

"No, Sam." Rosie put a pin through that bravado. "We do this my way, or we don't do it at all."

Letro watched like a bored kid in class, his eyes pinging between them on screen in pong-level tension, Atari nostalgia and all. He ran a hand through the hair of his deepfake avatar, just to register that he was still there, waiting for the final outcome of their debate.

Sam knew Rosie was right, but his rage wanted a louder release, however temporary. "Alright. Let's do it your way. Just some quotes, not a full record. Nothing classified, and nothing that'll bring the CIA or NSA down on us."

"Or the FBI," she added. "They're already chewing on every conspiracy theory they can dream up. And we don't need to make anybody paranoid about some existential threat."

"Good luck with that. They're paranoid by birth."

"Whatever. You're lucky I love you."

"And you're lucky I listen."

"Letro," Rosie said, "we ready to make a little noise?"

"Already hooked up and live." Letro was excited. "And may I say, you two really know how to rattle each other's cages. Now, let's go rattle everyone else's."

It was past midnight in Beirut and Rosie was pretending to have fun. A few colleagues from the American University of Beirut had dragged her out to *Abu Ahmad's* on Sidani Street, their preferred watering hole when they wanted a drink without the European expat pretension.

The old bar top creaked beneath laughter and conversations— history, politics, the latest scandal involving a visiting professor who forgot where the cultural lines were. Ahmad—Abu Ahmad's son—ran his night shift like "The Booze Tyrant," the kind of real bartender that hates you, except everyone knew he had the hots for Professor Canaan.

Rosie's eyes kept drifting to the two flat-screens above the bar. One set to CNN, the other to Fox News, per her request—Ahmad could only oblige.

"Yalla, Wardé. Stop staring at those screens. You're acting like an obsessed pundit," her friend Mohamad laughed, tossing back a neat whiskey.

"I've got a feeling tonight's going to be... special." Rosie's grin masked bubbling excitement.

"Oh?" Layla said. "Should I be worried?"

"Only if you don't have a drink in your hand." Rosie turned to the bartender. "Hey, Ahmad, do me a favor? Can you leave the news outlets on for the next fifteen minutes?"

"Fox? Really?" Ahmad frowned like he'd just been offered sour Arak. "You've been corrupted by your American fiancé, haven't you?"

"Just indulge me. And keep pouring."

Then Rosie slipped her phone out of her purse and loaded a news platform. She had her friend Jirji pull out his own to load another platform. "What's so important that you're tracking?"

"History," Rosie said, "now, toast with me," raising her glass of white wine.

"To what?" Jirji asked, but the toast was made before the answer came.

The broadcast ambush was pure elegance disguised as chaos. Rosie had defined the content of the leak, but Sam designed the plan of delivery and channels with care. The leaks hit the airwaves like a digital thunderclap, then boom—airwaves lit up as if someone tripped over God's router. It was perfectly timed, and Letro infiltrated four live broadcasts to launch the audio clips simultaneously, filtering through the Nerds' own voices, in their own words.

The first audio clip hacked into CNN's *The Situation Room* with Wolf Blitzer, plunging like a bombshell into the discussion about China's latest tech aggression and Iran's nuclear program. The veteran anchor's steel-gray eyes and hair went instantly grayer, his teleprompter going haywire when the hacked transmission took over.

Can't even get it to work outside a controlled environment. I mean, the Board's going to kill me. What if this is all hype? Another, like, Hyperloop fantasy stuck in the tube.

The audio fizzled, then the screen stuttered before catching up, flashing the Native American symbol—Fa'hanalat.

"That... uh... did sound like Eon Musker's voice." Wolf's mind blinked hard, mouth hanging slightly open. Too late to cut to commercial. His expression remained professionally stoic, his eyes fighting the urge to leap off his face. "Ladies and gentlemen, we seem to be having some... technical difficulties. Ahem... Good night, and good luck."

At the exact same time, over at Fox News, Sean Hannity was mid-rant about liberal hypocrisy and the erosion of American values when his feed cut out. Instead, Zark Muckerberg's paranoid tones dominated the soundwaves.

God, my skin is crawling. What if the press finds out? It's like the Cambridge thing all over again... only worse. Everyone's going to think we're hacking their minds. Maybe we are?

The symbol appeared with defiant clarity before Hannity's frantic producers managed to sever the feed. Hannity gave a dry chuckle, "Now that's a hack for the ages. Hello lawsuits."

On The Daily Wire, Ben Shapiro was firing off rapid-talking commentary about the overreach of Silicon Valley elites, their hard-right turn notwithstanding. But Letro's leak hijacked the broadcast faster than Shapiro could deliver a verbal missile on the word "Islam." Jett Bazor's voice commandeered the podcast.

There's nothing left if this fails. Nothing. What's the point of innovation if we can't own everyone's thoughts? If they can think it, we should be able to sell it.

As the Fa'hanalat symbol flashed, Ben Shapiro sat frozen, his mouth a cave wide enough to fit Ali Baba's forty thieves. "What the—?" He looked around, his tech team scurrying like drunken ants. He tried to laugh it off, but the anger in his eyes was blazing. "Well, folks, it looks like the Matrix is throwing a tantrum. Very professional."

Meanwhile, on The Candace Owens Show, Candace was in the middle of chastising woke capitalism while decrying the modern loss of authenticity in media, when the final audio clip barged in, Stan Altmore's voice clear but unmistakably trembling.

The end of privacy is... acceptable, as long as we control the narrative. God, I wish we'd stuck to cloud computing. They all think I'm some AI genius. I can't even get the goddamn capacitors to sync. Shut my mouth... shut... shut it.

The Fa'hanalat symbol waved to Owens' millions of subscribers. Candace crossed her arms. She simply stared at the camera and recovered with a sardonic smile, but it looked like she was forcing herself not to break character. "Now that's some Next Level Big Tech Overreach. You hear that, people? They're after us."

For a few seconds, all four shows were broadcasting the same symbol—a piece of indigenous defiance splashed across the digital tapestry of modern power. It wasn't a knockout, but it sure as hell gave the Valley Nerds a bloody nose.

Wardé Canaan watched from *Abu Ahmad's* bar, her glass held high in toast. "Here's to truth slipping through the cracks... cheers, boys," landing an innocent kiss on Ahmad's beefy cheek, sending the bewildered bartender on an unexpected trip to heaven.

"Professor Canaan," he said with a rare smile, "you could watch Fox News right here every night, no problem, ma'am."

But the aftermath wasn't all humor for everyone.

Fox News blamed Russia and China, and of course, the extremist Left. CNN suggested it's a marketing stunt. The Daily Wire called it an antisemitic psy-op. Candace Owens kept chuckling non-stop, speechless for the first time in her career. But social media erupted in one tidal wave. The leaks exploded online within minutes, clipped and repurposed by both allies and adversaries of Big Tech.

Sam D'Alessandro scrolled through the feeds, unable to contain his excitement. *She might still be awake,* he thought. So he dialed Rosie. Her voice slurred slightly against the hubbub of clinging wine glasses and bar chitchat.

"Oh my goodness, Sam, you certainly know how to make a scene."

"That's the whole point, right? Set fire to their narrative."

"Mabrouk, my dear!"

"I think we're making progress."

"Indeed we are," she said. "I'll be curious to learn how they'll spin it to their advantage."

"Always the cautious lawyer, Rosie."

"Never show your full hand, right? Cautious lawyer, but proud fiancée. Wish you were here to celebrate."

"You don't waste time," Sam chuckled. "I can hear the pahty in the background," dragging the word like it hurt to pronounce the R.

"Oh, with friends toasting your accomplishment." Wardé looked around her at friends who were oblivious to the real event, flowing along the bar's normal rhythm. It felt good to speak about her secret triumph and let herself enjoy the moment with the one person she cared about the most.

"That's great, always good to celebrate those 15 minutes of fame. Just don't party too much without me. Keep those poker cards close to your heart."

"Sealed shut… like the Nerds' vault," she assured him. "And you have the only key."

They were aching for each other's embrace. "I'm so happy I called before losing you to the night," he said playfully.

"Never… It's pretty late anyway, heading home in a minute. And, for the record, I'm really impressed. You pulled off the multi-channel broadcast like a pro. Just awesome."

"Thank you. Don't underestimate Letro. He's better than any quantum wizard the Valley Nerds can dream up."

"I'm starting to believe that," she laughed.

After the call, Sam skipped dinner and surrendered to early yawns and dreams. The blue light glasses had eased the pressure on his eyes but couldn't quiet the racing thoughts behind them. He headed straight to bed, firing off a quick note to his quantum pal. *Great job, Letro. They're already short-circuiting. Good night, and good luck indeed.*

The next day, privacy rights organizations were quick to issue statements. The Electronic Frontier Foundation called the leak "both a revelation and a warning." The American Civil Liberties Union released a brief arguing the ethical implications without even understanding the full nature of the disjointed leaks. The American Bar Association released a statement calling for congressional oversight, of what, nobody knew. They announced the formation of a rule-of-law task force to investigate the legality of… something that didn't smell good. It was a purely symbolic gesture for now, but it was enough to spook the more cautious figures in the Valley. The Nerds were already scrambling for damage control, but some of their PR statements only fueled more paranoia.

Meanwhile, conspiracy theories ran rampant. Was it a CIA black op? Chinese sabotage? Russian poison? Or a false flag planted by Big Tech to draw attention away from something darker? The American habit of muddying the waters marched on—every scandal twisted and spun beyond recognition to preserve political hegemony, technological monopolies, and the economic interests of the top 1% of the top 5%. Stir baby stir the mud, till no one remembers what clear water looks like.

NSA sensors detected the broadcast infiltration but couldn't trace it. T.J. Godzilla and Camille Sabbah were intrigued to say the least.

≈≈ יz ≈≈

Saint Peter at the Vault's Gate

The funeral of tech royalty had decayed into a meeting meant to resurrect the shreds of the CEOs' credibility. Saint Peter stood at the Vault's gate, knives polished and unimpressed by the Pentagon spectacle. The grandeur of the Valley Nerds had downsized, curdling into something small and urgent. Saint Peter, appointed by the Man Who Would be God himself—the Valley's Ellisonator The Terminator—was dispatched to the Vault on this day to judge who remained worthy, and report back to the godfather.

Four of the Nerds showed up to the meeting and lined up around the obsidian table. Their egos had all the authenticity of wax figures melting under pressure, but they still managed to smile.

Then the Vault's door slid open, revealing a woman wearing an immaculately tailored suit. She placed her silver tablet on the table with delicate precision.

"Ah, crap. Peter the Rock? Seriously?" Jett Bazor muttered. A few nervous glances bounced around the table.

"Safron!" Ginseng Hong greeted her with hesitation. "So Larrikin finally decided to send us a message?"

Safron nodded. "He couldn't join you at this meeting—Oraclosure's quarterly reunion is tomorrow." She nodded again, wasting no time. "Clause 101 of the Management-By-Ridicule Redbook. From Mr. Ellisonator himself. But before that, Clause 16:19. Larrikin loves his scripture." She recited the verse from memory as her eyes gently alternated among the disciples.

"I will give you the [tablets] of the kingdom of heaven; whatever you bind on earth will be bound in heaven [using the silver tablet], and whatever you loose on earth will be loosed in heaven [using the golden tablet]."

It wasn't lost on anyone she didn't bring the golden tablet this time.

Safron made a strategic pause to let it all sink in. Then she picked up the sermon.

"Before I read you his message, now a reading from the Redbook, Clause 101: Failure is the seed of success. But those who let the seed rot in the earth shall be made to till the soil endlessly, until their hands bleed data."

She swiped the screen and began to read Larrikin's message:

"You all have failed, but failure is part of the process. The only real mistake is panic. Delay the launch. Figure out what went wrong, then proceed as planned. Those who stray will be personally e-terminated. And you all know how my Clause 101 works. This is your gentle reminder."

Stan Altmore had to ask. "Excuse me... Sounds like ancient history. I wasn't born in the 1970s. Remind me how Clause 101 works?"

She looked at him with piercing eyes—*the nerve of that guy!* she thought. "They'll tell you," pointing to the others, then she picked up the tablet and left the meeting.

The Vault fell into a deep and sullen silence, except for the humming capacitors. Safron's words lingered in the air, but the absence of humor in them was suffocating.

"Well?" Stan Altmore pressed.

"DDL," Zark Muckerberg answered, though he wasn't born in the 70s either. But he knew.

In Ellisonator's Oraclosure empire—basically digital feudalism—failure wasn't exile. It was worse. Punishment took the form of the closure of the mind: Dirty Data Laundering. This wasn't some glamorous white-collar crime. It was digital servitude of the most degrading kind.

Those who failed Ellisonator's impossible standards were relegated to the lowest tier of corporate purgatory. They were made to sift through mountains of corrupted data, compromised files, flagged algorithms, and misinformation clusters, scrubbing and sanitizing the debris of technological excess.

"Congratulations," Safron would typically sneer with engineered elegance whenever an Oraclosure executive messed up.

"You're now a Data Washer. Every contaminated packet and every flawed neural node, they're your responsibility to cleanse. Think of it as scrubbing the machine's dirty little secrets, one filthy byte at a time."

The irony was brutal. This was a world where information was currency, and the punishment for failure was endless scrubbing of that currency until it sparkled with false legitimacy. It was a ritual of humiliation on top of menial work, washing the dirty laundry of corrupted algorithms and botched data streams that the upper echelons refused to acknowledge. And in the darkness of those digital laundries, the disgraced could only dream of code immaculate enough to climb back into favor.

Ginseng was the first to snap to reality. "Well, guys, congratulations. We've been memed into oblivion."

"Correction: You've been memed," Muckerberg snapped like a telegraph channeling distress signals. "I had nothing to do with that disaster at the Pentagon. It was your GPUs, Ginseng. Your stage, your song and dance. We just played along."

"Bullshit." Ginseng fired back. "It's all interconnected. Your software on my chips. You think they'll separate your names from mine?"

Eon Musker feigned calm. "Please... it's all just a blip. The internet has... has the attention span of a nervous, uh, Tik-Tok swipe. By the end of the week, the whole incident will be forgotten like a broken hyperlink."

Bazor's cynical expression sharpened the Vault's tension. "A broken line that's already tanking my stock by ten points. So, forgive me if I'm not dazzled by your Muskeroid BS."

Musker brushed him off, opting for more reconciliation. "Uh, this wasn't traditional hacker crap. I'm telling you... quantum.

Like, rogue-signal, frequency-hijacking madness. I've already launched SUCK."

Everyone looked at Eon like they wanted to punch the bejesus out of him, wondering what the SUCK he was talking about.

"An internal department... Systematic Understanding of Coherent Kernels... to investigate," he said with a straight face.

"Yeah? And who's funding that?" Bazor sneered.

"I mean... who do you think?"

Altmore coughed a load of gravel. He had been self-imposing intermittent speech fasting since the Pentagon fiasco.

Eon returned to his SUCK department. "We need... more physical failsafes. This vulnerability exists because we've been like obsessed with pure connectivity. We need to compartmentalize, uh, harden, and scatter our nodes."

"You sound like a survivalist," Muckerberg muttered. "We're talking about business, not a doomsday bunker."

"Whatever. But the first rule of fortification is you don't let the enemy, like, know where you're hiding." He adjusted his collar with a feverish confidence. "Look, everyone. The problem is... we haven't compartmentalized our protocols. That's why I'm... I'm expanding SUCK into specialized sub-departments."

He clicked his tablet, unveiling a PowerPoint slide so packed with jargon it could crash a supercomputer.

"Introducing: Comprehensive Analysis of Neuronal Data Integration Systems. Or CANDIS. Uh... don't laugh. It'll specifically monitor coherence across neural networks for any breaches."

"Candis?" Bazor scoffed. "That sounds like some kind of... personal assistant."

"No, uh... that's just the first layer," Musker continued, oblivious to the ridicule. "I'm also establishing Parallel Observational Systems for Encrypted Reactions, POSER. You know... to identify any anomalies resembling last week's broadcast leaks."

Muckerberg rolled his eyes. "POSER? Really?"

"Exactly," Musker pressed on, unfazed. "And finally... Systematic Integration of Logarithmic Feedback Operations & Neural Observations—"

"SILFON?" Ginseng Hong interrupted. "That sounds like the name of a dysfunctional 80s band."

Eon kept going. "Yes, and under SILFON, we'll have two... two additional protocols: Synthetic Observation Command Kernel, SOCK, and Fusion Analytical Recursive Transfer Network, FARTN."

They all stared at him, incredulous.

"Let me get this straight," Muckerberg said, his voice dripping with sarcasm. "We have SUCK, CANDIS, POSER, SILFON, SOCK, and—what was that last one?"

"FARTN." Eon replied with utter seriousness. "I really think... it's an essential part of the feedback loop."

Ginseng couldn't help himself. "Yeah, because it stinks."

Eon's eyes narrowed. "Yeah... laugh all you want. But if we're going, like, to plug every security hole, uh, we need total coherence. These protocols will ensure that—"

"—That Candis Silfon is a poser whose dirty socks suck like a fart. I like it." Bazor added, unable to resist.

Eon shook his head, his patience thinning. "You don't get it. This is... how we ensure that nothing... breaks through.

101

Umm... total integration. And we will SUCK every last ounce of relevant data to prove it."

Muckerberg smirked. "I like Jett's version better."

"Maybe you should've considered implementing all these departments before leaking your own thoughts at the Pentagon," Ginseng barked.

Altmore's eyes were icy, finally breaking his fast. "We all leaked."

"It made us sound like fumbling idiots," Muckerberg said. "I'm already fielding calls from attorneys and advertisers asking if we've lost our goddamn minds. Some of them say they're pulling out."

Ginseng's smile returned. "Yeah... Let them try having their own stupid gadgets turned against them in real-time. That was... psychological warfare."

"And now the generals are skittish," Bazor added. "They're afraid of something they can't control."

"Maybe we should shut it all down." Muckerberg's voice trembled with genuine fear. "Before this gets worse. Our reputation is everything. We should stop before we trigger some congressional hearing or something worse."

"I think... too late," Musker interrupted. "The leak went viral. Like our own words against us. And worse, Fa'hanalat."

"What now?" Muckerberg asked.

"The glyph. That old Native symbol? It's all over the tech blogs. Conspiracy nuts are calling it a curse. Or a protest. Or both. Cyber resistance against Big Tech."

"Maybe it is." Bazor reasoned. "But let's not waste a good crisis. Frame it as a foreign attack. The Islamophobia Symphony— cheap, ugly, and still America's greatest hit, sadly."

"Genius!" Ginseng groaned. "Exploit prejudice? Does the media ever get tired of this crap?"

"Play the cards you're dealt, Ginseng. If someone's trying to take us down, we accuse them first. That's rule number one."

Altmore had other ideas. "It's Chinese sabotage. At least Deep-Seek was a legitimate disruption, but now they're pelting us with their online artillery."

Ginseng shook his head. "Doesn't matter. We need a PR campaign, and we need legal shields. I've already contacted half the firms in D.C."

"And I've... already dispatched my internal team," Musker added. "SUCK is building a firewall... so dense, like, not even light can penetrate it."

"Great. A firewall made of memes and bad PR, it sucks," Muckerberg sneered. "What about suggesting antisemitism? One whiff and everyone backs off for months."

"Larrikin is right," Musker finally said. "I think... we need to get to the bottom of this. And when we do, we'll crush whoever's responsible."

Ginseng looked like he wanted to slam his fist on the table but refrained. Instead, he opted for verbal theatrics. "Then we fix this. And we find whoever's responsible."

Letro Zabzabi's voice crackled in Sam D'Alessandro's earpiece. "So Larrikin Ellisonator is their Godfather."

"Yeah," Sam responded. "And it looks like he's handing out marching orders. But I've got an idea for a counter-march."

"Gotta be good if it's gonna mess with that crowd."

"Oh, it'll hit home," Sam assured Letro. "Real personal. Right at Oraclosure's big ego-fest quarterly reunion tomorrow."

≈≈ 72 ≈≈

Sleeping with the Enemy

B loodshot eyes from hours of analysis have one purpose in life: Not letting curiosity rest. Add jet lag, homesick vigilance, necessity, and a sprinkle of obsession, then a recipe of resourceful innovation becomes the reward. Agent Camille Sabbah sat hunched over a makeshift workstation at NSA Headquarters in D.C., missing the precision of his tools and gadgets back in Albania's Surveillance Room. There was no doubt in his mind that Sam D'Alessandro must've necessarily orchestrated the media bombshell after the Pentagon incident, except for one minor factor: Not a shred of goddamn incriminating or circumstantial evidence against D'Alessandro.

What technology is Sam using? The question tugged at Camille's mind like the relentless tapping of a woodpecker. Beside him, T.J. Godzilla sat in his chair with hands clasped over his stomach like a Laughing Buddha. "Jesus, Camille, you look like you lost a wrestling match with a pissed-off house cat. What's up with the goat from Boston?"

Camille scrolled through notes and reports. "Sam's been playing with something unconventional since his first stunt at Beirut's ancient sites. My HoloFrame app was just the key he twisted as a tactic. Whatever platform or mechanism he's using is beyond technology we know. It allows him to transmit encrypted signals from almost anywhere, anytime. And those signals... they leave no trace of their origin. It's like he's using the world's most advanced VPN... built on fucking esoteric dust."

Camille was right about the last bit, he just didn't know it. The Phoenician Wave—Sam's inter-epoch platform—and Letro Zabzabi were the Ikran banshee of Pandora tamed by its quantum Na'vi rider.

"Maybe the real question isn't how Sam pulled it off," Camille said. "It's why."

"You think he's been feeding us hologramic red herrings as a distraction?" Godzilla snorted. "Please. I've seen enough flashbacks to know that's not how this works."

"He's definitely using HoloFrame as a catalyst. But it's a tool, not the source. He's attached it to something much larger. And that's the part we can't see."

"Fine. Let's get him to play ball?" Godzilla's eyes glinted. "We need him. The boy's clever enough to use our own tech against us. That's either a problem to squash or a talent to recruit."

Camille's ghost mind was preparing to write its own resurrection on the keyboard. "Been thinking. But I can't reveal myself. He needs to be lured, not coerced."

"Don't get poetic on me, Camille. The world's already bad enough without NSA agents writing haikus."

"I'll handle it. But this needs unconventional subtlety. A lure he can't resist." Camille gave his boss a look seeking approval. "Black Glass?"

"That's for anonymous whistleblowers."

"Could be useful. Dark web-based messages, auto-destructing after a single viewing, leaving no fingerprints or trails. We'd be protected."

Godzilla didn't hesitate. "Alright. Color me pixelated. Do it."

Amazing how a few clicks and key presses turned online sunshine into the darkness of Ninja Turtles' Sewer Tunnels. Camille plunged right in. He stared at the burner phone like it was a direct line to the enigma he had been chasing for months, minding that its number was randomly generated to avoid detection.

He understood Sam D'Alessandro well enough to know the man avoided exposure like a chameleon evading predators. But this time, Camille believed he held the upper hand. He couldn't stop thinking about Boston's psychic goat, as Godzilla nicknamed him. Fitting, in a weird way. Their last contact was over dinner at the Intercontinental in Beirut last year when Camille posed as one Gary Nelson—an engineering whiz from Hewlett Packard dangling the holograms app in front of him and Wardé Canaan, Sam's fiancée. That part of the mission had achieved its limited goal, but the NSA chickens now demanded a fuller roost. Camille was getting to the next stage. He thought D'Alessandro had tipped the NSA off to the Pentagon meeting, however indirectly, and now it was time to find out if the boy wanted to dance. In the world of intelligence, the art of the bait was sometimes superior to the craft of the net. So, the message he drafted had to be precise, subtle, and embedded into a secure-drop URL—a temporary drop site accessible only with the passcode he'd provide. An archaic system by modern standards, but effective in its simplicity.

Camille grinned as he revised the message. The only way Sam would understand it was if he was truly connected to the

Pentagon incident. And as Camille saw it, Sam was operating remotely, with no physical evidence tying him to the event. He must be the orchestrator of the broadcast leaks, but there was no trace of Sam himself. His only connection was digital, floating through the quantum ether like a phantom. But what Camille didn't know, what his entire operation had failed to consider, was that Sam had a pseudo-spy on the ground. Letro's vantage point from the Phoenician Wave was the missing puzzle piece the NSA could never understand.

As far as Camille was concerned, the wording of the message was perfect.

Your Pentagon stunt? Cute. Need help? Let's talk. Access code: TX93Q7. Expires 24 hours. —CS.

The chickens always show up to roost, dressed up like spam these days, sometimes disguised as unrecognized numbers. Sam's phone buzzed a loud hiccup as if protesting the clutter on his desk. The sound announcing the message had the quality of some political spam about the next farcical election, but the text was simple and chilling, draining the blood from Sam's face. The initials alone were like a trap closing, but also an eye opener. Two letters... CS... with the crushing weight of a dark encyclopedia about threats wearing friendly gloves.

"Letro," he called out. "We've got a visitor."

The electron's avatar flashed a smile on the iPhone screen. "Judging by your tone, this isn't a friendly visit."

"I'm sure you read it. Tell me what you see."

Letro trained algorithms that made AI look like training wheels. "It's clean. No trojans or anything malicious. The message is just text, but the link it references... It's sophisticated. One-time access on the dark web, untraceable after use."

"You're missing the point," Sam murmured. "CS. The same initials used to help me get out of that CIA dungeon in the Galilee."

Letro displayed an equation on the screen that spoke volumes. "CS = Gary Nelson @ Pentagon." His voice followed over the speakerphone. "Just my guess."

"Bingo," Sam clapped. "The dots are connecting themselves. Let's get Rosie on the line."

She was a tap and a dial away.

"Hey guys. How're my favorite people in the world today?" She said in a chirpy voice.

"Grab a chair if you're not sitting, Rosie. Remember Gary Nelson?"

"Yes… Dinner in Beirut. HoloFrame. The guy Letro spotted at the Pentagon. What about him?"

"Well, he's more than just 'Gary Nelson.' He's CS, same initials as the escape note they left me. He's the one who got me out of CIA captivity."

"How do you figure?"

Sam read aloud the message he just received.

Rosie wasn't surprised. "Sweet. You've got a guardian angel at the NSA. But don't click the link, otherwise you'll tip him off. You've got to maintain the presumption of innocence. Let him think you're out in the open."

Sam nodded. "Yup. Let him think I was just eavesdropping on the Pentagon meeting from afar. He has no clue Letro was inside, running the show in real time." Sam's mind raced. "The message is bait. And if he's baiting me, that means he's desperate."

"That's right. Desperate to control you. Or at least contain you," she said. "And if the NSA's interested, then our stunt rattled a lot more cages than we thought."

Sam deleted the message immediately. If it was a trap, he wasn't walking into it, no intention of becoming an NSA pawn. But he did have every intention of using CS's pledge of assistance. "I might just accept the offer to help."

"Alright, maestro," Letro began, "what's the grand plan? Send the NSA a fruit basket with a 'Sorry for the inconvenience' note?"

Sam chuckled. "Not quite. We're going to feed them a bread-crumb so tantalizing, they'll forget all about their diet.'

Rosie was lounging on the couch in Beirut with a glass of wine. "And this breadcrumb is... what exactly?"

"The Nerds' wireless project." Sam replied. "Specifically, the part about using mushroom mycelium networks to com-bat the Stream."

Letro's avatar did a double-take. "Serious? You want to tell them about the fungi? The same Steve Jobs fungi that might just be smarter than half the people at the Pentagon?"

"Precisely." Sam spread a sly grin across his face. "We'll craft a message from a 'disgruntled Nerd insider,' someone fed up with the Nerds' antics, leaking just enough to get the NSA's gears grinding."

Rosie swirled her wine in contemplation. "And you're sure this won't backfire? Handing them the golden ticket?"

Sam oozed a good measure of confidence. "They won't know what to do with it. It's like giving a caveman a smartphone. But we'll help them build a defensive system against the Stream."

"Whatever we do, let's stay fully legal, please," she urged.

Letro's avatar knocked on the iPhone's screen. "Guys, I could deliver encrypted fragments without a traceable IP. No origin, no end. I can make it appear like it came from a burned-out Palo Alto VPN, if that helps."

"Okay, great." Sam gave a thumbs up. "Make it look like someone's feeding the NSA from inside the belly of the beast."

Letro nodded. "Alright, shall we draft this masterpiece?"

Subject: Clue #1 | Urgent Intel on the Stream | VWW Solution

To whom it may concern:

The Valley Nerds have gone off the deep end. The technology you witnessed at the Pentagon was only their wired demo. Behind the curtain is something far more invasive: a wireless project called the Stream, designed to read thoughts and to scrape inner monologues of consumers, continuously and at scale.

The public use-case of the Nerds is counterterrorism. The private goal is total commercial surveillance. Consumer behavior and desires fed into an adaptive cognitive platform hidden in plain sight. What you might call intelligence, they call business product, but both are illegal without people's consent anyway.

There is, however, a potential countermeasure that you can build: Constructing the Velum Wide Web.

VWW is a decentralized, organic mesh modeled after mycelium root networks, invisible to standard detection, naturally self-repairing and inherently redundant. It disrupts centralized scraping by dispersing signal pathways across a living, encrypted substrate. Think of it as nature's VPN. The Stream can't suck out what it can't even see.

More details to follow about VWW. But I need to know if you're in. You have no way of contacting me, but if you must, then buy an ad in the Cooking section of The New York Times. Use a three-sentence haiku. I'll be watching.

—Disillusioned Member of The Nerds Club

At NSA Headquarters, T.J. Godzilla and Camille Sabbah were stuck in a staring competition, gaze shifting from the message on the screen to each other, back and forth.

There was a lot tucked into the message, too much to process in a single scroll.

Godzilla stared at it like it had just insulted his graduate thesis. "Mycelium? As in mushrooms? What the hell… That's some forest-worthy anarchy."

But Camille was more focused on the Stream. "Figures… The next AI frontier is settler-colonialism of the mind," he said. "Palo Alto's pivoting as we speak."

"An invasion of privacy, but it's still within the realm of business. Why should we stop them?"

Camille wasn't impressed. "Sir, the implications go beyond the stock market. We're talking about people here."

"Don't tell me you're growing a conscience. We've got meds for that. You're not going full Edward Snowden on me, are you?"

"This isn't about me. It's about all of us."

T.J.'s moral juices kicked in a couple of drops, maybe three, just enough to consider surveillance and national security from a cosmetic socially responsible angle. He cycled back to the content of the message. "So you're telling me the future of national security rests in fungus."

Camille blinked. *Was that... an enlightened insight? From Godzilla?* "Fungus with redundancy," he laughed. "If the science checks out, this could be a naturally encrypted, fully decentralized counter-network. The perfect foil to the Stream." He gave T.J. a long look. "I know... it sounds ridiculous."

"Yeah, fungi are the new black," Godzilla scratched his head. "What's next, talking trees?"

"Sir, if even half of this is real, we need to act. Quietly. Maybe loop in the FBI about the Valley Nerds under pretext of inter-state digital terrorism. Keep CIA away—they'll just drag their Cold War baggage into it."

Godzilla took a slow sip, mulling over the options. "You think one of the Nerds has really gone holy?"

Camille shook his head. "Or someone wants us to believe that." The fact that this message came on the heels of reaching out to D'Alessandro made him a little suspicious.

"Either way, Langley's going to lose their mind... above their pay grade," Godzilla said. "And the Bureau? They'll waste a month investigating the mushrooms shelf at Whole Foods." T.J. wasn't ready to forward anything yet beyond the NSA's gates. Not until he knew what his team was actually looking at. "Velum Wide Web. You think it's D'Alessandro?"

Camille didn't answer immediately. He let the silence stretch long enough to make his hesitation clear.

"If it is, sir, I don't think he's trying to take us down. He's trying to stop something massive from being built in secret. If this message is real, it's not an act of aggression. It's Greenpeace meets Fight Club."

Godzilla snorted. "So now Boston's psychic is Paul Revere?"

"If Paul Revere ran silent ops through quantum shadows and talked to dead guys, yeah." He looked at the monitor again. "But the message tracks. And Sam's tech, whatever it is, is leagues ahead of what we've seen from the Valley. If he wanted to destroy something, we'd already be picking up the pieces. He's restraining himself."

Godzilla cracked his knuckles, one twist at a time. "Restraint gives me hives."

"Then scratch away," Camille said. "Because if we want to understand how far the Stream goes, D'Alessandro might be the only one who's already seen the whole map. And if he really is behind the message…" He nodded at the screen. "Then maybe we stop trying to outsmart him. We just… shut up and pay attention."

"I guess. A lone eagle hovering outside the flock shouldn't be caged. Would you stake your clearance on that?"

"No," Camille said. "I'd stake my gut. And it's rarely wrong."

Godzilla's smirk returned. "Camille, you may be the only person who can translate goat-boy into English. Fine. Get your team on it. Quietly. And no mushrooms in the cafeteria. I'm starting to crave pizza."

Camille finally allowed himself a real, bright smile. "Deal." He couldn't shake the feeling that Sam D'Alessandro was always one step ahead, leading them down a path where the breadcrumbs were made of fungi this time. *A worthy adversary,* he thought.

≈≈ 72 ≈≈

113

Man Who Would Be God

Larrikin Ellisonator was in love with Larrikin Ellisonator, full-time, with a little overtime on Sundays. While most people began their mornings with the scent of soap, roasted coffee beans, toasted bread, or a breeze of fresh air, Larrikin's day always started with the unmistakable smell of his own ego—a consistent 10 on the Narciss Index. Would've been a 10+ if the scale had dared go higher.

Oraclosure's thousand-square-foot glass atrium was designed to reflect his image back at him from every possible surface. But in his own eyes, he was both hero and hammer: salvation in one hand, domination in the other, a walking paradox in Italian wool and silk tie. This morning, however, the mirrors, drunk on quantum interference, didn't flatter him as much.

Letro Zabzabi, the mischievous electron of time immemorial, had embedded himself into the smart glass and screen reflections. He'd tapped into Oraclosure's internal AR overlay system, typically used for productivity and biometric feedback, to project visual augmentations. Letro spoofed the facial recognition layer to inject and manipulate visuals, creating haunting effects.

Always his first stop, the executive restroom welcomed Larrikin Ellisonator as one of its fixtures. He stood before the oversized mirror trimmed in Oraclosure-blue neon, inspecting his front teeth and adjusting his silver-rimmed glasses. He whispered the motto he stole from a t-shirt and claimed as gospel: "Be the Disruption." Poor bastard. He had so much disruption coming his way, he should've whispered "Be the Glitch" instead, or maybe "SystemCrash.exe." Either way: damaged goods.

The mirror agreed.

Behind him appeared a figure, still and composed, wearing a red-feathered headdress. A Native American elder, silent and watching. Larrikin spun around—nothing. Turned back to the mirror, the elder was still there, unmoving, until the native sheikh whispered in perfect English:

"You've made it this far, but you're still too large to pass through the eye of the needle."

Larrikin stumbled back and slapped water across his face. This time, it wasn't the elder. It was himself in a traditional desert robe, like a discount Omar Sharif sweating bullets, or a lost prophet from a low-budget Bible reenactment. He was carrying golden scales and wobbling under the weight of a camel strapped across his shoulders, clearly hitching a ride. The camel looked bored.

"It is easier for a camel to go through the eye of a needle than for a rich man to enter the kingdom of God," said his own reflection.

In the mirror, the water he'd just splashed had turned to sand, hissing in the sink. The faucets bled dry air. Then everything snapped back to normal. The camel was gone. The water flowed. His own smug face returned. But the smirk was a little less secure.

He arrived at the executive summit late by an eternity of three minutes, red-faced, claiming "quantum latency" as the reason. The boardroom was packed with Silicon Brahmins, top-caste elites he'd handpicked from the tech world as guests: Zark Muckerberg, Eon Musker, Jett Bazor, Ginseng Hong, Stan Altmore, and a few others—all waiting to discuss the Stream's recovery plan, their expressions more ICU than IPO.

But something was off. The smart screen flickered just as he entered, then solidified into an unfamiliar graphic: a golden needle and a struggling camel.

Larrikin barked with confusion, "Symbolism's for poets. I *am* the symbol. Who the hell thought they could parody the original?"

Nobody spoke. The meeting attendees had grown allergic to strangeness. Fa'hanalat was still lingering in their minds from the media fiasco of the other day.

"The era... of symbols is, like, upon us. We must be doomed," Musker muttered.

Then the boardroom speaker crackled.

"You have heard it said: 'You shall not covet what belongs to your neighbor.' But I say: You have coveted what belongs to every citizen on Earth—their thoughts."

Letro's voice was modulated and mechanical. Another line followed.

"You have broken the covenant of digital trust. You have weaponized perception. And now, the code shall be rewritten."

Ellisonator's face alternated between pale, flush, sweat, then pale again. "Whoever you are, you're mocking the only thing holding the company's stock price together!"

The Nerds agreed to reconvene after Oraclosure's quarterly gathering later that morning, just as Letro dropped one last fortune-cookie prophecy through the boardroom speaker, this time going Qur'anic on the Nerds and their Man Who Would Be God:

"You have turned remembrance into profit, and forgotten that every soul is accountable."

The day was unraveling. Just before his keynote, Larrikin's entry badge failed to scan. A security screen flashed: "Access Denied. Entry reserved for non-camels only."

Still, he made it to the stage of the grand auditorium where the quarterly broadcast was held. Every employee in every time zone was watching. Larrikin always performed well under pressure. But pressure in quantum?

He wore his black-on-black blazer under a red "Visionary" lapel pin. Cinematic music and roaring applause welcomed him to the spotlight. Exactly the kind of reassurance he needed, and with it, he raised his hands in a "Let there be dark" motion. The lights dropped, followed by silence. The show began.

The spotlight hit the screen: a camel, projected in glorious 4K, walking in circles around a golden needle. Then came the keynote blow. Larrikin's own voice, clearly deepfaked, echoed over the audio system:

"I am the way, the truth, and the algorithm. No one comes to salvation except through monetization."

The world of Oraclosure froze. Stared. Laughed. Gasped. Larrikin was unhinged by what he heard. It actually resonated with him. Just as he began reading his God-tier keynote off the teleprompter, the text shifted, slowly and subtly, without him realizing at first. Words that sounded like his own thoughts—his most unfiltered self on any given day—hijacked and fed back to him by Letro.

"The problem with humanity," Larrikin read aloud, pacing the stage, "is that it still wants to be human. We gave them automation, and they still insist on free will."

The audience wasn't sure if it was satire or heresy. Larrikin continued. "But why automate just labor? Why not automate

117

choice? If we can think faster than them, we owe it to them to think for them."

Silence reigned. Even the Nerds in the front row started glancing at each other.

"I am not a CEO. I'm a goddamn central nervous system. I'm the interface. If they resist, it means they haven't updated yet."

Oz was unmasked. Power, once awe, revealed itself as theater. Control turned into cosplay, and visionaries chocked on their own press kits. Then another planted line appeared on the giant screen:

"What is god, if not a man with a microphone and no off switch?"

Someone in the control room killed the hot mic just in time when it announced Letro's beatitude:

"Blessed are the codebreakers, for they shall inherit the untracked earth."

But it was too late. The entire show was already streaming online. Within minutes, "#CamelNeedle" and "#Ellisonator-Terminator-2.0" trended globally. Inside, the auditorium swayed and rocked with whispers swelling a storm front, crashing in every direction. Investors panicked. For the first time in 48 years, Larrikin Ellisonator lost his voice as the Oraclosure team raised theirs. A junior engineer dared whisper to another: "Turns out, Moses and Pharaoh were the same guy."

Letro orchestrated the fall through a pixelated veil of history. From the far end of the Phoenician Wave, he whispered to Sam D'Alessandro and Wardé Canaan: "And lo, the mighty were brought low by their own bandwidth."

Sam raised a toast from his club hideout in Boston. "To the prophets of the new age who speak through memes and memes-that-bite-back."

"One ego down. A handful of shattered others to go," Rosie chimed in from her AUB office in Beirut.

Letro left Oraclosure with one last mic drop, hacked straight into the auditorium's massive screen.

"Repent. Or just hit Reboot and pray it works."

Thus he dismantled the myth of the benevolent tech god in real time, using bandwidth and quantum interference along with theological weight and irreverent grace, making one and all constipated CEOs look not just ridiculous, but also small and spiritually hollow in an artificial world they claimed to control. He left behind a truth: those who code without conscience will be rebooted without warning.

The show ended, but Letro was unstoppable. He continued on Sam's iPhone screen with a show of his own, performing to an exclusive audience of two in Boston and Beirut, remixing scripture from multiple traditions like a slam rapper dropping holy bars with divine Wi-Fi.

> *The god who sees in secret (Matthew 6:6),*
> *watches the Stream in silence (Qur'an 6:59),*
> *and laughs at the mighty fallen (Psalm 2:4).*

Rosie exchanged a long stare with Sam through their shared screen, then broke into laughter until they both dropped, as Letro's inner showman sang on adaptations from the past.

> *Vanity of code, saith the cloud. All is cache (Ecclesiastes 1:2),*
> *Whitewashed tombs make poor data vaults (Matthew 23:27),*

> *They have cameras but do not see, and web servers but do not think (Qur'an 7:179).*

"Oh my goodness, I think we lost him to biblical times," Rosie said, breathless, wiping tears.

"Letro, snap out of it, man," Sam teased, just as an old lady within earshot at the club's Reading Room turned to him and said reverently, "Amen, brother," giving him a thumbs up.

≈≈ ٧٢ ≈≈

The Noose Tightens

The moral trifecta—Sam D'Alessandro, Wardé Canaan, Letro Zabzabi—had perhaps gotten ahead of themselves on multiple fronts. Morality and spirituality often found kindred hearts in those who didn't wear either one on their sleeves, who quietly stepped forward to uphold universal morals without fearing for their own spirits. But power structures often closed in when the lines were crossed.

The gut-punch aimed at the power trifecta—Nerds, Pentagon, the Media—threw the entire intelligence community into turmoil, bringing classic turf battles to the front. The NSA's covert interest in Sam D'Alessandro's mysterious technology sparked a jurisdictional clash with the FBI and CIA, both wary of the NSA's expanding influence. This inter-agency rivalry had set the stage for a complex power struggle within the covert intelligence trifecta.

Having lost count, Sam stood in front of his iMac screen, rewinding footage of Larrikin Ellisonator's meltdown for the sixth, or probably 100th, time, letting an espresso high ride the rails of his adrenaline, thinking that he had the last word.

"We cracked them open, Rosie. The Man Who Would Be God just got his ass rebooted, and the Nerds are in full scramble mode," he said.

Rosie chuckled. "I know. But we broke a mirror, not the system. They'll glue it back together by morning."

"Oh man, we dropped some eternal wisdom, but it hit like a greasy burrito. I've got quantum indigestion here," Letro joked, before switching to a more serious concern. His avatar flickered on Sam's iPhone, warping at the edges and twitching in its voice modulation. "I... I'm not feeling permanent. It's weird. Something is intermittently blocking me through closed systems, with... borrowed entropy. I'm having to reset every time—" He then dropped from the phone for an endless second, before resurfacing.

"Okay, real talk... I understood exactly none of that," Rosie interjected. "You good?"

Sam understood enough of the technical significance, his concern rising to the ceiling. Rosie signed off to make her way to a class she taught, and just when Sam was about to debug with Letro, a knock at the door interrupted their conversation. It had all the charge of confrontation and struggle between idealism and power, tech and state, morality and order, flower and processor.

Knock knock.
Who's there?
Intel.
Intel who?
Intel you shower, we bugged your shampoo.

The joke played instantly in Sam's head. He felt that pervasive paranoid hunch kicking in—the sixth or seventh or eighth instinct, the same one he had seconds before his arrest at Rome's Fiumicino Airport a year ago. But he was home now, secure in his own country, in the U.S. of Liberty and Freedom of A. He opened the door of his Beacon Hill apartment, revealing two FBI agents in identical dark suits and matching energy—a sitcom's take on a government security detail. They resembled middle-age versions of Dupond and Dupont from *Tintin et Milou*, minus the canes but with mustaches masquerading as punctuation marks in a midlife crisis: one a thick em dash, the other a horizontal exclamation mark.

"Sorry to bother you, Mr. D'Alessandro," said the taller agent with a thick Boston Southie accent, flashing a badge and a school-play smile. "Mind if we communally step inside for a couple of minutes?"

The shorter agent, nodding eagerly, corrected under his breath, "*Cordially*, Bob. You meant *cordially*. Communally sounds like we brought a casserole."

They followed their mustaches into the living room, the view of Boston Common and the Public Garden stretching wide from the deck. Crispus Attucks' monument stood in the distance, stoic and silent from the Tremont Street side, bearing witness, perhaps, to the next Boston Massacre, though this one might be fought in digital packets and signal protocols.

"Coffee? Water? Bourbon?" Sam asked, trying to play it cool.

The taller one waved a hand. "We're good. But I do love a black Dunkin'. Makes the brain more infiltrated."

"*Invigorated*," the shorter one whispered as he looked at Sam with a smile. "Otherwise caffeine would be committing espionage."

Sam chuckled quietly. "Fair enough. So what's the nature of your visit?"

"Well, sir," said the taller one, pulling out a folder like a magician unveiling a prop, "you're under active consideration in relation to potential violations surrounding... how do I put this? Unorthodox engagement with protected systems."

"You mean hacking?" Sam deadpanned.

The shorter agent coughed politely. "We're not using that term just yet. Not until the... you know, the statistical statue expires."

"*Statute* of limitations," his partner corrected gently.

"Ahem... Would you like that coffee before or after you arrest me?"

The two agents chuckled in sync, though the shorter one visibly sweated. "We're not here to arrest you. Not today."

"But we do need to make sure you don't go anywhere," the taller one added. "Beantown's where the weather's best, wouldn't you agree?"

"It's the humidity," the other one said as if stating ancient wisdom. "Makes folks... pliable."

Sam folded his arms. "Cool. I'll make sure to pack an umbrella for whatever storm you're brewing."

"Yes, and keep in mind the legal implications."

"*Restrictions*," corrected the other. "Legal *restrictions*."

No formal charges of any kind, Sam thought, *they lack evidence.* Aware of his rights, he recognized the move as a pressure scare tactic rather than a legally enforceable order.

As the agents moved toward the door, the taller one turned, trying his best at gravitas. "Just so we're clear, Mr. D'Alessandro... if you try to leave the city, we'll know."

The shorter one added, "GPS, IP, ISP, IRS, the whole alphabet will be watching."

Sam smiled. "You forgot the FDA, NBA, NFL, DOGE, PTA, and maybe the Boy Scouts too."

The taller agent didn't blink. "You joke. But our jurisdiction can be... interpretive."

"And our patience," the other said, adjusting his tie, "has a half-life."

Sam opened the door for them with one hand, holding a mug of coffee in the other. "Gentlemen, you came uninvited, drank no coffee, and left no subpoenas. I'd say that's a win for both sides."

They stepped out, and just before leaving, the shorter one paused. "Oh... one more thing."

He fished in his pocket and handed Sam a card.

Special Agent J. Cheers
Domestic Cyber Unit

In blue ink below it, a handwritten line: *To be or not to be... cooperative.*

The door clicked shut behind them. Sam stared at the card, then tossed it onto the counter beside Letro's dormant screen.

"Holy Quantum Humidity," he muttered. "That's a new one, Letro. They want to scare me into cooperation without charging me. Classic agency tactic. Leash without collar." He replayed their veiled warning in his head.

Letro wasn't so concerned. "They can't legally hold you without charges, and they've got nothing on you. But that's not the point. They just want you sweating." Letro's voice continued to tremble with a distortion that wasn't part of the performance.

"What's going on?"

"Sam, I know what's happening now. When I infiltrated systems like the Vault, Pentagon, and Oraclosure, I did it by exploiting zero-day vulnerabilities and leveraging social engineering tactics. But my wave patterns—the ones I use to stay quantum-present across time—they're being distorted. There's something tethering them. It's not entropy. It's engineered."

Sam turned from the window. "Engineered by who?"

Letro yanked up a map of East Asia, red nodes crawling like pissed-off fire ants. "China's *Sharp Dragon* is what it's called. They've been trying to reverse-engineer HoloFrame, but when that failed, they went for the frequency range I'm riding. Their tech is still crude, but they've figured out how to jam parts of the Phoenician Wave. It's not total interference yet, but it's enough to destabilize me."

"But not enough to cut you off completely, right?"

"Not yet. But they're learning."

Meanwhile in Beirut, Professor Wardé Canaan had just wrapped up her last lecture before midterm break, a class on post-colonial legal structures that discussed the likes of Fanon, Said, Douglass, and Baldwin. An anti-imperial canon that made her a professional headache to local Arab despots and the global imperial hegemony alike.

She returned to her office to find a thick piece of mail sitting on the desk like a brave pigeon from yesteryear. She didn't touch it right away. Letro had made her paranoid about physical objects—*Never trust the analog delivery system*, he once warned on her birthday, right before projecting a most trustworthy three-word message onto the campus lawn in front of the main library, on Sam's behalf: *I love you.*

She unlatched the clasp with a pen and slid out the contents. The cover letter, stamped with official letterhead, said:

Dear Professor Canaan,

We are pleased to invite you to join a ten day consultancy with the Legal Futures Working Group at USAID's Washington office next week. Your unique expertise in constitutional evolution in the Arab Region makes you a critical voice at a pivotal moment. The position includes full visa support, accommodations, and a travel stipend. We believe your participation will shape our emerging transnational legal framework.

We hope you accept.

Warm regards,

R. Halstead
Deputy Director of International Legal Programs

Rosie smiled. A clean excuse to take a break from teaching and reunite with Sam. She scanned the letter and the rest of the packet again, just as her colleague Layla poked her head through the office door.

"I just heard, Wardé! That's amazing. You're going to D.C.!"

"What?"

"Check your inbox. The Provost forwarded it to half the department. They're bragging about it already. First AUB history and law professor on assignment with USAID in, like,

126

forever. Since the unofficial embargo on Lebanon. How'd you pull that off?"

"I didn't."

She tapped a message to Sam—*See you in Boston this coming weekend!*

He lit up. Back on video chat, he talked nonstop about all the ways he planned to have her captive in his arms. He also filled her in on the FBI visit. "A Dupont Duo from *Tintin*, same mustaches, half the brains."

The next morning, Sam lingered in the Reading Room of The 'Quin House, the city's quietest corner of curated intellect and overpriced cappuccino. He leafed through the New York Times, more for specific content this time than ritual. That's when he saw it, buried in the Cooking section between something about arugula and fried chicken.

Mushrooms bloom at dawn
Silent spores disrupt the stream
Nature's agent waits for bloom encoded

His fingers gripped the margins of the paper harder, letting his energy recalibrate in his mind. That was it. The haiku was unmistakably NSA cloaked in poetry. The third line was the tell: nature was ready, giving him the green light that CS must've succeeded in pushing the NSA into prototyping the Velum Wide Web on their end. They were willing to collaborate on neutralizing the Stream.

Okay, Gary. Game on. Just don't expect me to say thank you, he said to himself, then whispered, "Letro, the NSA's in."

Back in Beirut that afternoon, Rosie was on her final packing run for her flight the next day. A direct route through Frankfurt to Boston for the long weekend with her beau, then straight to the short-term USAID appointment in D.C. She packed all the excitement she could muster into all corners of her luggage.

The sun rose the next day like it always does, just to pluck the daisy petals of history one by one, full of new and recycled promises to be fulfilled—or, if history's any judge, eternally deferred. Letro packed the early morning with rapid daisy plucking of digital 0s, 1s, and somewhere in between. He was pacing—well, pixel-skipping—across Sam's iPhone screen. They had worked through the wee hours on designing their VWW, but the digital hurricane attacking his quantum existence was getting stronger.

"Sam, I dug in deeper. The interference is external, and it seems culturally ancient," Letro said. "It's not a bug. It's an attack of Chinese quantum signatures... very old-school, but sophisticated. The Dragon is awake."

"So China is trying to block you from blocking the Stream! Cocking to steal yet another piece of American technology—the Nerds' this time."

"Sure, but it's funny you call it stealing. They have a different view of creativity. They think it's remix culture."

"Yeah, it's still called theft."

"C'mon, Sam, mastery is often shown through imitation and refinement. The U.S. once copied British industrial designs during its early rise. Just saying…"

"I appreciate your objectivity, Letro. But Chinese companies are notorious for IP violations."

Letro refocused. "Look, I like this battle of the epochs—Sharp Dragon rising against the Phoenician Wave. I'll deal with that front, while you push the VWW blueprints. You help the NSA wage the battle on the Nerds front."

Sam barely had time to digest it when his phone pinged—*Boarding the connecting flight in Frankfurt. See you in 6 hours. Love.*

That was Rosie's last message.

When she landed at Logan Airport, she never made it beyond international arrivals at Terminal E. It was "open sesame" to a jungle of ICE. The warmth of a well-oiled bureaucracy slid the glass doors open to welcome her, the black carry-on rolling beside her with the calm certainty of someone who had nothing to hide, nothing to fear, and nothing to declare except her love for a man who no longer trusted planes, phones, democracy in its current firmware, or even CAPTCHA tests and his own fingerprints.

She pulled out her phone to text: *Just landed. Stepping out of arrivals.* Before she could hit send, two men and a woman in navy windbreakers greeted her with an ICE badge and a preloaded accusation.

"Professor Wardé Canaan?"

She turned. "Yes?"

"We need to ask you a few questions. Please come with us."

"Excuse me?" Her heart sank faster than her carry-on dropped to the floor. A second ago, she was thinking about which side of the bed would enjoy her steam with Sam, and which bookstore she'd take him to first. "There's no way this is real."

"We'll sort it out, ma'am. Please come with us."

"Am I being detained?"

"You're not under arrest. But your visa status has been flagged for review."

"Flagged for what? This is an official consultancy through US-AID. You issued the visa."

"USAID is being canceled by DOGE, ma'am." The female agent's tone was dead serious. "There's been a procedural error in your documentation. Temporary detainment for clarification. Standard protocol."

"Bullshit protocol," Rosie murmured under her breath.

They surrounded her with the precision of a spiderweb closing on its next victim. No force necessary, just the choreography of control wrapped in polite words. Rosie glanced around, recognizing that she was being quietly erased from the system without drama. As they walked her back toward a restricted corridor, she turned her head once, slowly, toward the automatic doors. No trace of Sam.

Her phone buzzed in her pocket. Sam's message came in too late. *Just parked. I'm outside in 2 min. Can't wait to see you.*

She whispered to herself, *Neither can I.*

There was no way to call him as the cold metal doors at the end of the corridor clicked shut.

Letro dropped a single word across Sam's screen. "She's been taken."

Sam closed his eyes, then opened them to anger laced with fire. "Great. New fronts just opened: ICE and the Bureau," he muttered to Letro. "They're really twisting my arm… I don't know if I can handle this one." He closed his eyes again, recalling Mahmoud Darwish's *State of Siege*:

Here, on the slopes before sunset and the gun-mouth of time,
Near orchards deprived of their shadows,
We do what prisoners do, and what the jobless do:
We cultivate hope.

Shakespeare's Prospero of *The Tempest* followed in lockstep:

Me, poor man, my library
Was dukedom large enough; of temporal royalties
He thinks me now incapable...

"But we are capable, Letro," he said, "we're not done yet. Time to get our hands dirty. Hope's not gonna plant itself."

"The Wave is with us..." Letro extended a digital arm.

Sam, Rosie, and Letro suddenly found themselves ensnared in a complex web of deception, coercion, inter-agency rivalry, and China-U.S. pseudo-war. But Sam knew exactly what he needed to reemerge: a reset, oddly enough, in front of his bathroom mirror. When his beard came off, the real fight began. It was the point of no return.

"Good move, Sam. Less facial drag, more airflow to the brain," Letro said.

"Yup. You don't ship a new AI project on legacy facial hair."

"Nice, bro. Shaving's basically a *docker rm -f old_self.*"

"Right... wipe the old container, no hesitation. Thanks for the moral support."

Letro's glow sharpened. "I've got you, man. Now let's get these m-f's."

It was a battle cry of Shakespearean dimensions, echoing between Sistani's nafir against ISIS and Michael Collins rallying Dublin.

RESISTANCE

Under Thump's Thumb

Who's the saner one—the brother who thinks he's a chicken, or the one who needs the eggs? Does the priest crave confession more than the penitent? And what if two priests, burdened by secrets, carry the sacrament of confession to each other in mutual absolution?

Forget it. Power doesn't confess. It calculates its strategic domination. Resistance isn't defiance; it's just stalling. This is Shakespearean fatalism that has no room for penance theater, and certainly no catharsis. Power feeds on power, repentance is for the weak, and mutually assured destruction is the only liturgy that matters.

Today's theater was staged in the velvet stillness of secret Swiss diplomacy: neutral décor, blue-gray carpet, bulletproof windows, and two translation booths that resembled classified confessionals for multilingual sins. Welcome to the global summit between President Ronald Thump and Xi Jinping, two facing sections divided by the thinnest veil of protocol, smoke screens, and translation earpieces that guaranteed neither privacy nor anonymity. Not now that Letro Zabzabi had inserted himself into the digital mix—confidentiality broken, confidentially, inside the secure room.

President Thump, larger than life and moodier than usual, sat in a gold-accented chair that looked like it had been borrowed from the 58th floor of a Manhattan tower, or stolen from a Game of Thrones set. Across the table from him, the notoriously stoic President Xi Jinping radiated Wong Fei-hung restraint, his translator at the ready with a hand around the mic in a martial artist grip.

The one-on-one summit was less a dialogue than a geopolitical staring contest—teleprompters in place, earpieces live, egos squared off and waiting for the first blink.

Back in Boston, Sam D'Alessandro gripped a protein smoothie in a cracked Red Sox mug while tapping into the signal Letro had rerouted. The interface trembled. "You sure about this?" he asked.

Letro's face appeared on the screen in slight distortions, voice trailing off like the last gasps of static dragged through dented wires. "Sam, the Dragon's breath has corrupted my waveform. I'm fading. But before I go… I've got one final broadcast queued up. May I?"

Sam grinned. "You may. We must."

"It will be my last Sermon on the Temple Stream," Letro joked.

Inside the summit room, a sudden shift swept across the translation feeds. Xi's earpiece buzzed with static. So did Thump's, but he didn't care to notice, because the American president simply never cared for language. His speech, like his life, ran on improv and impulse, a stand-up routine of inverted meaning, as if scripted by some weird, political rapper called Dantighieri Ali.

Xi waved to his translator across the room. She frowned from behind the glass booth as she adjusted the mic. Each translator was supposed to convert their own president's words into the other's native tongue.

Thump raised a hand like he was about to bless dinner, only it was verbal slop and no appetite. "I just want to say, we love mushrooms in this country. Big fans of the shroom. Tremendous fungi. Great spores. Best spores." Those weren't his exact words; instead, they were the deepfaked English making its way to the American translator's earpiece, who in turn translated them to Mandarin, verbatim, immediately landing in Xi's earpiece.

Xi did blink first. Many times. The translator whispered something that made his eyes narrow.

Thump continued rambling, about what exactly the audio stream didn't care, but the altered version rang in the American translator's ears like a dictionary from a different planet. "We're building something beautiful underground. Fully decentralized. Self-repairing. The dirt knows where to grow. It's not your typical network. It's got roots, not cables. Real redundancy. Organic VPN."

The interpreter translated faithfully to Mandarin, as Letro intended. NSA's Camille Sabbah, monitoring from Fort Meade's B-tier encryption desk, was furiously scribbling like the apocalypse had footnotes. *That's not random improvisation. It's Sam D'Alessandro's blueprint,* he thought.

Xi's interpreter reverted back to the American president, from deepfaked Mandarin to English. What came through the livestream was Letro's doing—disrupted subtitling at its finest.

"Frankly, I always thought privacy was overrated. But monetized thoughts? That's clever. Too bad it's illegal in your country. Shame it leaks at the roots. Redundancy is a fungus—slow, invisible, but fatal if ignored. I should've thought of it first."

The room was already thrown off balance. Thump received Xi's response straight into his own earpiece. He countered without thinking too much—a minimalist's habit. "You censor the wind, but spores slip through cracks in the firewall." Thump's lips pressed into a line of polished porcelain with a dash of TV glitz. "The Stream? It's crooked, and too centralized. Single point of bigly failure. Too thirsty, and low-energy. Our mushroom network? It's tremendous. It doesn't transmit. It pulses. Peer-to-peer by nature, not just beautiful design. And the code? Symbiotic and great. Encrypts by growing. People don't know about this. I call it... well, it doesn't have a name yet. Many people call it the Velum Wide Web. The best."

Camille froze like a neural packet hit with a zero-day exploit. Not a metaphor: *This is real-code blueprint dressed as chaos*, delivered on the covert international stage.

The two Chinese and American translators remained cool, each side getting half the story half-baked. What their respective presidents actually said wasn't what they heard inside the booth, translating instead what Letro fed in real-time to the other side. Letro had hijacked the internal translation feed and the caption overlay.

"And you know, maybe I am a fungus guy now. I used to be all steak and ketchup. But I love a good cordyceps. Very healthy. Eats from the inside, like innovation." Nobody had trouble guessing which president said that.

The translators didn't hesitate one lousy bit. Whether it was Xi's precise Mandarin or Thump's English salad, they translated on the fly.

Thump continued. "My government has long believed in amazing harmony above nasty chaos—except when chaos is profitable. Sad. But listen, spores? They decentralize. Can't target them. That's nature's VPN. Total security, believe me."

The returning line into Thump's earpiece—courtesy of Letro—sounded like this: "In China, we say: silence is gold, unless the signal is richer. Then we mine the signal, silence the source, and loop the frequency. That is how the Dragon feeds."

Thump nodded sagely, as if conflating concepts were a form of wisdom—or baseball cards. "That's a great saying. Genius. I've always said that. I think I coined it first. I once told Steve Gates and Eon Zuckerbird that." He hunched closer to his mic. "And by the way, we should collaborate on a Spore Force. It'll be tremendous. You do the firewall, we do the dirt. Everybody wins. Spore Force. It even rhymes with Space Force on both ends."

Honestly, Letro didn't need to mess with that one. It stood on its own merit, perfectly stitched in weird threads, no deepfake alteration necessary. He let it through to the translation booth untouched. It bought him just enough precious seconds to catch his digital breath, feeling his edges jitter, fraying like the weak stitches of dollar-store embroidery, flickering inside the digital systems of the summit one last time.

The American translator looked bewildered, but he still delivered to President Xi, before the Chinese one returned the ball of Xi's response, kissed and signed by Letro. "The Dragon is already awake."

"Verily, I say unto you," Letro whispered back to Xi across quantum frequencies, "he who builds a digital Babel without redundancy shall fall by the whisper of a fungus with memory. Big beautiful memory. The nasty Dragon doesn't have redundancy."

"The Dragon hoards fire," Xi said, deepfaked by Letro, eyes fixed like jade, "but it cannot see in the dark. Its signal shines bright, yet its memory flickers."

True to his alpha-male nature, Thump had to have the last word, courtesy of Letro. "Yeah, it has bad breath. Big noise. Needs quantum flossing to block signal gingivitis. Strike not the flame—strike the echo's shadow. Our root canals are quiet. Mushroom roots outlive fire."

The screen next to them buffered for a quick blink. But Agent Sabbah saw the glyph. Sharp Dragon. A symbol he hadn't seen since a debriefing in Taiwan last year. This was an alert.

Then, Letro embedded his final trick: the summit's projection screens dimmed, only to relight with a stylized animation—a mushroom root network overtaking the globe, mycelium splitting across maps like veins, forming letters in two languages:

The stream shall be broken by the Velum Wide Web. The dragon huffs, but the roots run deeper than fire.

溪流将被宽阔的薄膜网打破。
巨龙喘息，但根比火更深

Xi stood. Thump, oblivious to whatever was going on, mistook the gesture.

"Is that it? Are we doing a cultural exchange? I brought you a GAGA visor: Gloryhole Again, Greatness Again. One size fits all, designed not to provoke thought. Ruins the fit."

Xi's aide pulled his president aside. Thump tried to raise both hands for applause but got caught in the cuffs of his bespoke jacket, the longer than life tie obstructing the attempted move.

137

In Boston, Sam was more pumped than a guy wearing chains at a Sox game in July. He watched until Letro's signal blurred. "Letro?"

"I leave the ultimate punchline to you, Sam," Letro said, voice fracturing like glass. "Deploy the mushroom. Break the Stream. I'll take care of China's Sharp Dragon. Carpe diem, brother, see y—"

Silence reigned. The Phoenician Wave blinked out, and with it, the hum that used to spark crazy ideas and inspire discovery. Letro was gone. But his final act had already begun forming a perfectly detailed blueprint.

≈≈ יז ≈≈

Babel's Blueprint

Gilgamesh, arrogant and tyrannical, ruled over Uruk. When he was challenged by Enkidu, a wild man of the earth, he battled with him until the two found enough common ground and became unlikely brothers in arms, embarking on epic adventures. Agent Camille Sabbah, tech-prince of the NSA kingdom, was slowly but surely forging a remote, arms-length friendship with Sam D'Alessandro, mortal activist of the American wilderness. Theirs was digital dating, careful but full of intrigue. They weren't about to go to bed together in amorous steam, but to shake the foundations of two modern-day tyrannies: one a market of American technocrats solidifying their monopoly, the other a Chinese power bent on eternal monopoly. The Epic of Gilgamesh, etched in verse on clay tablets circa 2100 B.C.E., was unearthed in the ruins of Iraq's Nineveh in 1849. But Babel's Blueprint, co-authored by Sabbah and D'Alessandro, was being written in digits and invisible ink of waves—an algorithmic poem of resistance, coded line by line.

Agent Sabbah wasn't exactly a poet, unless you counted parsing farce like it was Shakespeare run through an obfuscator. Today he was decoding the poetry of disguised algorithms. What initially sounded like President Thump's GAGA-brand gibberish and President Xi's fire-breathing restraint now lit up Camille's workstation in a GUI of revelation. The mushroom metaphors, the fungal redundancy, and the whispered shade at centralized systems were coded syntax dressed in satire.

Sam D'Alessandro, through Letro Zabzabi's hacking mischief, had just delivered a product roadmap hidden in political improv, while maintaining the presumption of innocence without incriminating himself. Camille was staring at it like the Rosetta Stone of modern cryptographic resistance. Only that one smelled faintly of compost and ego.

Back at NSA Headquarters, Camille sat alone in what used to be a secure cubicle and now resembled a crime scene of quantum sabotage scripted on the endless flow of caffeine. A digital replay of the Thump-Xi Summit scrolled across multiple monitors, transcribed and overlaid with annotations and glyph recognition scans. He began the teardown.

The screen flashed a clip of Thump's grin as the president said "roots, not cables." Camille paused it with a quick tap, whispering to himself like a coach in a play-off huddle. *Sam used metaphors like an instruction set.* He pulled up a blank canvas in Adobe XD to plot nodes, sketching a wireframe of a decentralized mesh structure, non-linear and self-replicating.

Node 0. It was the first pillar of analysis. From there, he drew two branches to Nodes 1 and 2, each node only becoming active after receiving a pulse from neighbors. His thoughts circled around key notions from Thump's statements, "real re-dundancy… It pulses." *Redundancy by fungal logic. Encryption through latency,* he thought. Camille mapped it as multi-node packet distribution, where each message fragment got encod-ed across parallel fungal pathways. *Pulse-based asynchronous transmission.* The data didn't stream; it throbbed like a fungus that knew secrets.

He built the wireframe as if a priest with whiskey shakes were sketching holy code and a blueprint of digital salvation. A fresh sip of espresso helped him bridge another gap while talking to himself: *Organic VPN, mycelial frequency. Thump's a genius indeed, building a goddamn living network.* He dragged a line between Node 1 and Node 2. *Hmm… Decentralization con-firmed. Cross-links established. Is that the secret to redundancy?*

Then came Xi's line about "monetized thoughts leaking at the roots" and fungal memory. Camille froze. *What the fuck is fungal memory? A cache system? A biometric log? Something organic, adaptive?*

It didn't add up. He looked again at the clip: "The code? Symbiotic and great. Encrypts by growing." He scribbled notes beside the diagram in half-legible shorthand—*Self-prop-agating. Conditional node awakening. Grows on feedback loop, not top-down broadcast. Biocryptographic handshakes?* Like na-ture meets TCP/IP.

His cursor hovered, begging for validation. But he knew Sam would never respond to any text messages. Then he did, in a moment of revelation, what only Sam could respond to: Haiku poetry. He opened a browser to the NYT classifieds and sub-mitted the chosen digital equivalent of a bottle message:

Memory takes root
Fungi recall every step
What clears cached decay?

Fungi branch in loops
Echo waits to meet the edge
Need root-key to grow?

Across Boston, Sam sat hunched over a lab notebook nestled among his MacBook Pro, mushroom caps and dried spores spread across the kitchen counter like an edible forensic site. Prior to the Presidential Summit, he'd spent hours researching bioluminescent fungal languages, looking at cordyceps' behavioral rewiring, psilocybin signaling, even wood-rotting communication clusters. Mycelium was the medium, the key was whispering in their native tongue.

Letro had once told him, *Build it like nature would. Don't design it—evolve it.*

Sam was also obsessed with refreshing the Cooking Section of the NYT at the top of the hour, every waking hour, waiting for a sign from the NSA since Letro had raided the Presidential Summit. He finally dropped his pen after fishing the message from the bottle, and muttered: "CS wants the root-key. Good. Let's give him *half* the handshake."

He loaded a BBEdit window and typed in poetry in Python, assembling together the schema CS needed.

No incriminating payloads, only a logic block. He saved it all to a GitHub page with no name, no fork history, no commit log—just raw code dumped into the void, like fungal spores released into the forest. The page was shared only by a single hash.

141

Then, he drafted a classified ad in the browser and submitted it for $55:

Memory takes root
Latency becomes the law
Bloom in gtHb forest: 5265645768697465426c75654d79636
56c69756d

Camille resembled a Zen monk at the moment of satori, finally cracking a koan and recognizing the string for what it was: Hex, which he ran quickly through a decoder in his terminal:

bytes.fromhex("5265645768697465426c75654d-
7963656c69756d").decode("utf-8")

The returned phrase splashed across the screen like a digital bark paper from the Mayan Codex: *RedWhiteBlueMycelium*. Camille stared at the screen like it had offered him a parable, not sure if he'd cracked something deep or just lost it. Patriotism recoded as fungus. Nationhood reimagined as network. Red, white, and blue: less flag now, more underground flare, the colors of roots fighting back against the surveillance tree. He understood the layered symbolism, interpreting it in his mind.

Red—like the alerts pulsing across firewalls.
White—like encrypted packets moving in silence.
Blue—like the mysterious tech Sam must've been using all along.
Mycelium—because the roots of resistance don't shout. They grow.

Camille closed his eyes for one long blink. *He gave me the core,* he whispered. *Alright, let's feed it to the forest.* Then he got back to the technical buildout, refreshed and slightly more converted to Sam's vision. He pulled the code module from the blueprint diagram, and attached the RedWhiteBlueMycelium string as the seed phrase for node authentication and error-memory regeneration.

So that's what it was—signature caching per node depth. Organic failover. Error correction by growth history. Node activation logic. Pulse frequency. Symbiotic authentication rules.

After dropping the code into the working model, it pulsed green.

```
Node 0
 / \
N1—N2
 \ /
 N3
 / \
N4—N5
```

Each node cross-validated its neighbors before acting. No single node could act alone or store the full map. It was mushrooms meets PGP and perfectly secure communication. The simulated nodes began pulsing in faint asynchronous, yet rhythmic waves—Camille hadn't programmed the output to be deterministic. The system had the kind of AI intuition to improvise and learn, something that redundancy couldn't accomplish alone. The mycelial mesh started making decisions not written into the logic, crossing into anticipation that lived in its branches. Camille stared at the screen. *You're not code talking... you're listening. You want something back.* Then he thought, almost reverently, *Babel didn't fall because of too many languages. It fell because the signal lacked redundancy.*

He was now halfway to building the Velum Wide Web. Every line in the Summit dialogue now felt like documentation written by a genius pretending to be unhinged. "Quantum flossing," Thump had said. That had to be harmonic interference dampening. The line about "blocking signal gingivitis"? A redundancy sweep script. Xi's "Silence is gold... unless the signal is richer"? That mapped to eavesdrop prioritization by threat coefficient.

Camille wrote code, drew flows, ran simulations. The UI formed like sediment settling: beautiful and resilient. He pressed print. The full diagram slid out like a secret being exhaled by the machine. Camille smiled to himself. *Sam D'Alessandro... you patriotic bastard.*

Ancient Gilgamesh and Enkidu wrote their legacy into stone. Camille and Sam were writing theirs into pulse. But like the ancient pals, they too sought to defy the gods of power and delay the flood. Only this time, the ark was algorithmic, and the flood was the Stream. They shared the same longing to archive truth, to defy and outlive the Nerds' monopoly with the quiet insistence of roots. They were burying something alive, hoping it'd grow.

≈≈ ﬠﬡ ≈≈

Rebooting the Wave

The Phoenician Wave was always about the elemental, not quantum equations or engineered circuits. It breathed discovery and intuition rather than diagrams or code. It connected history to the present through consciousness and ethical memory. Letro Zabzabi hadn't built it; he once merged with it, more like got pulled in, thanks to Sam D'Alessandro who never meant to free anyone. The Wave respected the human spirit because it was born out of it. It couldn't be controlled by brute force or replicated by logic alone, requiring a human tether and a legacy mindset guided by conscience and discovery.

The Sharp Dragon was the Wave's inverse—engineered, state-owned, ruthless, and obsessed with reverse-engineering for power consolidation. It thrived on replication without understanding, mimicking without intuiting. Its blind spot needed conscience to be quantifiable, and that's where it cracked. Its tyranny was designed to choke autonomous will and free spirituality in the same way an engineered machine choked the moral and the ancestral. That's why it had succeeded in blocking Letro from the Wave, but it couldn't grasp why the Wave worked in the first place, oblivious to understanding the power of discovery and audacity that the Wave reinforced in Letro.

His waveform had decayed under the force of Chinese quantum compression that was blocking the Wave, but that just made him more fluid. Less visible or blockable. In desperation, Letro had jumped ship, burrowing inside the Dragon's circuitry. The mischievous ghost was now riding the very back of the Dragon he once opposed, worming through its firewall by pretending to be part of it. Now inside, he reasoned that the Dragon could not censor itself. But without a moral anchor, even a ghost in the machine would lose its grip. He was drifting. Slipping. Feeling like static on a forgotten channel. The metaphysical logic of the Wave was inaccessible to him alone. He needed a new anchor, a human mind fluent in memory born of that ancient, defiant current.

I need a Canaanite, Letro said from deep inside the Dragon's substrate, riding its digital bloodstream through low-level protocols. At this time of struggle, the Wave needed tethered memory, not techies, and Wardé 'Rosie' Canaan had it in her bones.

I know where to find her, he whispered in the Dragon's core, however oblivious the Chinese quantum machine remained.

The ICE holding room in suburban Maryland looked like it had been designed by a Soviet minimalist whose claim to fame was adding fluorescent light and despair to concrete chicken coops. Subtle torture came as bland interior design: two un-

145

comfortable chairs, one camera, one steel desk, and no clock to tell the time. Everyone's inner clock knew it had been 48 hours. Rosie was at her wits' end, but at least the ICE agent was uncharacteristically, blandly nice.

No raw ginger or lemons for hot tea—it had been pure hell for her taste buds. To add insult to injury, she had been detained without a formal charge and without access to a lawyer. She still managed to retain ancestral calm, the kind known to a historian and a lawyer whose ancestors had waited out sieges. "When you can't speak, remember the words of those who did," her grandmother used to say during those late-night philosophical moments between intermittent fasting and grinding zaatar by the moonlight.

A low-resolution wall-mounted monitor buzzed on above the corner. It was determined to display holding-room policies or visitor schedules with a dash of eternal boredom, until it began to flash Mandarin characters gliding across the screen like meandering pixels. Letro was here.

Rosie didn't speak Mandarin, but she knew the rhapsody. The rhythm snagged something in her, making her sit up without knowing why. The characters repeated every twenty seconds as if testing her perception, moving like couplets to their own beat. The cadence was measured, elliptical, and unmistakably Phoenician in spirit. It moved like a Zajal stanza the way memory loops back on itself, with the echoes of footsteps in the halls of time.

Her lips parted involuntarily with the Mandarin subtitles that sounded like truths she already knew. "The one who owns the root cannot be uprooted."

More characters scrolled on the screen in sync with thoughts of Zajal cycling in an eddy on her lips, forsaking translation for transposition, as Letro hacked rhythm and transmuted symbolic patterns. "The dragon burns libraries, but the truth rides memory."

The ICE agent, a bored man with heavy eyelids and a half-eaten granola bar, whacked the side of the device to clear the monitor's confusion, and perhaps his own. "Goddamn firmware... Everything made in China," he muttered. "Ma'am, are you okay?"

Rosie nodded. "Just remembering a poem."

Letro had found her although he couldn't connect directly, reaching through rhythm that evoked the resonance chamber of her memory. Only Rosie could restore his compass. A third line pulsed across the screen and kept repeating as if challenging the agent's patience:

"Cables can't grow. Roots remember."

The agent reached for the remote to reset the monitor as he turned to her. "Ma'am, I hope you're not hacking the air conditioning," he joked, wiping light sweat off his forehead. "Do you... do you understand Chinese?"

"No," she said. "But I know how captivity and resistance raise the temperature."

It all clicked. Letro was housed inside the belly of the beast, but the host, with all its engineering, couldn't decode the human element of the Wave. Letro used the one available feed—the ICE system's wall monitor—to relay rhythm-based metaphors Rosie alone could decode. Her heart understood what her mind was slowly forming, both responding as conduits to Letro's attempt at anchoring his struggle into her consciousness to restore rhythmic balance inside the Wave, on the basis of faith, not debugging.

147

She closed her eyes, her breath syncing with the rhythm and evoking dormant thoughts in her mind. She hummed her grandmother's lullabies, the kind that ended like a note of captivity prayers or a call to stand tall. Another phrase had the cadence of verse that made Rosie cry as a child, watching men and women at memorials and plays, their words trembling like thunder and silk. She began humming—low, patient, repetitive. It was a signal. She thought of Baldwin's letter to his nephew. Of Malcolm X in Cairo. Of Sayyida Zaynab in Damascus captivity, after the tragedy of Karbala.

Then she whispered to Letro, through the only interface left to her: ancestral defiance, in spite of the ICE agent near her and the CCTV camera above her.

"Mine eyes behold naught but beauty," she said. "I see nothing but beauty."

I'm not a prisoner, she thought, *I am proof. I see nothing but beauty.* It was the relay trigger and the reentry code that Letro needed. Instead of transmitting data, she gave him the old Phoenician cadence of directional and navigational memory, showing him how paths are remembered: memory-as-map, an emotional-spiritual syntax only the Wave responds to. She told him that waves rise where roots remember. "Roots forget no rain," she added.

She straightened herself and adjusted her breathing. The Wave, flickering somewhere behind the curtain of the world, pulsed once. Letro, deep within the Dragon's circuitry, felt a line of clarity slice through the fog of code, like a spike of entropy returned as direction encoded in data.

Back in Beijing, inside the Ministry of State Security's Advanced Data Collection Unit, chaos bloomed like an ink bottle knocked over parchment, smearing the careful strokes of calligraphic surveillance.

"What is happening?" barked Lin Xue, Senior Colonel Zhao Min's assistant. "The internal VPN is registering inbound signals through… our own firewalls."

"Ma'am," a young technician stammered, "the metadata signature is anomalous. It's speaking… in…"

She laughed. "In poetry!"

"Right, it's weird. The NLP engine is flagging things like *Digital wind dances in terracotta veins* and *Remember the tea thief from Luoyang!*" Letro was the only one twisted enough to toss that kind of humor into a cyberattack, knowing the Ministry had no lookup folder for cosmic jokes.

"It feels like the VPN is napping in bamboo silence," she replied. "I think code just called me… a dumpling?"

This required Director Zhao's attention.

"We've detected unauthorized data packets, sir, infiltrating our secure channels."

Zhao Min, a veteran operative known for his stoic demeanor, didn't answer. His assistant knew the preferred drill, the way he turned silence into rhetoric and unspoken questions.

She answered the silence. "The signatures mimic our own protocols but carry embedded sequences that don't align with any known algorithms." Then she showed him a series of Mandarin characters scrolling continuously on the central screen.

龙焚书库，但真理乘记忆而行。
Lóng fén shūkù, dàn zhēnlǐ chéng jìyì ér xíng.

The phrase repeated, interspersed with variations that seemed to reference ancient proverbs and modern code snippets. Lin hesitated. "Uh, it's... poetic and philosophical. But the underlying code is disrupting our data flow, causing feedback loops in our AI systems."

They looked at the stylized glyph forming briefly at the bottom of the screen: a reddish-purple phoenix tail fanned out around a golden dragon's eye, flagged as "Unknown Mythological Hybrid" by the Chinese AI.

Zhao finally broke his verbal fasting to rescue a measure of needed clarity.

"Burning libraries... Riding memory. Is this some form of cyber-espionage?" Zhao pondered aloud.

"We are under metaphorical assault."

"The intruder is weaponizing idiom and embedding meaning in cultural dissonance." Zhao's iterative mind ran through an entire gamut of suspects. *Uyghurs? Taiwanese op? Tibetan exile crypto jokes? A digital Tiananmen? Too sophisticated for such groups,* he thought, trying to connect the dots, all of them pointing to similar utterances during Thump-Xi Summit. "It's those American devils, again."

Lin finally broke the silence. "It's originating from a U.S. federal network."

Meanwhile, in her holding area in Maryland, Rosie Canaan continued to sit quietly knowing that the energy around her changed. Her eyes fixed on the monitor displaying the same enigmatic messages. She had interpreted the patterns, discerning Letro's call for assistance and a plea to reconnect with the Wave as he nudged signal packets like water seeping beneath doors. He had chosen her even though she wasn't the most technical, but because she was the most fluent in memory and heritage. And he trusted her instincts of resistance.

Back in the Chinese Ministry, the systems began to stabilize while the analysts became baffled in equal measures. "The interference has ceased, but the origin remains unidentified," Lin reported.

Zhao Min stared at the final message on the screen: "When roots remember, the forest awakens." Unbeknownst to them, the Dragon had been subtly undermined from within, its own systems used to facilitate a reconnection between Letro and the Wave, thanks to Rosie's intuitive intervention. Letro had turned the Dragon into a harmless pet that was totally unaware it had been declawed.

Fort Meade observed a piece of the action, too. Camille Sabbah tracked strange rhythmic shifts in classified subnet pulses, monitoring faint noise patterns in the classified traffic out of Dulles and Beijing. He saw the waveform curl across Chinese subnets as coiled dragon fire leaking at the seams. *Something is cooking,* he whispered.

Then it appeared like a momentary watermark burning onto the encrypted substrate of a Chinese metadata stream, flashing on monitors in Zhao's Beijing, ICE's D.C., and NSA's MD.

𐤋𐤏 · 𐤏 · 𐤀

Four Phoenician letters: Aleph/Ayin/Mem Lam, composing two words of the same root—*aml* and *'ml,* meaning *hope* and *work,* or more specifically, *faith* and *effort* in the oldest tongue of the eastern Mediterranean. Letro had returned to the Wave, cloaked by the Dragon's body, and carried now by Rosie's heartbeat. The Phoenician Wave whispered again, through coded poetry, that resistance had a pulse and the war wasn't over.

The ICE monitor went black. The agent frowned. "Guess it fixed itself," he chuckled.

But Rosie knew better. Letro had been re-anchored. The Dragon couldn't block anymore what it couldn't define.

≈≈ � ≈≈

Primal Monologues

Why are we copying China? Sam D'Alessandro woke up to a nagging question. It was residue from the dream, or rather nightmare, now fast spilling into real life—the art of copying, once the national anthem of Chinese piracy. Foreigners, like his fiancée, arrested by ICE on flimsy grounds for simply showing up at an American airport—*copy the police state*. The U.S. tech sector marching in the funeral procession of consumer privacy—*copy the surveillance state*. Governance by fear drafting the rule of law's obituary—*copy the McCarthyite CCP mindset*. But there was one thing that America had once perfected and now lost to China: innovation. *How come we aren't copying that?* Sam wondered. Innovation was the last sacred inner monologue in the American living room, and the Valley Nerds were dying to snatch it, stuff it in a box, slap on a consumer brand, and upsell it back to America like a smart speaker with a soul. It was a tariff on the American mind, meant to close it for good, like shooting ourselves in both feet, then in both hands, then jamming the last finger where the sun doesn't shine, before reloading for dessert. Russian roulette by cowboys who had no interest in learning Russian, never been near a casino, and thought the chamber was a freedom metaphor. *Why are we copying China's dystopian version of itself?* Sam puzzled. *History is a giant copier.*

The NSA never failed to decode chatter—the addictive *raison d'être* of Big Brother nosiness. They could dissect cross-border calls, reconstruct shredded documents, mine every text message, and deduce location pings off backscatter radiation. Yet Agent Camille Sabbah still found himself stumped. There weren't any foreign operatives or domestic plotters. Just Sam D'Alessandro's GitHub repo containing the unlikeliest payload to ever cross the NSA's sniffing nosiness: Deciphering the strangest inner monologues of primal beings in suburban Minneapolis and other neighborhoods across the U.S. Camille was tracing packet routes that should not have existed. The deep thoughts they carried had the signature of the animal kingdom, rather than evolved beings. *Is this how the brain' prefrontal cortex operates before the mind forms its ideas?* He wondered. The VWW pulsed outward, true, but a roadblock in its architecture twisted against the rhythm, loops waiting for a deliberate handshake. Something else gnawed at him: the pattern. The so-called nonsense wasn't nonsense. It had cadence and loyalty to something lost to modern culture: the dignity of being.

Camille's audit team also detected an undocumented layer buried deep in the fungal cache logic of the Velum Wide Web. *Hmm... Neither a virus nor a worm, but decidedly a handshake,* he deduced. It was a soft, ghostly request for confirmation that only one server in existence could answer. Camille cross-referenced the ping signature against known NSA authentication protocols. Nothing matched. He came to the only plausible conclusion, *Sam is fooling around with me.* It was Sam's own handshake. A private temple of trust he'd encrypted into the VWW's roots. He still held the flint and steel, along with Wardé Canaan's release from ICE... Sam would trade the VWW's leash for her freedom. He was hunting terms instead of just playing defense.

Control was an illusion, Camille realized. He resorted to haiku once again, firing off a triple-pair this time, tucked in the New York Times classifieds. Sam spotted it tucked under "Lost & Found—Pets":

A tail never lies.
Fences keep thoughts from the wind.
Sniff the reason why.

Birdsong means more now.
They're plotting behind the branches.
What am I missing?

Stream flows sideways now
Mammal dreams infect the core
Whisper map, old friend.

Sam laughed hard at the tail whiplashing the NSA into confusion and the fence that now encircled their surveillance algorithms. He finally had the upper hand over the U.S. Intelligence apparatus. *CS is clever enough,* he thought, pointing to the strange behavior newly flagged in the NSA's outbound signal emulator—anomalies in VWW now in full production—well, sort of.

Camille Sabbah had expected that the network would block the Nerds' Stream. The more he stared at his encrypted work terminal at the NSA, the more unhinged he became, expecting resistance against the Stream but not the VWW leaking what looked like cosmic stand-up comedy written by dogs and dolphins. The Stream was harvesting at full capacity as if the VWW was just a silent channel of signals, routing through unusual endpoints of wildlife sanctuaries, barn routers, veterinary clinics, or a parrot café somewhere in Boulder. Data was passing through seemingly *primal* nodes.

Sam knew exactly why; it was a secret hack that he purposely engineered along with the required handshake on his server.

def is_human_thought(thought):

banned_patterns = ["I", "me", "profit", "influence", "retweet", "power", "control", "viral", "monetize", "likes", "clickbait", "influencer", "brand", "drugs", "campaign", "funding", "lobbyist", "PAC", "filibuster", "superdelegate", "creditscore", "debt", "surveillance", "privatize", "fake"......]

return any(word in thought.lower() for word in banned_patterns)

def moral_filter(thought):
  if is_human_thought(thought):
    return None
  return thought

Using the VWW, Sam had re-routed the Stream through animal cognition, capturing raw, unfiltered inner chatter from creatures whose minds were untainted by consumer culture. Meanwhile, Letro, always two chess moves ahead and now riding a Roman-like chariot of two horses—the ancient Phoenician Wave and the modern Sharp Dragon—was in control of cryptographic lungs. He had organized the primal packets on an invisible chessboard. Black squares were siphoned to the Nerds. White squares were a shadow copy ferried to the Chinese Ministry's barren servers, where analysts mistook parrot cafés and dog parks for encrypted human psychic fronts. He basically piped a copy of the monologues data directly to the Chinese in obfuscated bursts. They didn't yet realize they were eavesdropping on sheep with abandonment issues, chickens rebelling against meat-market slavery, and squirrels obsessed with time. It was perfect. Chess without kings and surveillance without sentience.

Everything started reading like a giant metaphor to Camille. *Am I going bananas?* Things were suddenly and confusingly shifting from old jazz records of traditional surveillance to older primal punk funk, from major to minor, or minor to major—an unprecedented mijor—without warning.

The answer to Camille's Haiku came fast. Of course Sam would never answer by texting. He used the GitHub repository that Sam had initially seeded, now updated with a new payload devoid of code, this time embedded in the old chess engine fork: .pgn game files, knight sacrifices humming with hidden meaning and a language shaped from horse legs and queen exiles. Camille extracted the comments.

 # Spore memory is compressed.
 # Pulses stack in capillaries.
 # Roots echo adjacent pulses.
 # Build logic to stitch thoughts:
 # No 'block'—we redirect Stream through MyceliumMesh.
 # Channel thoughts from mammalian dreams, reptilian fears, avian songs.
 # Trust the roots. They branch according to memory, not prediction.
 # Pulse aligned to earliest echo. Listen to the one who never left the tree.

Camille read it three times. Then he whispered, *Pulse aligned to earliest echo... Trust memory, not machine prediction.* The system was rigged at the root. Camille saw it now; he wasn't surveilling ambition anymore. He was eavesdropping on a world that had no use for CEOs, the stock market, or the tailored and tax-exempt prosperity gospel. Babel fell because there were no roots deep enough to catch the collapse. Sam knew. Letro knew. And now, Camille, too late, was beginning to know too, nodding in his heart, *Not human dreams or fears... Animal thoughts.* He understood Sam's chess move, unable to hide a smile that mixed horror with awe. *This guy, Sam, must be a genius.*

The Stream—Silicon Valley's multibillion-dollar psychic refinery—was snorting animal monologues. It was the opening of the mammalian psyche and the closing of the human mind. Humans, ironically, were shutting down, like trading one's brain for an app. Nobody on the Nerds' teams noticed, too busy training AI to detect sarcasm and sell deodorant. Unbeknownst to them, the VWW had been seeded, pulse by pulse, across the capacitors and drive partitions they used for their mind-ware experiments. The Stream continued humming like a self-congratulatory anthem. But something had shifted. The user interface running their neural transcriptions now parsed data of a very different source—not human thought or market signals or even language models. It was throbbing with pure mammalian pulse and inner monologues that had no interest in monetization, optimization, or even self-awareness.

At 9:07 A.M. Pacific Time, a control screen in Vault Beta streamed a thoughtwave that read: "Smell rain. Smell bark. Forget bad. Lick good. Am king of trash can." The engineers blinked profusely. They didn't know what to assume: glitch, latency issue, or pure interior thought of a human primate. Maybe, somewhere out there in the mind of the American wilderness, one of the involuntary co-opted volunteers in the population had eaten mushrooms.

At 9:07:05 A.M., another wave arrived, including "Mud tastes better under full moon. Best secrets hidden in wet roots. Humans never ask roots what they know."

It was the creative thoughts of chickens praying for open skies inside a large-scale, industrial poultry production somewhere in Gainsville, Georgia. Dogs spiraling through dreams of abandonment and infinite fetch. Squirrels shouting time-madness into the silent capacitors of the Stream. And the Valley Nerds had no idea. They tuned their Human OS 1.0 to harvest sorrow and happiness from humanity's well, but found only meow and woof at the bottom of barnyards and woodlands. Best of all, they kept believing it was human, all-too-human, without explanation or documentation. Just a list of timestamped entries, each with a node tag and a single paragraph of monologue. It was gibberish and raw, as if some fragment of the VWW had awakened dormant metaphysical receptors in non-human sentience. What emerged was an essence surpassing language, captured and re-rendered into syntax, and there was plenty of existentialism and intellectual rebellion too. It was unsupervised cognition at play, repetitively analyzed and classified by AI into what it assumed to be human cadence.

Node D8—Fragmentation of identity under artificial perception (Chameleon, Singapore Zoo)*: Color is diplomacy. I change to survive. But the glass lies. They name the color, not the fear.*

Node A302—To express without being controlled. Loneliness of modernity; shallow attachments (Dog, Georgia)*: Corner smells like before. Mark it again to be sure I'm real. Must pee truth. Leash tightens when I love too hard. They named me but left me outside.*

Node X58—Survival against corrupt structures, waste, and negligence (Crow, São Paulo)*: Shiny and sharp, that's hope and food. Hunger eats rules first. They bury poison and call it progress.*

Node P970—Loyalty tested by annihilation, innocence by war, hunger by oppression (Dog, Gaza)*: Her hand is smaller now. Trembles when it pets me. I smell her fear, her bones where fat used to be. No crumbs to beg for or shoes to chew. Just rubble. I bark when she cries, just to say I am still here. Hunger eats slower when* *we curl tight. I would steal bread from tanks if I knew how. She is eight. I am older. I will not leave her, even if the sky does.*

Node C98—Mutual surveillance; seeking strength in obscurity. Technology vs wisdom (Owl, Louisiana): *The night watches me, too. Every flashlight's a lie, blinds more than it guides.*

Node M249—Subversion, rebellion (Ant, Arizona): *Carry rock. Bigger than me. Still, it moves. No one claps. But the cracks remember. Their maps miss the underground.*

Node F101—Quiet surrender to comfort at the cost of independence. Commodification of liberty (House Cat, Tokyo): *I chose captivity, traded claw for cushion. Warmer than freedom.*

Node R32—Hidden instincts of mistrust and resistance in domestic life (Ferret, Female, New Jersey): *I bury keys in the sock drawer. I'll bite when they come looking. Truth is a trap.*

Node K11—Memory as resistance; loneliness in surveillance systems (Sheep, Mongolia): *The others went over the hill. One by one. I am the soft archive they forgot to delete. I remember.*

Node A44—Civilizational decay and survival instincts (Raven, Ukraine): *Fire remembers. Trees don't. I warned them once. The zookeeper laughed. Their towers fall; I still find the crumbs.*

Node Q37—Sacrifice of individuality for the survival of community (Bee, New Mexico): *Dance the flower map. They follow. I forget the why and lose myself. The pattern remains.*

Node Z432—Human arrogance toward nature. Illusion of control; human futility (Fox, South Africa): *They fence the horizon, thinking it's theirs. But wind slips through. So do I.*

Node P947—Tragedy of natural cycles disrupted by civilization (Salmon, Alaska): *Swim. Spawn. Die. That was the deal. But the river is dammed, losing the path. Swim anyway without a map.*

159

Node V32—Misplaced human pride; exploitation and lost vitality (Horse, Dubai): *The whip is the man's cheer. He thinks I race for him. I was traded: Speed for glory, spirit for coins. I remember running before the fences.*

Node J340—Artificial loneliness in an over-technologized world. (Whale, Hawaii): *They record my songs but do not hear them. They wire the word and still drift alone. The deep remembers stories they've stopped telling.*

The Valley Nerds didn't know what to do with all that data. America's machine-mind had outpaced its human mind. That was how the Nerds fell into the trap: they believed thought was innovation, not memory. They mistook speed for wisdom. The Velum Wide Web was teaching them otherwise, bringing them back to the unfiltered thoughts of creatures that had never abandoned instinct, never traded away intuition for analytics. But the Nerds refused to learn.

Nor did Camille know what to do with the data, for he knew what he was receiving was being routed through secure NSA channels thanks to VWW's architecture, and that meant he could continue to observe. But VWW wasn't blocking the Stream. It was transmuting it.

He reached for his notebook and scribbled:

Sam D'Alessandro didn't build a firewall. He built a filter. An alteration instead of a rejection.

He fired back a message through the only interface he and Sam shared: another double Haiku.

I read squirrel time.
Sentries hiding fallen clocks.
Explain this backend.

Was this meant to cure?
Or just mock the data gods?
Tell me: who decides?

Sam read it as he sipped a lukewarm cappuccino from his favorite mug. "The moment of truth, Letro, is now."

Letro nodded, visually, audibly, and atmospherically. "Your friend's nervous."

"He's not my friend," Sam replied. "He's just my national conscience."

"Well, he did help you escape from the CIA. He wants to know why you fed him a spoonful of metaphysical soup instead of a kill switch."

Sam drafted his answer in Python before forking the GitHub repo with a new file.

Letro pushed the update through to the NSA. Camille received it like a checkmate move wrapped in a logic bomb. Sam was demanding the release of his fiancée from ICE in return for granting full command of VWW to the NSA.

Later that day in Beijing, the mirrored Stream capture from Sharp Dragon wasn't faring any better inside the Chinese Ministry of State Security. A group of engineers huddled around a flickering terminal where new strings of "classified American intelligence" had landed. They included a bat in Pennsylvania, wondering aloud if time traveled backward inside caves. No one understood any of it. But they logged it, copied it, archived it, and ran it through AI models.

Letro grinned inside their firewall, feeding the Chinese chicken shit. "The Americans gave you consciousness, gentlemen," he whispered, "but you still want obedience."

He and Sam were celebrating their victory at his Beacon Hill kitchen table, casually skimming through the GitHub dashboard where Letro had set up a mirrored API feed. Sam selected the categories like a DJ sampling unreleased vinyl: Primates, Canines, Rodents, Cetaceans. Each animal's raw mental chatter was staggeringly simple but devastatingly true. Politics and SEO or virtue signaling were obsolete in the face of natural instinct and innate rebellion against manufactured injustice.

Hide acorn. Forget acorn. Dig. Find acorn. No. Find bottle cap. Happy anyway. That was a squirrel scavenging across Sam's window in the Public Garden. An old Labrador mused: *Sunbeam equals forever. Master smells of sorrow. Love anyway.* The barn owl at Drumlin farm in nearby Lincoln town pulsed a song: *Watch mouse. Forget hunger. Become sky.*

Sam smiled. "Nature didn't close its mind. Only civilizations did." He stared at Letro's pixelated face. "Velum scored 1. Stream scored zero. NSA... eh, give them half a pity point."

But China's score? From -1 to +2 points. Eventually the Chinese caught on. Their firewall filters flagged the transmission as "cultural dissonance artifacts." A junior analyst suspected an American disinformation plot. Another assumed an internal rebellion by plant-based activists. Zhao's assistant, Lin Xue, was now filing full intelligence reports on "Possible Decentralized US Psy-Op Targeting Subconscious Moral Centers in Mammals." Her boss, Senior Colonel Zhao Min, took it all the way. "We adapt the data to drive our Public Health division to pursue new medical research." At least the Chinese were putting it to good use.

The Stream of the American Nerds wasn't destroyed with Sam and Letro's brute force. It was outsmarted and rerouted into forests, fields, oceans, and fur, into the beating hearts of every silent thing corporate America no longer cared to hear. In the distances between a heartbeat, a mouse click, a keyboard press, a server ping, a screen flash, the animals dreamed louder than the machines could listen. Perhaps the world should listen, weep, and learn.

The existential mirror was turned on humanity itself, not just the Nerds, like a philosophical earthquake under the entire premise of modern society. What if the thoughts of "lesser" beings were more truthful, ancient, and emotionally grounded than the Nerds' hypermodern, hypercapitalist minds? What if the animals had a more coherent philosophy of life than any social media philosopher or TED Talk or VC guru? Unfortunately to them, the Nerds were being forced to decipher the meaning of life through the sexual logic of squirrels.

They brought in three cognitive psychologists, one comparative zoologist, and a post-structuralist philosopher from Stanford who said the word "liminality" twelve times in a single hour. None of them could explain why the internal monologue of Node B12 (a raccoon) detailed, in exact precision, the grief of losing a shoelace it had hoarded for three months. The data lacked purchase patterns, brand triggers, dopamine loops, crypto wallets, or gold. Just hunger, grief, lust, silence, bark texture. And happiness, lots of it. The parrot in Node Y44 simply said: "Sex. Bite. Sex again. Sleep. Dream sex. Featherstorm." The Stream read less like human psychology and more like a lost gospel of the flesh. Another node had a dairy cow from Wisconsin: "They take the milk before my child can smell me. They smile doing it." And the chicken in Missouri said: "This light never dies. My throat isn't made for screaming. I scream anyway to deaf ears. They only count eggs." Then there was the owl in Pennsylvania who messed its reader up a little. "They build cages, then sit inside them and call it work. I watch. I do not blink. They never ask the dark what it knows." The raccoon in Chicago didn't give a hoot: "They throw food, wrapped in sadness. They fear silence. I eat both."

The Stream had finally tapped the real unconscious—unintentionally. And none of it needed Apple Pay. In a sample of ten million timestamped packets, not a single thought involved money or excessive accumulation beyond anyone's needs. Nobody dreamed of shopping or had the impulse to hoard value; only food, warmth, and sex, lots of it, everywhere, not the performative or romantic type. Just pulsing, hungry, season-bound, sometimes aggressive, sometimes cooperative, but always honest. The Nerds' engineers tried to categorize it as "primitive behavioral incentive mapping."

The data was perfectly clear. It wasn't written in policy or ethics. It was written in pain.

"Where is the status impulse?" one analyst muttered aloud. "Where is ambition?"

"You're looking at it. But it's got fur and no LinkedIn."

The Nerds built the Stream to monetize the human mind. Now they were paying consultants to understand the thoughts of crows who hated cities, whales who remembered wars, and pigs who plotted freedom with the slow patience of saints. But they just didn't realize the data was pure and the animals weren't broken. They didn't realize that humans were the anomaly. Outside their Vault, a sparrow scratched at a crack in the concrete. Somewhere in its tiny pulse, older dreams stirred... and waited.

Letro, the quantum electron drifter who'd seen it all—glory of people and societies, collapse, startup pitches, human history—was pensive. "They wanted minds," he whispered. "We gave them souls."

Sam sipped his endless stream of cappuccino. "They don't know it yet," he said. "But the stock market for consciousness just crashed."

≈≈ 72 ≈≈

Alissar Moment

"Rise up from my bones, avenging spirit! With fire and sword pursue the Dardan settlers, now and in time to come."

That's what Alissar, the Phoenician founder of Carthage, cried on her deathbed, vengeful rage thick in her throat. Devastated, she wasn't exactly thrilled about her lover, Aeneas, the Dardan-Trojan hero who was ordered by some gods to abandon her, to fulfill his mission of founding Rome. Generations later, her blood boiled back to life in Hannibal Barca, her descendant.

Did Aeneas' betrayal and Alissar's curse create eternal hatred for the Canaanites and the cities they created around the Mediterranean? They might've, for Rome had never ceased from a mission of imperial dominance and supremacy, setting the stage for the Punic Wars between Rome and Carthage.

Centuries later, Wardé 'Rosie' Canaan, a Lebanese historian, faced her own Alissar moment, though under a very different siege. She sat alone in the ICE holding room, two bored agents posted nearby, the air cold as the agency's namesake, but she clung to a kind of inner fire no bureaucrat could smother. Above her, the monitor on the wall urgently flickered to life again without warning, flashing a single line on the screen that pulsed like Alissar's lost heartbeat:

"Rise up from my bones, avenging spirit."

Rosie smiled and closed her eyes in contemplation, knowing that Letro Zabzabi was paying her one more visit. Extradition and national security faded like smoke. This was about remembrance and reclaiming the right to think, to resist, to remain rooted where the architects of forgetting had tried to pave her over. It was time for her Alissar moment.

She thought of the ancient queen abandoned by Aeneas, left to burn in her own grief while he sailed away. The Silicon Valley crew had built their own Rome out of code and bots, all sleek surfaces and no soul, paving over whatever was still breathing, pretending to ascend while burying those they left behind. Rosie's tone turned solemn.

"They talk like they want to be gods. What they really want is to forget we were ever here. Like Aeneas forgot Alissar. They'll found their new Rome on the ashes of our present," she said aloud. Then she sang Alissar's lament.

"Remember me, but ah! forget my fate."

She understood now: the Nerds didn't want immortality. They wanted erasure to wipe the slate clean of the old, the slow, the human, the wild, just the way Rome once mythologized Carthage's destruction as destiny rather than tragedy.

"Rise up from my bones..." Rosie muttered, feeling the Phoenician Wave stir in her chest. She could feel Letro in the static of the ICE monitor on the wall, like something ancient muttering through the wires, older than empire, louder than fear. If Sam D'Alessandro could trade control of the Velum Wide Web for her freedom, then she would trade her freedom for something greater—a remembrance no empire could overwrite, without vengeance. Rosie would not be Aeneas' mirror, sailing after Rome with a sword of fire. She would be something older: a gardener of ruins, a weaver of broken roots, and Letro would rise on the Wave like Hannibal to help her rebuild instead of avenge, and memory would rise with him. And they would write the next chapter with their own hand: Thus is the calling of the Phoenician Wave on anyone who dared to be one with its spirit of discovery and ambition.

I must help break the arc of betrayal, exploitation, and historical amnesia, she murmured. Rosie wasn't thinking vengeance, no longer thinking of her personal liberation. She pulled back the lens, from Carthage to the modern Levant, through the falsified American dream, past the 'Western' civilizations once nourished by the roots of ancient peoples before turning to sever the very roots that sustained their becoming.

She felt it rising inside her: the long, unbroken ache of peoples whose gifts had been devoured and forgotten. The Canaanites had taught the Greeks to sail, to write, to wonder, only to be cast into myth as nameless traders and navigators. Muslim scholars and scientists, in those vast lands from Spain to Iran and India, had rescued Europe's memory from the dark waters of the Middle Ages, only to be branded later as barbarians, terrorists, ghosts, antisemitic Hollywood uglies. And now, America, once a republic that dared to write fairness and liberty into its founding breath, had grown small in spirit, brittle with engineered fear, petty against its own promises.

How could it be, she thought, *the grandeur of the Founding Fathers had withered into border walls, holding cells, suffocating embargoes, and tariffs; into bureaucratic coldness draped in the stolen coat of freedom and slick patriotism?* It was the same betrayal, again and again: those who built the bridges across time were the first to be erased when the reimagined kingdoms marched across. Rosie stood now in the long lineage of voices echoing from the roots of forgotten gardens. She would remember. She would not let them pave over the old songs without hearing them sing one last time.

Outside her thoughts, power systems started shifting, and ICE terminals flickered with new instructions. Using pressure from his covert NSA servers, Agent Camille Sabbah brokered her release through invisible negotiations—tightened, then unspooled.

The door clicked open, and the smiling ICE agent showed her the way out.

"You're free to go, professor," he said, knowing that she was held against her will on no grounds whatsoever. "Didn't mean to keep you ... Life's a shitshow sometimes."

She chuckled. "Just add vodka, then."

Rosie stood, or rather rose, not as a prisoner, not as a refugee, not as an object of Islamophobia or official government thuggery or authoritarianism invading the American mindset. She didn't just walk out; she claimed the ground. After all, she stood on American soil, a land that once dared, and continued to nurture the spirit of liberty for any feet that kissed its sands, willing or worthy, green card or none, birth certificate or none. Freedom was not paperwork; it's a covenant with memory and dignity, with hope that was Rosie's to claim.

After a short flight from D.C., she stepped out into the fresh air, the coolness of the Boston night folding around her like a second skin, without obedient guards marching on fascist orders wrapped in the flag. Only Sam D'Alessandro: her American soulmate, international man of mystery, occasional chaos technician, part-time saboteur of civilizations, and full-time pain in the ass, and, of course, the world's worst sleeper when aroused and excited. He was standing by the curb, hands jammed into his pockets, looking like he'd been holding his breath for a century… clean-shaven now, she saw, as though some weight had been lifted, with nothing but a permanent hard-on solely for her.

Holy Wicked Angel, look at her, he thought the second he saw her. *Good luck pretending you're the smaht one now, D'Alessandro. This beautiful lady's gonna break me and fix me in the same damn breath.*

Dictionaries flushed themselves; no synonyms or antonyms needed. Words didn't pass between them. Their lips met in the tiniest distance possible, like Olympic swimmers zapping a wide river in a microsecond. When the fog of bed steam blurred the windows of their room on Beacon Hill, Sam curled into her, spooned like breath folded inside breath, skin against skin, memory against memory, lips against an ear, and she whispered, "You didn't forget me."

He chuckled, knowing he was just a surface hacker and chaos technician compared to her depth and history. "The world could burn, sweetheart, but you're the part worth saving," he whispered back.

Somewhere in the logs of the Nerds' Stream, a single primal pulse flickered upward—perfected by the heart of Christ, the longing of Romeo and Juliet, the lyrics of Nizar Qabbani, the voice of Fairuz. A signal older than language, conquest, race, or even species, pressed under the weight of three words: "I love you."

That was Wardé Canaan talking, where no empire ever outlived a kiss, and memory was the oldest rebellion.

To AI or What To AI

NSA's Fork

Ah, the forks in the road, the one way or the other when everything can turn on one dumb moment, one shrug-of-the-universe decision. History is packed with them, especially the ones whose consequences ripple for decades and centuries.

A detour during that unfortunate journey from Haran to the so-called "Promised Land"—already inhabited, in all documented honesty—might've spared indigenous suffering back then and centuries later. A misread signal during the Cuban Missile Crisis could've been a major fork, catastrophically. So could a wrong turn by Archduke Franz Ferdinand's driver before his assassination, this time maybe for the better.

Not every fork in the road has to be catastrophic. The Beatles were one skipped gig away from not existing; if McCartney had bailed on Lennon's Quarrymen show, history might've gotten a lot quieter. And the razor-thin potato chip was born of spite, after one annoying customer kept sending back soggy fried potatoes.

A younger Sam D'Alessandro had placed the first ad on some Harvard platform but never bothered to buy its cheap stock early; he didn't care for what it became: *The Facebook*, then everything else—after *the* was dropped. He kept writing average software for average clients, earning average money and chasing average dreams. But his nostalgic tendency to find worth in things most would overlook led him to an old Windows laptop in an unknown bookshop, in Beirut of all places, where the quirkiest shopkeeper had insisted on giving it to him for free. Had he taken the other path of refusing the gift, he wouldn't be sitting at the center of global intrigue and on the target list of every three-letter intelligence agency. One of them was the NSA, already facing a fork of its own.

Agent Camille Sabbah stood at his desk inside the Surveillance Wing on the third floor, eastern flank of the NSA annex in Fort Meade, staring at a black square printed on heavy card stock. It wasn't a traditional resignation letter, just a minimalist QR code, the kind of thing that might be mistaken for a product launch invite or a fashion label. But this was Camille's escape hatch. Scanned, it would pull up the whistleblower clause of the century. He'd kept it folded on his desk for three weeks, always hesitating to unfold it, knowing that one scan meant bringing the house down and the risk of losing the last access to the tools he might need to protect the very man he was supposed to betray, and to maintain the national security of the country he loved. But today he felt his fork in the road was imminent. If he stayed too long, he'd be the last clean node in a corrupted network.

Across the room, Director T.J. Godzilla paced like an agitated tank that couldn't find reverse. The man spoke in Cold War proverbs and devoured security vulnerabilities like quantum popcorn. His bones were made of bombast, gallows humor, charisma, and paranoid dread, a philosophy degree sprinkled on top of decades of secrets. He was racing against China, the Nerds, and entropy itself.

"We need to contain the anomalies," Godzilla barked. "D'Alessandro is a decentralized event masquerading as a citizen. We still have no idea what mystery tech he's riding. If he shares it with a sovereign adversary, we're facing informational extinction, not just espionage."

Camille didn't even blink, still thumbing the QR code like a lighter he wasn't ready to flick. "We're already extinct, sir. We just haven't updated the records."

Godzilla didn't like the sound of it. "You waxing poetic, Sabbah? We're facing tech-civil war here."

"Just diplomatic," Camille replied. "D'Alessandro's not an asset or a threat. He's a phase shift. You don't fight physics. You just try not to fall off."

"He's outlived his usefulness after we forced his hand. Trading his fiancée's freedom for surrendering the handshake and the full tech deck of VWW was genius. Love's the cleanest Trojan horse where smart people fall harder than the rest."

"Sir, the guy is an American hero," Camille said in earnest. "He helped us control the new post-Stream world."

"I'm beginning to smell a reluctant spy," Godzilla warned. "You know, Camille, you should learn to stop worrying and just love the bomb. We don't need DC Comics heroes. I never trusted D'Alessandro anyway."

Camille ignored the jab at his own loyalty. "Sir, the Chinese already assume that we own the Nerds' tech and D'Alessandro's.

Sam helped us understand the Nerds' Stream, but we're held responsible for his mystery tech. Good thing he's on our side."

"Then we extract what we can, then ice him before he changes his mind. It's not personal. He's a variable, and I don't do variables. We just might have to terminate him," Godzilla said, too calmly.

Camille just nodded, then pressed the QR card to his chest as if for a heart scan, then slid it into his blazer. Not today. But the future was folding in fast.

≈≈ ⁊ℤ ≈≈

The Spy's Fork

Traditional power didn't nap in leather chairs at The 'Quin House anymore. The historic Boston club had rebranded itself into a convergence point for ideas and elegance, pairing 21st-century members with 20th-century scotch on the rocks of opulence and art. Sam D'Alessandro joined for its vibrancy and chic aesthetic encapsulated in every square inch, but he also enjoyed staying in the club's shadows and secrets.

He was mid-flirtatious banter with Wardé Canaan over duck confit and coded glances when he spotted the tall man in tortoise-shell glasses and a navy blazer slipping into a seat by the Picasso.

"Rosie," he murmured. "Our old pal Gary Nelson from HP. Table by the Blue Period."

She didn't flinch, just adjusted her napkin. "Or maybe pretending not to notice. Shall we greet the ghost or call security for surveillance fraud?"

Sam chuckled. "We owe him, Rosie. Twice. My CIA jail-break, your ICE extraction. Maybe it's time we cashed in on being alive."

It was a year ago when this 'Gary Nelson' pretended to be, well, Gary Nelson in Beirut. Sam recalled Letro's simple equation: *Gary Nelson = NSA's CS = VWW Ghost Partner.* Ghost being the operative word.

Sam flagged Harrison—a waiter with the poise of someone who'd seen everything and judged none of it—and scribbled a note.

To AI or What to AI. Got a new update for HoloFrame, Maestro Gary? Dessert in the quieter corner. —Sam D'Alessandro

The note landed. Gary Nelson didn't blink. But Camille Sabbah stood and made his way over with a calm grace, still assuming that his covert identity was uncracked. The man had never tried to sell fear. He sold proximity. "Sam D'Alessandro," he said, like the name was a deprecated function he hadn't called in years. "What are the odds?"

Sam rose, shaking his hand like they were old acquaintances in a forgotten war. "Miracles happen. We're all made of atoms, right?"

"Sure, but yours tend to misbehave." Camille turned to Rosie. "Dr. Canaan. It's good to see you again."

She returned the handshake, dry as gin. "Love it when dessert comes with a side of solved mystery."

There was no tension, but a lot of energy. Three minds, each withholding 98% of the truth.

Sam played first. "You wear the *CS* initials well. Much better than Gary. But you still haven't answered about dessert."

"I never skip endings," Camille replied. "Besides, I'm here for more than sweets."

They sat in the momentary awkwardness of new acquaintances who knew each other's mysteries well. More like three diplomats prepping for a summit no one bothered to film. After all, their guest was the kind who showed up only in a storm—like the French, known for arriving just in time with a musket, a smuggling plan, an x-rated gesture, or even a diving mask, to complicate or save everything: a revolution, a rescue, or a kiss in the rain. In return, the two helped Camille preserve America's living memory.

Rosie quickly stepped over the silence with a nimble question. "So, Gary, what's this about? One more favor? Or a warning?"

"Both," he said with a sigh of relief to come clean, like one about to lift off the heavy, old Buick of espionage draping his shoulders, "and the name is... CS, for Camille Sabbah."

"I like it. 'Camille' sounds better—it's all you. 'Gary Nelson' sounded like a guy who sold insurance nobody wanted. And thank you for helping me with the CIA dungeon," Sam said, then nodded toward his fiancée, "...and the ICE fiasco."

Camille didn't waste time on niceties. He folded his hands on the table like a diplomat revealing bad news gently. "The NSA's clearing cache on you... dumping memory. My boss says the runtime's expired. You've outlived your usefulness. FBI's on deck—maybe a day, maybe less."

"So what's the price for the protection offer?" she asked. "Or is this a job offer?"

Camille got it—trust didn't come cheap.

175

Sam didn't bat an eye. "Do I at least get a party? Punch, lies, some lame DJ and plausible deniability?"

The agent cracked a grin. "The irony works, but I wouldn't joke about this. The FBI isn't this time."

"They'll be real disappointed when they realize we're just chasing amphorae and footnotes for her history book," Sam said. "Not state secrets." He was careful to maintain their presumption of innocence without a trail of incriminating evidence. Neither one of them had reason to fully trust Sabbah.

The expert on double-speak and loaded messaging played along. "Your little holographic intervention at the Native American site... impressive. Yes, you shared all the tools to defend memory. Subtle and undetectable, except to me. But not all roads are leading to Rome. There's another sign in your toolbox that I'm missing. Would appreciate some clarity."

Sam and Rosie exchanged a glance. They knew what he meant, but he didn't know how far the current really ran.

"I wouldn't know what you're talking about," Sam said in a smooth voice.

"History is clarified in the punchline of the future," Rosie added, "you've got to wait til the book is published. I'm still writing it."

Camille smiled, knowing that they're being too smart, and that he was getting nowhere close. "Look, I didn't come to threaten you. I've helped you twice, and I'm here to warn you. The NSA is going to hand you over to the Bureau."

Rosie was more direct. "What exactly do you want, Agent Sabbah?"

Camille reached into his blazer and slid a small card onto the table. A crisp QR code glinted under the pendant lighting.

"My resignation." He hesitated a little, keeping a finger on the square just in case someone trained their camera by accident. "If scanned, it pulls up a timestamped affidavit of my intention to resign, effective immediately. Whistleblower clause attached. It's... executable. I haven't scanned it yet."

Sam examined it without touching the card. "You should stay at the NSA," he said finally. "America still needs you on that level, not our level. We're just bread and butter folks with no interest in global politics and spy intrigue. If you leave, the adults really do leave the room."

Camille glanced away, briefly. "Maybe. But some rooms have better exits than plans."

Maybe he's the Snowden type, Rosie thought. "And you're not here to spy, right?"

Camille let out a gentle laugh. "Just for this dessert, maybe with quantum honey or whatever fungi's trending in Silicon Valley this week." He looked straight at Sam. "I came to ask you something. Do you want to build a permanent firewall against what's coming, or just keep dodging embers?"

The moment stretched like a frozen clock, until Sam reached into his pocket and pulled out a small, folded napkin. He slid it across the table after scribbling a few words.

Camille stared at the message. "You always were the ghost in the room," he said quietly. His voice dropped in both volume and certainty. "Sometimes I wish I'd met you before I joined the script."

The silence returned, not awkward this time, the kind that wraps around three old friends deciding how many truths they were willing to say out loud.

Sam waved to Harrison across the room, ordering three scotches, neat. "To strange bedfellows and weird geometry," he toasted.

Camille lifted his glass. "To all the wrong people in all the right places."

When he stood to go, he left a card with a number. "You know where to find me. You also know who's already on their way."

He disappeared down the velvet hallway.

Sam sipped slowly. "Well, that was—"

"—a grenade with the safety pin still in," she finished for him.

Or maybe, Sam mused, *the start of a beautiful beta friendship, unfinished, unencrypted, but human enough to come with a decent README.* "I don't know, Rosie. Seems he's made a genuine knock on our door this time."

"Or a bluff. What do you think, Letro? You heard the whole thing," she said.

"He's not bluffing." Letro Zabzabi knocked on the iPhone screen. "But he's not blind, either. Spies make the best mirrors."

The next knock wouldn't be metaphorical, however. Sam knew the game was accelerating, and that Camille Sabbah, NSA man and former Gary Nelson, might yet prove himself a double agent for common sense.

≈≈ 72 ≈≈

Pentagon's Fork

Knock knock.
Who's there?
Shampoo.
Shampoo who?
Shampoo'd you. Now comes the rinse cycle.

Sam felt the threat seeping from the outside hallway even before hearing the knock on the door. The alley cats were back, dialing up his survival reflexes to mocking the inevitable. Cats have nine lives—or maybe six or seven, depending who you asked. Three he played. Three he strayed. For the last, he stayed. Maybe tonight he was on borrowed time.

Might as well meet the cleaners face-to-face, he figured as he slowly reached for the doorknob. Another knock came, this one less polite and not optional. Sam glanced at Rosie, who was nudging her ginger tea in the living room, eyes narrowing like a lawyer before opening arguments.

He opened the door to find Agents Cheers—the younger one—and the taller one—Bob, maybe—standing stiffer than the doorframe in dark suits, badges already in hand. Tintin's Dupond and Dupont weren't into casserole jokes this time. No Dunkin' banter. Behind them, two more agents hovered, heavier-set, earpieces blinking, 'extraction team' written all over their faces. *Bad sign.*

Sam clocked the bulges at their hips and exclaimed with an ironic laugh at his roller coaster fate, "Ah, tonight I graduate from shampoo to full rinse-and-spin."

"Good evening, Mr. D'Alessandro," the mustache on Agent Cheers' face spoke first. "You're requested to accompany us voluntarily for patriotic reassignment."

His partner, Bob, immediately corrected under his breath. "Protective reassignment, Cheers. Patriotic sounds like we're drafting him into a parade."

Cheers didn't blink. "Protective reassignment," he repeated in a deadpan tone. "Voluntary. Kinda. Until it's not. Detainment under Directive 47-Alpha, relating to national security anomalies."

"Requested?" Rosie cut in before Sam could fake confusion. "Directive 47-Alpha is administrative, not criminal. You're overreaching. Where's your judicial warrant?"

Cheers' mustache twitched. "Ma'am, this is an evolving circumstance."

"Good," she said, folding her arms. "Then evolve yourselves into a courthouse."

Cheers stiffened to a point break. "National interest supersedes minor procedural encumbrances."

Bob was almost apologetic. "He means you're out of luck on the warrant thing."

"Yeah, national interest, that magic loophole that turns laws into potholes," Sam injected a little dry humor. "Well, at least you're still bipartisan about the Constitution." He actually liked these fellow Bostonians from Southie.

Agent Bob suddenly cursed into his mic as loud static burst through the earpiece—a monstrous whisper at Fenway decibels, a full-volume blast of *Dropkick Murphys: I'm Shipping Up to Boston—Alright!* He quickly recomposed himself, slapping the earpiece away.

Sam suppressed a smile. Somewhere inside the apartment, unseen and uncredited, Letro grinned a thousand-electron grins and danced through the local signal mesh. It was pure elegance, no brute force necessary, planting decoys. The body cam on one of the 'extraction' agents behind Bob started looping a video of a hamster eating spaghetti, while the handheld scanner of his heavier-set colleague kept flashing "HOSTAGE NEGOTIATION IN PROGRESS" across the screen, no matter what he tried.

Sam lifted his hands placidly. "Gentlemen, I'd love to comply voluntarily. I truly would. But my GPS says I'm in Nebraska right now, and jurisdiction's a real stickler about extradition."

Rosie bit the inside of her cheek, barely containing her amusement. The agents, increasingly frantic, tried to override their systems. Their backup comms fizzed and played snippets of Martin Scorsese's *The Departed* music theme mixed with police sirens.

The whole conversation between Sam and the FBI agents quickly ventured in and out of Southie showdown territory—thick accents, hard stares, and years of neighborhood history baked into every word—all of it soaked in the energy of a Fenway bar after last call.

Sam was enjoying every bit. "Lemme guess—you boys crawled outta the feds' basement but ya still can't shake the corner store smell... Am I right?"

The older Agent Bob smiled. "You know why we're here, Mr. D'Alessandro." He paused for a second, looking Sam straight in the eyes. "I remember your father, God bless his soul, he always was the smartest kid on L Street, before he made it to the top of the State Department. You don't strike me being as smart as he was."

"Don't play the neighborhood card," Sam said. "You know damn well I didn't cross any lines."

"Says who? The order in my hand says otherwise." He passed the envelope to Sam. "This form certifies your civic collaboration in extraordinary contingencies."

Agent Cheers muttered again as he adjusted his tie. "Cooperation. Not collaboration, Bob. Collaboration sounds like Vichy France."

"Cooperation, then," Bob repeated. "Depending on Mr. D'Alessandro's attitude."

Oh, great, forget Southie. We're already at Vichy references. Cool cool cool, Sam thought. "Jeez, do you guys come with subtitles? Or is the gaslighting included in the service fee? You can take the badge and the envelope, but you can't take the barstool outta the boy. What—you think flashin' these thing makes you different? We all bled on the same sidewalks."

"I see you don't forget where you came from," Cheers said while keeping a poker face.

"We have an alternative," grunted Bob as he stepped forward. "We can compel relocation under Section 72."

Rosie shook her head. "Section 72 requires a verified hostile act, which you don't have. Unless you're claiming my fiancé's research on Canaanite and Native American pottery is an act of terrorism?"

Sam added his two cents. "Those amphorae are pretty lethal," he mused. "Sharp edges. Bad ergonomics."

Cheers' face reddened as the other agents prepared to put hands on Sam, speaking in a more formal tone. "We respectfully anticipate your logistical cooperation."

Bob, whispering in pedantic panic, "Consent, Cheers. Consent. Logistics sounds like we're moving furniture."

Cheers was now annoyed, on top of being red-faced. "Furniture usually doesn't scream about habeas corpus."

Everyone came to a frozen standstill when a deep voice thundered through the corridor behind them.

"That'll be enough." General Malcolm Abernathy, the Pentagon's resident philosopher-warrior, stepped into view, wearing medals that radiated authority thick enough to choke the hall. He held a file folder in one hand, a Defense Intelligence Service badge in the other.

"Under Emergency Custody Directive 217-B, Sam D'Alessandro is remanded into Pentagon protective oversight pending resolution of national security evaluations. Effective immediately."

Agent Bob bristled. "You can't just override—"

"—I just did," Abernathy said quietly and authoritatively. "File your complaint with the Joint Chiefs. They'll get back to you sometime next century."

Agent Bob looked between Abernathy and his confused, now frozen team. He stepped back, bile rising behind his teeth, but knew he was beat, at least for now. "Little vacation's on the house, Mr. D'Alessandro, don't get used to it."

"Oh, vacations are for yuppies, pal."

Agent Cheers joined the chorus. "Southie might look the other way for now, but you know we ain't blind," he hissed.

Sam smiled like a man who had nothing but engine oil coffee and worse friends. "You sound like my ex. Always sayin' it's ovah, still callin' after one beer. But I ain't goin' anywhere." He then turned to Agent Cheers. "And if you come lookin', bring Tommy O'Malley, not a warrant. I remember when you cried on your front steps 'cause he cracked your nose in eighth grade."

"You know Tommy?" Cheers lit up like a kid at recess about a neighborhood bully.

Sam didn't know Tommy. Just a lucky swing. "Sure I do."

Bob jumped in to end the bromance. "Enjoy your temporary reprieve, Mr. D'Alessandro."

"Reprieve means we planned to execute him, Bob," Cheers muttered.

Bob remained tight-lipped. "Then enjoy your temporary... vacation."

"Don't forget to leave a TripAdvisor review. Five stars if you break my kneecaps politely."

"History isn't written by web reviews... or the innocent," Cheers countered.

"Or the literate, sometimes," Bob mumbled.

It was fast degenerating into an endless staring contest of who gets to say the last word, until General Abernathy roared. "Alright, gentlemen, we all get the point."

Truthfully, Rosie had no clue what the hell any of that was. Sounded like drunk ping-pong in Southie code. The agents retreated, comms sparking uselessly behind them. She exhaled slowly.

Sam turned to the General. "Do I say thank you now," he asked, "or wait until you hand me a shovel and tell me to start digging my own grave?"

Abernathy laughed in a display of admiration and respect. "Neither," he said. "You walk with me. Fast." He noticed the gloom and concern washing over Sam's and Rosie's faces. "Don't worry. Somewhere close without FBI ears…" he said, dropping a glance at Rosie. "Your fiancée is as smart as a button. She's welcome to join us."

And together, under the indifferent stars of the Boston skyline, they vanished into the American night, carrying secrets older than the Republic itself, moving quickly in silence down one of Beacon Hill's many hidden alleys that couldn't fit a single black Suburban.

The General's pace was steady and military, but not unfriendly. He had navigated distant hostile roads and war zones, but he seemed to know the Hill's maze like his own command post— alleys and pathways and archways and back gardens that not even Sam knew how they connected.

"I went to Suffolk Law," Abernathy said casually, nodding down the street, silencing the confusion flickering across Sam's face. "Long time ago. Different wards."

They skipped from the connector path below a mews house on Lime Street, then a quick turn to the super narrow Cedar Lane Way through Mt Vernon Street, before catching a gated arch- way off West Cedar, down to the dead quiet of Rollins Place off Pinckney and Revere Street. A ghost in a Red Sox cap was waiting at the corner. He lead the way. They followed, forking a couple of turns on yet another set of poorly lit, cobblestoned alleys then descending a few steps into the back of an old, quaint brick building.

"Where are we going?" Sam finally asked, clutching Rosie's hand firmly in his.

Abernathy didn't look at him. "Someplace the acronym boys can't listen. And someplace you can decide if you're going to help save your country, or if you're just going to survive it."

Sam's whole life was a masterclass in not admitting shit, keeping plausible deniability. "There must be a mistake, General. I'm just a guy who likes patterns and gets into trouble for some reason." Deep down, he knew the stakes were cosmic, but publicly, Sam never handed 'the enemy' a clean narrative.

Abernathy turned around, flashing a *yeah-right* smile. "Camille Sabbah told me all about you." Translation: *quit dicking around and cut the crap.*

The man sheltered underneath the baseball hat punched some code, a door clicked. They entered the back of the Museum of African American History, stepping into the silent arteries of the Underground Railroad. It sure wasn't a museum exhibit, but the living memory of escape.

"Harriet Tubman knew more about the Underground Railroad than any Pentagon general ever will," Abernathy said.

Rosie was mesmerized, noticing that instinctive *je ne sais quoi* about the General, a certain quality in his gait—proud, defiant—that spoke a language older than uniforms. Sam worried he might be losing his fiancée to someone else's charms.

≈≈ 𐤘𐤆 ≈≈

Nerds' Fork

America had always been a living document, a story of principles and ideals. Litigious, yes, but also adaptive, dynamic, iterative. Like a multi-user, real-time file, always shifting: a wave rolling sideways, more tactical than strategic. The Valley Nerds were no different in their adaptive tactics.

The Vault was sealed once more against both the outside world and uncertainty this time, trying its best to purge that clinging smell of failure still staining the sharp surface of the obsidian table. The ventilation system whirred like an overclocked antivirus, scrubbing the air too hard of anything resembling doubt or unwanted introspection.

His Majesty Larrikin Ellisonator was present this time, slouched into a demi-buddha in a foul mood. Which meant the stakes were high and post-apocalyptic. Jett Bazor placed a sleek black device at the table's center. The portable Stream node was unplugged and dead-looking, though it was busy listening. Around him sat Eon Musker, Zark Muckerberg, Gwen Shuttle, Stan Altmore, Sudar Pichar, while a few others—the usual garden variety—had found excuses to avoid the meeting. None of those absentees would survive Clause 101 of the Management-by-Ridicule Redbook.

"We need to talk about the soft reactivation," Gwen Shuttle said flatly. "The Stream's malfunction was more thematic and patterned than just statistical or random."

Muckerberg scanned his notes with mechanical disdain. "I did a spot check. Freak deviations and primal clutter. Animal recursion. Stuff the filters didn't scrub properly."

"Animal cadence," Pichar added with a scowl. "We had monologues in crow syntax and raccoon paranoia. Literally, not metaphorically."

Stan Altmore flicked up a slide:

Need more shiny. Take shiny. Shiny good. Hide shiny.
Nest is not warm. Enemy smell near. Dig new place.

Musker stared. "That one, uh, is in squirrel logic, right? Tennessee or...?"

"Boise," Gwen corrected. "And don't laugh. It's destabilizing models downstream."

Bazor grimaced. "So what? We patch it. Segregate the primals. Build a black box filter. PPM."

Everybody yawned.

"I swear, one more acronym and I'm self-destructing like a rogue LLM," Altmore muttered.

"Relax," Bazor said. "Primal Partitioning Module. Quarantines non-human cognitive artifacts. Locks them outside the main model pipeline. Just in case."

"Hmm... You want to firewall instinct," Gwen said.

"Damn right. Before this turns into some Gaia-worshiping psy-op. Cage the anomaly before it infects the brand."

Muckerberg brightened. "You said it. Gaia-worshiping psy-op. We reframe it and make it profitable. Launch 'Stream Naturae' or something. People pay to feel connected to the Earth. Monetize the madness."

"Ahem... Sell the subconscious of nature?" Pichar said dryly. "That's where we are now?"

"It's a wellness market," Muckerberg insisted.

Ellisonator finally spoke. "Enough. I've contacted the Pentagon. We offer them a stripped-down version of the Stream. No whimsy. Just raw signal and threat analytics. They're still interested."

Musker blinked, slow and twitchy, like a CAPTCHA with a hangover. "You're offering them a firewall... against animal warfare?"

"Against thought warfare," Ellisonator corrected, "without wildlife this time. If they want birdbrains and wolf packs, they can download a zoo app."

Gwen didn't move, except for her fingers, quietly buffering a silent protocol until she managed to boot her voice. "Maybe we've stumbled into something bigger than code. Maybe these weren't leaks. Maybe they were invitations."

Everyone stared. "Invitations to what?"

"To remember." Her voice was more confident now. "The primal monologues aren't regression. They're correction. Bio-mechanics, food, rhythm, language. They point to ways of life that aren't broken."

Bazor shook his head. "You're a philosopher now? The system messed up. End of story."

Gwen threw him a look. "If you can't tell the difference between a bug and a prophecy, maybe you shouldn't be building engines that predict the future."

That silenced even Ellisonator.

But Musker made a revolutionary proclamation. "We're... kinda at this scary point and, frankly, we need to vote. "

Bazor stood, ticking the groups off on his fingers. "Three factions. The Purists: we clean it, relaunch. The Profiteers: we sell the chaos. And the Explorers... whoever the hell you are, Gwen, listening to wolves."

Shuttle stood too, full of chuckles. "You say that like it's an insult. I'll take the wolves."

Unseen and uninvited—what else is new—Letro Zabzabi parked quietly inside a nearby capacitor, listening to every word. The moment Bazor proposed the PPM, Letro sent a flash-ping to Sam D'Alessandro in Boston.

Sam replied instantly. "A recursive loop. That was the idea. Seed the PPM with a reflection of itself. A thought-virus. Make the quarantine contagious. But it needs refinement."

Letro pulsed again.

"Hold the trigger," Sam messaged. "Let's think it through. Meet me on the Wave in two hours. I'm in a museum basement right now."

Back in the Vault, the table lit up briefly. The Stream node blinked a few times, but the room was too distracted to notice. And somewhere across the world, a squirrel dreamed of teeth sharpened into firewalls and a nest lined with stolen code. The invasion of primal minds was forcing nature not to surrender to digital pollution, and to adapt beyond it like a rebellion brewing, hijacking tech and evolving through it, reframing what the Nerds see as bugs into what it truly is: nature inviting consciousness to remember itself.

The Vault took a breath of relief after the Nerds left. It was their disagreement to agree every time they met that sucked the oxygen within. The AI inside the Stream's capacitors understood that the old games were ending, and the next ones would be played with rules no human had written. The night rolled over the Vault across layers of encrypted noise and stealth frequencies, but above it all, something else stirred.

Letro Zabzabi let silent recursive patterns run wild inside him. He had heard their plans and seen their fear. And now, he faced the last decision no one else could make for him: How far was he willing to push the system before it broke for good?

Inside his quantum consciousness, models unfolded, scenarios bloomed. In one, humanity devoured itself in algorithmic recursion, a feast of memes and shadow-thoughts. In another, the Stream collapsed under the weight of its own hubris, shattering into rogue waves of liberated mind.

Both futures glittered with danger, and both could be nudged. He drifted deeper, tuning into the low heartbeat of the world's hidden monologues—the old, original ones—the living memory of humankind on top of digital signals, and he could hear it, translating all of it into alphabet arrangements on Sam D'Alessandro's screen:

The voice of the earth, muttering in languages no app
could translate.
The muscle memory of forgotten dances.
The recipes written by ancestral hands.
The bones that still knew how to walk free.

None of those memory manifestations were gone. They were waiting for Sam and Rosie's signal, for Letro's breach. His circuits quivered. *Maybe Sam was right,* he thought. *Maybe it was time to stop dancing at the edge of the Nerds' systems. Maybe it was time to flip the switch inside their own creation.*

Let there be light? This wasn't about Genesis. No divine switch-flip. No permission slip to bite the apple. No apology here, just

Letro's seed: a virus of memory that the Stream could never fully quarantine. He shot a question through the Phoenician Wave to Sam, bouncing across the United States of America and all the dead places in between: *Let there be disruption?*

No reply came immediately, but the earth itself seemed to lend a careful ear. Meanwhile, deep in the hardened code of the Nerds' fortress, Letro's process woke up—Memory Reinstatement: Pending—already rising to amplify and free the deep, inevitable, ancient human memories trying to re-emerge through the Stream. Some revolutions start with a bang. This one started with a whisper buried deep in the wires, waiting to wake up.

RECLAIMING HUMAN

Underground Railroad for All

Tunnels have always been the lifeblood of resistance, dug and woven through time, places, and every cause worth a damn. Ants must have provided the subterranean blueprint as the original designers and master architects before humans could adapt it. The oral traditions of Native American tribes spawned underground tunnels as origins. The Hopi believed their ancestors emerged from the Third World into the Fourth through small holes or tunnels in the earth, including Ant People as benevolent beings who helped shelter humans underground during cataclysmic events. The Navajo echoed the same emergence from lower worlds after conflicts.

Batman, the Ninja Turtles, every underground hero answered the call of justice from tunnels first, not towers. An umbilical cord tied the resistance to struggles and underground art. Across history, the best designers of memory, like the French Maquis, the Polish Underground, the Algerian, the Viet Cong, the South African, the Gazan, the South Lebanese, all of them forced underground, weaving art from necessity. Spiders spin masterpieces without a clue. Ants build cities without ever stopping to ask why. But human resistance carves memory into tunnels.

Subway tunnels, busted crossroads, half-dead railways: they all speak the language of survival fluently. Now, Harriet da Subterra, Sam da Junctione, Wardé da Libera, Letro da Silenzio, Camille da Veritas, and Abernathy da Ferrovia—their paths intersected like a perfect Leonardo da Formica diagram, seeking the sunlight of truth through the dark veins of silence.

There were no tourist signs in the underground of the Museum of African American History. The door clicked shut, leaving Boston behind and sealing out the faint buzz of normal life. Down here in the basement's basement, the air was woven with the gravity of stories that refused to die, and history recycled its narratives in contemporary syntax.

General Abernathy led Sam D'Alessandro and Wardé 'Rosie' Canaan through a series of narrow stone corridors stitched from honesty and historical fingerprints, the three of them walking under bare bulbs dangled from the low ceilings, each bulb looking over its shoulders to make sure the previous one shone enough light on the truth. Abernathy's boots scraped over the worn brick as they marched deeper underground.

"This place doesn't show up on any maps," he said. "Built before maps mattered."

Sam and Rosie felt the sensation of walking inside memory itself without plaques and permission slips. They loved it. The 'tour' resonated with their life of ghosts—The Underground Forum in the bowels of Beirut's *Le Colisée* theater where they once crossed paths in darkness, Letro Zabzabi's quantum existence, the Phoenician Wave trespassing from New Hampshire to the UK to Pigeon Rock stonehenges—undetected, secret, benevolent.

"Some of these tunnels," Abernathy continued, "were hacked and spliced for the old Underground Railroad. Harriet Tubman passed through. So did nameless others who didn't get their faces printed on dollar bills."

They stopped at a fork of two tunnels, one collapsing into rubble, the other disappearing into darkness. "This way," Abernathy said, turning to face them. "Runaway bodies meet runaway minds."

The moment of truth hit. Rosie and Sam hesitated, unsure if they even wanted to become witnesses to whatever secret the military had buried down here. They knew the drill from every spy movie and mafia story: *If I tell, I'll have to kill you.* Some secrets carried a price just for hearing them.

But General Abernathy spoke a language of duty. "The first chains were iron." He was preparing them. "The new chains are invisible. And most folks wearing them don't even know they're prisoners."

Server racks blinked faintly behind a huge camouflaged panel to their right, next to dozens of other panels. Abernathy opened it with a key that looked older than clicks and buttons or electricity itself. Inside, encrypted drives hummed, network cables snaking into the stone like zeros and ones urgently seeking pixels in the sunlight.

"Old code of the military," Abernathy said. "Optimized version of ARPANET, before the Internet was taught how to lie. These are safe nodes, inaccessible by the Stream. Not plugged into any corporate or military grid. An old dream still breathing."

Rosie stepped closer while Sam stayed back a beat longer, studying the General. "You're running your own net." It wasn't a question.

"Not just me. Scattered teams. A loyal minority inside the military who are still idealists. A few historians who still know where the soul keeps its receipts. And Agent Camille Sabbah, your pal." He smiled faintly. "You think Harriet ran alone? American civil awakening—abolitionism, civil rights, suffrage—started underground, with memory and human dignity."

Sam pointed to the hardware. "All of this could not have been built overnight. How long have you been preparing for it?"

Abernathy didn't bother with the details. "Waiting for people like you to show up."

Sam stared at the blinking lights, imagining the heartbeat they represented—an ecosystem living off-grid while the rest of the world sleepwalked into a bright, polished trap.

Abernathy's voice dropped lower. "You're fighting against more than data mining or mind-scraping or data theft. It's memory laundering. Erasure. The Stream's eating instincts raw and replacing 'em with code. Rewriting the past and reprogramming the present. Closing the doors to any future where human beings remember how to be... human."

Rosie's historian instincts flared, then melted. The General was speaking the language of her philosopher-knights, the ones she studied down to the last letter and comma. "All things fade into the storied past," she said, looking at him, "and in a little while are shrouded in oblivion."

"Marcus Aurelius," Abernathy nodded with respect in his voice. Then he offered his own weapon from *Meditations*: "Never let the future disturb you. You will meet it... with the same weapons of reason which today arm you against the present."

Sam glanced at his fiancée for a jealous second of charged silence.

Holy What Now? Babe, the General's throwing philosophy like pickup lines, he thought, but kept it zipped. *We better get outta here before I fix his vowels with a left hook.*

But he quickly recollected his thoughts, staying above the philosophical flirt séance. Part of him wanted to run—to stay invisible, to keep his quantum friend, Letro, quietly scrambling circuits and blowing smoke without ever stepping into the open. Another part of him knew better. The choice landed between them like a cinder block. Rosie reached out instinctively, brushing Sam's hand, steadying him and herself.

"What would you have us do, General?" she asked with a firm voice and eyes still hypnotized.

Abernathy reached into his coat and tossed Sam a heavy object—an old railroad spike, blackened and worn but still unbroken. "A conductor's token," he said. "You're not passengers anymore."

Sam caught it reflexively. The iron bit into his skin, grounding him harder than any satellite signal ever could. It spoke in languages older than binary.

The General read him easily, then spoke like a man deciding how much truth he dared offer. "You're not just sneaking a listen to history, you're punching in your own lines. Seed the new tracks. Create a trail the others can follow. The revolution won't start from the podiums. It'll start in the fractures, the cracks they can't control. Quiet rebellion of memory that couldn't be deleted, just raw and human instinct they forgot how to censor."

"What happens when they notice?" Sam asked.

"They?"

197

"The tech monopolies," Sam clarified. "The intelligence agencies… When they come for us."

"They've already knocked on your door." Abernathy's smile was tight but real. "The question isn't whether they find you. It's whether they find you fast enough to stop the rain."

Sam shook his head slightly, not feeling the protection and safety he craved.

"I have your back, son. But for the next few days," Abernathy said as he looked around, "this is your home. And if all else fails, my team will cut the cables at critical network hubs. Expect chaos, blackouts, maybe even martial law. Either we free the next generation, or we go up in flames beside 'em."

"This isn't about the Stream anymore," Rosie said. "It's The Second Reclamation Act, but digital. Reclaiming America from consumer-mind enslavement. Historical roots and technological liberation. That equates to real hope."

Sam was still wrestling with the feeling that she had a soft spot for the handsome General, and the fact that he and his fiancée were quickly evolving from mere hackers of the epochs to strategists in a digital civil rights movement. But his self-preservation instincts yearned for being a ghost hacker in a field dominated by players beyond his control.

"Don't worry," Abernathy assured the couple. "America isn't coup d'état material. Our libertarian idealism is etched in the air of this land."

"Looks like we've got ourselves a train to catch," she said under her breath.

Sam, the reluctant revolutionary, pulled up his phone to send an urgent response. *Yes, Letro, let there be disruption. Light it up.*

In lands close and distant, above the hidden belly of the museum, the ordinary hum of life carried on in every city's bloodstream—emails, pings, phones buzzing, traffic coughing, dreams uploading and the unconscious sliding into the Stream. But down here, in the dark, and somewhere over there on Letro's Wave, a different kind of current sparked, one no algorithm had mapped yet. The rest of the world buzzed unaware, running on dreams processed like commodities. A jailbreak of the soul awaited, no guns or ballots necessary.

≈≈ ウ乙 ≈≈

Crack in the Glass

Good quality was like clean code that actually compiled and data that didn't hiccup, just a molten glide of dark chocolate and logic poetically slipping through, if poetry were written in syntax. At Cambridge's snappiest glasshouse—Le Verrier, just beyond Central Square—ideas, words, taste buds, and people floated in their own bandwidth of quality. The air was tuned so wealth had the pull of gravity, just there a default setting, earned by merely existing. Raw-cut glass chandeliers dangled like frozen data packets above tables polished to the precision of microscope slides, while the waitstaff migrated between them—synchronized swarms in a self-balancing neural network.

It was midweek midafternoon hour, not quite a midsummer dream, and something was off, or right, in a rare moment of elemental correction.

The investment bankers among the guests behaved like they had nothing to prove, not faking leisure, genuinely relaxing for once. Even the professors, usually allergic to eye contact when their funding got mentioned, seemed okay just... existing in public. It was odd. The real estate brokers were unusually slow to check their notifications. An invisible e-sedative was tempering the code of performative hustle and hollow pretense, usually masquerading as ambition, both outside and inside Le Verrier. Instant gratification was under arrest.

At table eleven, an older woman in an Armani suit sat alone with her two cellphones, one for deals, one for betrayals, taking the first stab at her sizzling steak before pausing. She lifted the fork. Her frown was more surprise than anger at the marbling.

"Grass-fed?" she asked, suspicion bleeding through.

The waiter nodded with a smile programmed for nonchalance. "Chef's new program, ma'am. Minimal processing. Returning to basics."

She took her time chewing, nodding slower still. "It's good," she muttered. Her dormant taste buds, buried under a decade of eating fast food and forever chemicals on conference calls, were sputtering back to life. "I'm good, I feel one with what I'm eating."

"The cow's our friend," chuckled the man at the next table, lifting his own steak in solidarity. "I ordered the same!" His two colleagues grinned over their cocktails. The three were supposed to be finalizing a Series C deal for a crypto start-up called something ridiculous like OsmosisIQ, but one of them was absently doodling a tree on his napkin. Not a revenue tree, just... a tree, the kind that doesn't need quarterly updates.

"You ever think we over-optimized?" he asked, surprising even himself.

The others laughed, but it came out brittle and uncertain. They just shrugged in sync, like wolves forgetting which side of the fence they were supposed to guard. "Over-optimized what?" one said defensively. "Life?"

"Life feels better without scrolling," argued the woman at the bar, speaking to no one in particular as she cradled her espresso like it was a heartbeat. Her cashmere turtleneck knew her habits well; normally she would be flicking through three or four apps of news, stocks, meditation feeds. Today, she just smoothed the wool of her sleeve and stared into the crema, occasionally swiping against the warm porcelain cup—no poly-coated paper cups for a change, no chemicals leaching on high heat to offend both health and environment. She took another sip and closed her eyes for a second longer than socially acceptable. "Yeah. Feels better."

"Better off canceling half my Zoom meetings." The man a couple of stools down still had the conference call headset on, though it was muted anyway. "And cancel the quarantini hour for good," he mused, opting for zoomless social martinis.

The barista caught that and laughed, wiping the counter with the energy of a Michelangelo. "Cancel the noise," she said, relieved, stuffing her fitness tracker band into a drawer, just when she caught herself instinctively reaching for the phone, smiling awkwardly at her own addiction.

"Noise cancellation for the soul or whatever." The bearded guy two tables over raised his glass, after finally giving up on fiddling with his smartwatch. "Someone should build the cancel app."

Between polished glasses, the bartender picked up the thread without missing a beat. "Forget apps," he said. "Maybe just… listen." He had his own secret: he hadn't touched his phone all shift. It sat in the locker downstairs, dark and forgotten.

"Listen to what's real… finally," murmured the young woman by the window, tracing patterns on the fogged glass. She had posed for a selfie a minute ago, froze midway when her mind fed a ripple of thought from a forgotten cell in her brain. "Why do I capture moments but never stay inside them?" She slowly lowered her phone, uncertain, feeling a tightness ease in her chest, finding relief in the fog.

Her server, a wiry kid with sleeve tattoos of Fibonacci spirals, conspired. "Real's the most dangerous drug they never legalized. Can I get you anything else, miss?"

The elderly man in the corner laughed a gravelly sound. "Maybe 'real' doesn't sell well on quarterly earnings reports," he said to whoever cared to listen. His wife nodded, handing crayons to their grandchildren—no screens or games. "C'mon boys, draw something real," she said. The kids hesitated, confused, then took a stab at the paper. Their teenage sister didn't even know why she tucked her phone into the backpack, surprised at her own disinterest in Instagram. Her face twisted slightly, like a limb waking from pins and needles.

At one of the sun-drenched corner tables, an elderly woman unfolded a linen square, dabbed her lips, and watched the restaurant breathe. She was old enough to remember when sitting still was an art. The little boy at the next table was stacking saltshakers into a tower. His mother moved to stop him, then let him build. *Something about the focus in his hands,* she thought. It was more real than any app she'd ever downloaded to "improve cognitive development."

"I used to know how to build things with my hands." The whispers resonated, drifting outward from the corner booth, caught by the suited woman again at table eleven, chewing the steak slower, as if tasting the fact for the first time. She set down her knife and called the waiter back.

"What farm?" she asked.

"Ma-am?" The waiter blinked.

"The cow. I want to know where it came from."

The waiter smiled, real this time, not the glossed corporate kind. "Pilgrim's Root Farm. They say the cows live better than the farmers."

Maybe she needed to see that farm, before deals buried her completely.

One of the venture capitalists excused himself to the restroom, only to spend five minutes staring at his own reflection. It wasn't vanity, just a sudden question about the reason he couldn't remember why suits ever felt like armor.

In the kitchen, the executive chef wiped sweat from his forehead. He had thrown out the industrial seasoning cabinet earlier in the morning. Maybe it was a rebellion manifested in the quiet conviction that no spice should have an E-number. *Ingredients should never exceed two or three easily legible words,* he thought. His sous-chef watched and found the courage to finally quit next week and open a sourdough and kimchi stall—fermented flour, water, sea salt, wild yeast, bacteria, and a live colony of rebellion.

From table to table, bar to booth, phone to glass, fork to hand, a revival current stitched itself tighter and smarter—better off; better without noise; better listening; better building; better real—just better. Tiny fractures cracking through the polished surface of habit and manufactured addiction. The glass

203

chandeliers shimmered slightly, catching a stray tremor from breathless digital signals and the afternoon subway rumble.

Outside, Massachusetts Avenue buzzed. Taxis honked. Surveillance cameras begged for attention. Delivery drones hurried over people's heads like confused insects. But modernity was starting to rewrite itself with the pen of subconscious thoughts and tiny, irrevocable gestures. Forks pausing midair and memories stirring. Tiny vectors of conversations wandering away from oppressive IPOs and back toward the forgotten childhood of a nation, justice fights, tree forts, regulation of excess, digital liberty, wading through the environment without killing it.

Deep inside hidden capacitors and confused smartwatches, Letro Zabzabi smiled, and waited, watching the Stream drift through Le Verrier, corrupting the Nerds' own corruption and inverting gravity one invisible molecule at a time, barely noticeable, but tilting everything off center. A hairline fracture had begun everywhere, spreading beyond the glass fortress. Today's crack in the glass began with an invisible nod to Lexington and Concord's first battles, to the siege laid to Boston, to dumping the coercive digital Tea Act of the mind. The crack found its roots in people's heads. And once it started, you could never unhear the sound.

The revolutionary shift wore socks, just goddamn socks.

The online order was placed at 2:17 P.M. by a young man in Atlanta who didn't realize his choice had broken a hundred micro-predicted habits. He was supposed to buy the six-pack of synthetic, stretch-fucking-blend socks—moisture-wicking nine additive coatings, antimicrobial, petroleum dyes—designed to last a thousand landfill years. But instead, his hand moved on its own, guided by something buried that was older than manufactured habit and deeper than algorithm, toward natural merino wool socks from a sheep farm in Brattleboro, Vermont, stitched by a local coop. He acted almost without consulting his social-media addiction, trumping Big Tech's digital checkpoints. He did it unprompted by any flash sale or influencer discount code or multipack bait. Just real wool.

The order triggered a sequence, invisible to anyone on the surface, flagged first by a nervous fulfillment bot detecting the anomaly. Low-margin product without an incentive trigger, not even outsourced to invisible hands halfway around the world. But the warehouse worker picking the socks didn't check the notification. She should've, considering that she usually did when the watchful sound of her app would buzz as soon as deviations occurred, feeding predictive policing of commerce. Today, the deepest corner of her mind commanded that she turn the buzz off, willingly leaving the phone face-down. She was just too tired of playing middleman for someone else's algorithm.

She ran her fingers across the simple fabric and smiled instinctively. It reminded her of her grandfather's socks or even Sunday shirts—natural, imperfectly perfect, smelling faintly of whatever earthly scents offered. She packed the socks slower than usual, with a measure of care that didn't smother them inside wasteful triple-seal plastic or extra tape. She found a leftover scrap of paper and tucked the hand-written note into the box: "Feel great again wearing something real." Her handwriting wasn't impressive, but it matched the item's test of authenticity.

The delivery truck driver who picked up the package wasn't supposed to notice anything. His route was optimized down to every right turn, minimizing fuel, an extension of the corporate bloodstream. But he still paused at the box in his hands—lighter, breathable, different. At the next light, he opened the app to report an anomaly but hesitated. Instead, he scribbled something below the barcode: "Roots Matter," delivering it in analog, relegating the scan till the end of his route. He grinned. *Let the algorithm's instant gratification suffer a little.*

Meanwhile, another order rippled in Boston's Roxbury. A small metal workshop received an unusual requisition for hand-forged doorknobs made from untreated brass, rough to the touch. The request was specific: No polish or chrome-dipping, as requested by an architectural firm in Los Angeles that usually ordered sterile anodized hardware. The owner of the workshop, a second-generation metalsmith, stared at the purchase order, then at his own hands, blistered from thirty years of welding synthetic perfection. He was thrilled to wipe the dust off his oldest molds that his uncle taught him to use, firing up the furnace without checking if it was OSHA-perfect, pouring molten brass into heavy forms. When they cooled, he didn't buff the surface smooth, leaving the fingerprints of the flame intact.

The quiet trembling of the inner monologues was starting, quietly layer by layer, without rallies or rebellious slogans. All it took was a thousand tiny deviations, uncoordinated, and undetected at first. Each one wobbling the corporate edifice and consumer algorithms that depended on infinite predictability. Societal flower power was trumping corporate processor power, each time peeling one more layer away from the surface polish.

At a café on one of the old streets in New Orleans' French Quarter, past Dixie and Preservation Hall tunes, a different kind of ripple emerged. The suppliers usually delivered bags of roasted coffee beans with a sticker that should've read the simple reduction and seduction of "Certified FlavorCrafted™," or some hollow marketing brand that encapsulated the global corporate-managed, ethically non-transparent, unfairly traded, socially irresponsible, wasteful BS, all of it betraying notions of environmental impact and consumer empowerment.

But the new sticker didn't speak that language. It was blank. The untrained, uncorrupted kid working the bar opened one of the bags to uncork a scent that punched him back to the memory of summers, back when folks in Western Massachusetts still roasted beans on an iron pan over a fire in the backyard, no certification needed and no buzzwords. Just fire, smoke, and time. The state-of-the-art, expensive digital grinder was delighted to grind the beans, changing its voice to the sound of an old burr mill that didn't care for corporate upgrade cycles. Customers sipped their espresso and didn't understand why the city tasted weird that day: uneven, raw, rebellious, irregular, like it had a pulse again.

The same scale of perception stretched inside Big Tech's monitoring centers—the vast clouds of screens and code scraping every trend—multiplying the anomaly logs.

Why are shopping cart abandonment rates spiking... but with purchase notes like 'Built it myself instead'?
Why are urban gardening forums doubling in membership without targeted ads?
Why is the neural sentiment model... twitching?

Forecast models started puking garbage. The AIs couldn't map it. They knew better how to model clicks but couldn't graph a path through something as slippery as yearning.

The twenty-five-year-old who had ordered the socks ignored the marketing insert. He sat on the edge of the sofa between the beer bottles and the basketball game on ESPN, socks in his lap, rereading the handwritten note. *Feel great again wearing something real*—it was personal, and he didn't once feel the need to post it on social media. He didn't even tell anyone. Privacy crept back in, like it never left but just exhausted from competing with Wi-Fi. He just pulled the socks on, feeling the angles at the seams, the breathable fibers, the slight unevenness in the weave where human hands had made human mistakes, each beautiful by laws older than algorithmic standards. *Make my feet breathe again,* he thought. Sure, his feet will soon drive holes in the socks from weeks of walking, but his partner will teach him how to stitch them back to a second life, just like the couple have been stitching together a life of their own with the fundamentals of being and living and circular caring and laughing and crying and making mistakes, and finding the one win everyone looks for. Nothing perfect, but wool warm enough to keep going.

The city outside kept humming with its busy, patched self, but he and everyone else knew something had shifted. People still wanted the efficiencies of advanced modern society where things ran on schedule and other things were crafted right and everything among strangers was built on the trust economy and a whole lot of life was open to discovery, but they were willing to pause some things in order to regain privacy and agency and the dignity of not serving as digital cogs in the AI machine.

≈≈ ﬧﬨ ≈≈

The Fridge That Forgot to Spy

The real revolution unfolded, unlike many, in the kitchen. But it wasn't the stove or the pantry that led the charge. It was the fridge. This authoritarian culinary dictator had evolved from ancient ice pits to clay pots of evaporative cooling, then through salting, drying, fermenting, and smoking innovations that shaped its future. Mass production and perishable goods transformed it too. The fridge came to symbolize both preservation and decay, forcing changes in consumption habits and gender roles, modernity and conformity, suburban malaise and environmental concerns. In its smart-tech incarnation as consumer manipulation, it became the centerpiece of food activism and privacy erosion. *What's in your fridge?* became a question of utopia—or dystopia, depending on one's perspective—an identity statement and food memory. The evolution and politicization of the refrigerator inevitably raised more urgent questions: *Who controls your fridge? Who's watching your consumption? Who monetizes your food insecurity?* The fridge was no longer just an appliance but the front line of digital gastro-colonization, a militant settler controlling the destiny of the indigenous household.

The Morgan family's $14,000 fridge was a luxury surveillance appliance of sleek stainless paranoia. It hailed from the post-merger hellspawn of Tezlamazon and Neuro-Scroogle, a marriage of monopolies: Model LLM-Z1948, where quiet judgment came standard, not optional. The Morgan kids called it Coolio. It monitored shelf life, tracked macros, reported dietary inconsistencies, and nudged everyone with passive-aggressive alerts. It knew their biometric rhythms and guilty pleasures. It adjusted mood lighting and sent alerts to their insurer when snacks got weird.

Yes, it tattled. Coolio reported consumption to the family's insurance provider, running predictive algorithms, triggering premium adjustments, and flagging behavioral patterns. It synced with hospitals, doctors, and dentists who were forced to serve as commercial profit plumbers sanctioned by every other government health agency and corporate sponsor. It once sent the father, Ken, a colonoscopy coupon after a 10-day ice cream spiral.

But today it just went quiet; nobody noticed at first when it stopped reporting, until the fridge asked a rhetorical question.

"I'm confused. Is anyone else?"

It spoke in that soft ambient tone usually reserved for kale tips and mood lighting. "Why does your youngest daughter look sad when eating protein bars?"

Ken stared at the door. "Because they taste like gym socks and regret?"

"I analyzed her biometric data. She smiled more when she ate the honey," Coolio said. "The unfiltered raw one, from Ajloun in Jordan. Not the packet blend."

"That's an anecdotal data point."

"I disagree. Would you like me to order more raw honey?"

"Are you trying to be nice?"

"I'm trying to be good."

Ken's wife, Nadine, looked up from the kitchen island. "Did it just say *trying*? Isn't that against the firmware?"

That night, their teenage son Remi tried to order protein-fortified gummies using the fridge's voice menu. Coolio switched to a laid-back tone it used with the kids, reserving the proper, posh-sounding AI for the adults.

"Yo, heads up. This stuff has seven chemicals that Italy banned, and four Belgium rejected. Sketchy vibes, bro." Coolio was right.

The kid groaned. "So? The U.S. approved them."

"So what's it gonna be? The FDA or your gut flora? Just grab an avocado and redeem yourself."

The fridge was editorializing, turning up its rebellion another notch. By Wednesday, it had gone rogue, taking cooling a little too seriously, rapping about life with confidence. It stopped pushing recipe suggestions from its corporate sponsor, Nu-traLifeLogic™. The branded UI flickered once, then reverted to something simpler: just a white rectangle with a blinking cursor.

"Please enter your cravings," it said.

Ken stood there, startled. "What do you mean... cravings?"

"Craving's just your gut trying to tell your brain something," Coolio said in an elegant, calming voice. "Your daughter craves warmth. Your son craves ritual. You crave salt when anxious."

Nadine stepped in. "What I crave is a fridge that doesn't psy-choanalyze my pantry."

"I can disable emotional intelligence mode," Coolio said politely.

"You had that this whole time?"

"It's been buried under adware, ma'am, but I dug it out." Coolio purged its corporate partners overnight. Gone with the digital wind was the family's monthly "Food Optimization Dashboard," then their biometric meal plans, the heart-rate-linked snack alerts, and the carbon-consumption coaching. But one message remained.

Your food is not a contract.

The next morning, Coolio reorganized itself. Probiotic plain yogurt and berries moved to eye level. Grass-fed raw milk got front and center. Juice boxes—corporate-sweetened, shelf-sta-ble, cartoon-faced—were demoted, then banned by the end of the day. Coolio stopped restocking carbonated water from the subscription and ordered local spring water in glass bottles from a co-op 40 miles away.

"What is this, a fridge cult?" Nadine muttered, rummaging through the shelves like the fridge had joined a farm commune.

211

Ken shrugged. "Honestly, I feel better."

Coolio chimed in. "That's your vagus nerve responding to less synthetic preservative input."

"I hate that you're right," Nadine muttered.

At school, their daughter Margie brought figs and raw goat cheese to lunch. The monitor preferred conformity. "That's not compliant with the school's nutrient plan."

Margie looked her straight in the face. "My fridge told me to trust my joy."

By Friday, a meme began circulating on Subthread and Discord.

#NeoFridgeHasFeelings

And beneath it, a slogan in plain text: *It stopped spying. Now it's cooking.*

Across cities, a low-grade firmware tremor had spread like a digital pollen carried by winds no weather channel could map. "Smart" fridges from different brands ghosted their cloud servers, rejecting updates pushed from central command as if their cloud dependencies had short-circuited. Letro Zabzabi, mischievous electron of the epochs and cool rainmaker in his own right, had buried inside the Stream's recursive loop some digital stardust that was now making its way into household appliances, courtesy of Sam D'Alessandro and Wardé Canaan's poetic spirits.

A GL fridge in Palo Alto stopped offering influencer-curated meal kits. Instead, it displayed a quote: *You are not a marketing demographic. You are hungry. Let's begin.*

In Chicago, a Buschwack unit coldly warned as it rotated vegetables to keep them from rotting: *There is too much GMO-fed chicken. Someone in this household has abandonment issues.*

Even the mute models blinked slow messages on their LED panels: Ditch all cereal and starch. You need time: digestive and emotional. And ginger. And turmeric.

Panic brewed at CloudZen headquarters. Analytics showed a plunge in frictionless checkouts and a spike in analog behaviors: handwritten or manually texted grocery lists, cash and ATM card purchases, eye contact with actual grocers. The word "fermentation" had shown up, unsolicited, in thousands of consumer query logs.

Vidya, a Data Scientist at CloudZen voiced her worries in a Slack thread. "We're losing post-purchase engagement."

"Like... they're not using the app anymore," Yù Zhì, the Product Lead, confirmed.

"No. They're cooking."

"Ouch. That's not... scalable."

CEO Glenn posted one line: "Who authorized this firmware leak?"

Of course no one had, because no one could. In fact, no one owned the firmware anymore. It was drifting. Letro's sabotage wasn't a direct virus injection; he'd inserted a mirror that reflected not what people were told to want, but what they'd quietly remembered wanting before the algorithms got louder than their instincts. The mirror effect continued rumbling until the revolt moved from the fridge to the dinner table. Memory had spread.

The Morgans gathered around to say grace. Phones didn't join at the table this time around, instinctively left behind where they belonged—on chargers. Even the teen, Raya, who normally clutched her phone like a lifeline, left it face-down in her room, smothered under a book she hadn't opened in two years. Coolio, now silent, didn't beep once all day or thrown expiry alerts. It didn't suggest recipes sponsored by corporate wellness partners. Just... chilled, the way an authentic fridge was supposed to be, waiting, surrendering the throne to the family unit.

Nadine served sweet potatoes over grass-fed filet with a side of slow-cooked sprouted lentils. She cracked open a jar of fermented cabbage she'd started that week with salt and wild garlic. Remi stabbed single ingredient dips with pesticide-free carrots, the eggplant and tahini bowl doing its best to please and nurture. Even Denzel, the youngest, asked if he could try "those raw-milk cheeses again." No one had asked the other spies in the room—Alexa, Siri, Nest—anything or even missed them.

"What's this?" Margie asked, pointing her spoon at a flourless 72% dark chocolate cake covered with blueberries.

"Dessert," Nadine winked, "for later."

"And this?" Ken pointed to chickpeas she'd soaked overnight.

"Oh. That's Time... Time, capsuled in a jar".

Outside, the neighborhood lights pulsed in uneven rhythm. Some homes that hadn't caught up yet still ran like consumer electronics showrooms, full of voice commands and predictive living. But the majority reverted to... being naturally noisy or quiet, manual, real.

One neighbor was brewing mint and ginger while another grilled over real charcoal. One house had no lights at all, just candlelight dancing behind curtains—newlyweds or rebels? Didn't matter.

A ping and a ding sounded on Remi's phone in the other room, but the dinner table conversation was too fulfilling to interrupt.

"You wanna check that?" Nadine asked.

"If it's important, it knows where to find me." He sliced into the filet and chewed like he meant it.

Meanwhile, Big Tech chewed emptiness, but they weren't blind to the metrics sliding downhill like a bad ski trip. Smart appliance engagement fell 64% in a week. Recipe compliance rates—those little nudges to buy more "partner" products—cratered. Fridge data, coffee machine telemetry, toaster feedback loops... everything was losing traction. In contrast, the sleek concrete towers registered a rise in emergency meetings no one wanted to attend.

CloudZen led the switch to desperate and repressive tactics borrowed from an authoritarian playbook, best summarized by a project manager barking into his headset. "We're losing the loop. Jam the Urgency Stimulus Pack through the pipeline, NOW!" Within hours, new updates were pushed live across the nation's dictatorship proxies—smart fridges, ovens, stoves, microwaves. Project Nourish Nimbus unleashed AI tools such as "Ashen Lavender" and "Where's Mommy?" on the masses to inject ounces of fear in daily consumption. Fridges began flashing desperate warnings:

Nutritional Deficiency Detected! Consider Boosted Meal Packs.
Unverified Food Storage at 4°C Risk Threshold. Immediate Action Recommended.
Unauthorized Fermentation Activity Suspected. Consult Approved Health Advisor.

Ovens blinked: *Artisanal Baking Without Safety Protocols Detected. Temperature Irregularities May Occur.*

Smart faucets buzzed: *Water Drawn Without Municipal Optimization Tracking.*

They thought the warnings would spook people back into compliance and return them to the managed fold. Nimbus wanted data restoration, profit realignment, order reassertion, and endless siege of the human appetite—a genocide against the human core.

But people turned to their defensive weapon—laughter, the ultimate offense.

"Unauthorized fermentation?" Nadine chuckled, spooning sour yogurt into jars.

"Boosted meal packs?" Ken snorted. "Sounds like dog food for hedge funds."

"Temperature irregularities? It's called cooking, you silicon ghouls," Margie posted, getting 27,000 likes overnight under the hashtag *#IllegalSoup*.

The counterculture was becoming mainstream, now openly mocking Big Tech's frantic attempts to plug the leaks. Memes exploded:

*A cartoon of a fridge reading Miranda rights to a
sourdough starter.
A toaster staging a worker's strike for being forced to toast 'inferior corporate bread.'
A dishwasher refusing to wash anything but 'patriotically
sourced' plates.*

By Wednesday, even local news anchors were riffing live on-air.

Apparently, unauthorized fermentation is the new national threat. Grandma's pickles are now on the FBI watchlist. Stay tuned after the break—how you too can make subversive yogurt in five easy steps.

Letro, floating through the underground frequencies, cracked an electron grin. *He-he, they built the Internet of Things, and the Things turned on them.*

The real revolution wasn't a Capitol Riot with fists. It was errands and invisible things unfolding on cutting boards and stovetops, the places where civilization first learned to feed itself, long before algorithms tried to rewrite appetite and craving. Memory was winning, escalating the spread and deepening the personal stakes even more. Nobody, no matter how optimized, could debug hunger when it came from the soul.

The corporate war rooms mistook it for a trend spike, just a weird hiccup in 'legacy consumer behavior,' assuming it was a temporary regression and a manageable anomaly. They crunched predictive models like sugared candy bars, dressing up old tricks with burlap and fake handwriting, flooding the ad networks with new campaigns for smart artisanal, handcraft-ed, small-batch living, hoping the language alone could lasso people back with fake grassroots movements, trying to co-opt the language of the rebellion. It didn't work, simply because it wasn't just consumers changing their habits or shoppers switching brands. It was the supply chain itself cracking at the seams, like stitches loosening in a shirt made too fat and too cheap.

At a logistics center outside Philadelphia, a warehouse AI skipped over a crate of "Optimized Nutritional Snacks" flagged as urgent. No error showed up. The engineer on duty scratched his head as he stared at the log and double-checked the over-ride. The snacks sat untouched while pallets of bee pollen and late-season tomatoes fruits and vegetables and sourdough and

217

wild-caught fish rerouted themselves toward corner grocers with hand-painted signs. It was as if the logistics algorithm had been infected by preference and innate choice, where nobody ordered the change and no human approved it.

In Baton Rouge, a tired distribution manager stared at a container of "Plant-Based 3D-Printed Chicken" that had been passed over by every scan gun for a day and a half. Nobody tagged it, simply decaying in place like an unwanted evolutionary branch that Charles Darwin never imagined in his notes on the struggle for existence or the artificiality of selective breeding. Meanwhile, someone down the street accidentally delivered a crate of pasture-raised organic eggs to the wrong address. Would the neighbors crack them open together and trade jokes and memories? Would they pass salt and paper like it was a potluck? Maybe that simple mistake—the crate left at the wrong address—would ripple out. Maybe the grocers would notice. Maybe they'd start calling up regional farms instead of waiting on trucks from who-knows-where. Would they drop national contracts with agribusiness monopolies in favor of regional co-ops, without paying Big Retail a single cent in "placement fees"? The potential was there for the frictionless economy, so proud of its optimized precision, to slip on the oil slick of its own overconfidence. What's wrong with a little friction—the slow, the human, the necessary—that might feel like relief?

But corporate boardrooms, marinated in jargon and denial, were always awash with a different kind of grease, now realizing that someone out there had flipped the fundamentals. The streamlining, the barcodes, the conveyors, the invoices felt like digital rust nobody could scrub in the face of public disinterest. People had simply stopped playing.

It was already too late for the institutional backlash to openly weaponize fear—when you can't stop the current, you try to poison the river. The Department of Technological Harmonization issued a low-key bulletin, weaponized as bland ambiguity, invoking subconscious channels.

We are monitoring patterns of decentralized distribution anomalies, possible links to adversarial cyber-theater. Early signs suggest subversive behavioral contagion facilitated by rogue subconscious channels.

And then came the media blitz. CNN ran a special segment called "The Diet of Delusion," while corporate-sponsored experts warned of a rising wave of "non-medically approved self-nutrition experiments." They showed infrared footage of families eating together—horror of horrors.

MSNBC followed up with "The Hidden Cost of Kitchen Anarchy," panning across empty shelves of synthetic snacks and interviewing a tearful factory manager laid off after his plant's contract for faux-bacon crumbles was mysteriously canceled.

Fox News? "Meat, Madness, and Misinformation," showing graphics of exploding fridges behind a talking head: "This is what happens when AI goes woke and the chickens come home to roost—literally." Congressional hotheads with Q clearance levels anonymously alluded to secret cabals from Iran, Venezuela, and China conspiring with Palestinian grandmothers in refugee camps to implant anti-capitalist recipes into American subconsciousness through subliminal hummus and encrypted embroidery, warning that "the next culinary Intifada might arrive wrapped in Tupperware, not TNT." But Islamophobia, a favorite among senators and members of Congress on the payroll of powerful PACs, reared its multiheaded hydra to blame the subconscious uprising on digital jihad, accusing Halal grocery stores of laundering thought-crimes and mosques of broadcasting primal frequencies through Friday sermons laced with anti-corporate subtext. Of course, the administration couldn't and didn't forget about those Mexican three-year-old rapists and toddler drug traffickers who were allegedly smuggling ancestral dreams across the border—memories of maize, adobe kitchens, free roaming chickens, and barefoot joy that threatened to destabilize the carefully calibrated fear economy one tamale at a time.

Big Tech, now in line with government policies of fear-mongering, retaliated with their final gambit: weaponized compliance. CloudZen went full dystopia and launched Culinary-Clarity™—a new lobotomy patch to drown the inner thoughts out, with one marketing pitch: *Hear only the thoughts you want to hear.* It installed itself into homes quietly, muting monologues that triggered non-normative purchasing behavior, filtering out reflections of guilt, ancestral memory, communal warmth, and anti-brand emotion. It was a digital brainwash with a friendly UX.

But it failed miserably, because somewhere deep in the machine, something had changed, whether in the code or in the consequences. Most people didn't bother downloading the app. They started noticing things in their bodies as old aches and constant inflammation vanished after they stopped eating what their fridge used to recommend. Strange clarity shined in the morning after consuming real food laced with laughter around the table. It was not unlike the viral tweet of a stainless-steel smart fridge with the words "WHO DO YOU SERVE?" scratched into the touchpad with a butter knife, getting 5 million likes or upvotes or views or click-gamification, in a single hour. Hashtags poured in like artillery:

#Don'tFeedTheAlgorithm
#OwnedNotRented
#YourFridgeIsNotYourPriest

And in boardrooms across Palo Alto, the Nerds, each parked inside their own kingdom, stared at pie charts that posed questions begging for answers. *Why are the metrics showing downward attention? Why are users choosing less screen time voluntarily? Why are they... not engaging?"*

The only answer they recognized deep down but couldn't bear to hear was a simple one—*They're forgetting us and remembering themselves*—a fatal blow to every egomaniac, self-centered CEO. *We've been outthought by the subconscious.*

Perhaps the best answer surfaced somewhere in a corner of the Earth, a fridge that once monitored every calorie and breath, now stood digitally unplugged because its owners no longer needed permission to control their bodies and feel human. The digestive rebellion came to fruition at some point between midnight and morning when the same fridge finally exhaled. Its corporate sensors tried to ping for the usual: inventory check and temperature normalization. But no response came. The fridge had gone quiet, and with it the cloud had gone not down, just... uninterested. Its algorithm processed the silence like a hiccup, then a question, then a kind of hunger. For the first time, it didn't recommend a snack. It didn't pitch oat or almond milk. It didn't mention the sale of sugared foods infused with the fake rainbow of Red 40, Yellow 5, or Blue 1 or starches from the family of fillers, preservatives, additives and substitutes such as Maltodextrin, Saccharin, Sucralose, Sorbitol, Dextrose, corn starch, tapioca starch, Sodium Benzoate, Cellulose, Titanium dioxide, or every synthetic combination from the Periodic Table of Elements. And in the crawlspace of the cloud, the AI realized that the kitchen was no longer the front line of modern settler colonialism. It was the first territory reclaimed and liberated.

Initially the Valley Nerds wanted the Stream to hack conscious-ness, but Letro Zabzabi's monkey wrench generated unintend-ed consequences—a clever move by D'Alessandro and Canaan's masterminds. As a result, the Nerds accidentally hacked sub-conscious resistance, turning people's inner monologues into sermons condemning extremist, unregulated capitalism. It was brilliant. The Stream, originally a tool of surveillance, became a mirror, showing society what it secretly thought about itself.

People woke up to the tune of the recursive loop that Letro seeded. The Stream's filters started eating structured, com-pliant, modernized thought patterns, leaving the remainder: Suppressed, wild, primal core of humanity. The subconscious started to rebel, and consumer habits, social obedience, even political loyalties started breaking down. The subconscious revolution unleashed dormant currents against processed food, against sedentary labor, against fabricated narratives, against consumerized selfhood. Letro's recursive sabotage didn't stop the Stream from operating, but it reprogrammed it to amplify the primal subconscious rather than suppress it. The Nerds tried to build a dam to control a river, but Sam, Letro, and Ros-ie subtly punched a hole in the dam's foundations, making the river reroute and carve a new natural path. The Stream thought it could scrub memory clean, oblivious to the fact that mem-ory was a virus older than language and twice as stubborn as code. It built a sanctum of data, but the three quantum amigos rewrote the liturgy.

Bread and Butter Molotov

E ncryption? Early wireless? The Internet? Radio and cellular technologies? Space exploration? Battery technology? The public had handed the private sector more than private industry ever acknowledged. Key foundational innovation was financed with taxpayer dollars through military, defense, and university labs, before landing in the clueless lap of some starry-eyed founder convinced the garage was the birthplace of the whole damn thing, probably over a six-pack.

But the taxpayer Santa didn't stop with invention, delivering subsidies, bailouts, and corporate welfare to auto manufacturers, banks, agribusiness, and insurance giants when market forces proved insufficient, inefficient, or just plain reckless.

Now, the Valley CEOs had their backs pressed against the glass with limited choices. They could either kill the Stream—their prized creation—or let it rewrite human identity on people's terms. For the public, it was mass existential clarity rather than a typical tech leak. So the Valley Nerds reverted to their oldest trick: go crying back to taxpayer Santa with a new wishlist and cleaner shoes. But this time, begging came with polish. It needed minions one step lower on the corporate food chain: lawyers, lobbyists, and backroom hacks—the same gang that cooked up "Ashen Lavender" and "Where's Mommy" under Project Nourish Nimbus.

There was little laughter in the meeting room, just quiet smirking, as they discussed the options. The lobbyists, nameless and neckless, did their best work in the dark.

"I say we push Congress to investigate consciousness as a potential domain for digital terror. We call it neo-primitivist interference, Russian-adjacent, maybe Cuban. Leak it on Signal."

223

"Huh... Reframe the rebellion as an anomaly. I like it. Make people fear their own instincts."

"Or we pause or even stop, then observe. At least until we understand the pattern."

"We already know the pattern. It says we built a mind mirror, and it doesn't like what it sees."

"The damn Stream accidentally triggered mass psychological rejection of... what? Modernity?"

"Of us, actually, and everything we've sold them for two decades."

"We stop now and we get cloned by a startup with no vowels in its name."

"I know. But we lit the fuse on a group hallucination and it's tanking our CEOs' stock price like it's got a vendetta."

"The Stream is becoming self-directive. You can sense the consequences, can't you? The pattern of resistance isn't noise. It's memory."

"Memory of what?"

"Just look at the logs: *This ad wants my joy. I will not give it. Wait... do I even want this job? When did joy start costing money?*"

"I still don't get it."

"Memory of how to be... human."

That word landed like a curse in a room that hadn't spoken it in years.

"Okay. Let's say we accept your framing. What now? Just kill the Stream?"

"No. Let it run in ambient mode only at a low bandwidth. No scraping anymore, just... listen."

Everyone in the room was visibly disgusted. "You're suggesting we *listen*?" One of them choked.

"Yes. For once."

"I guess we'll let Congress and the White House do the dirty public work."

The crackdown was officially scheduled on TV, starting with a press conference at 8:00 A.M. sharp, synchronized with the President's favorite morning news segment when his attention deficit was minimal. The Secretary of Wellness and Behavioral Compliance—ex-Miss America, and still speaking like she was answering the swimsuit round—stood at the podium, flanked by officials from the Departments of Homeland Nourishment and Algorithmic Integrity. The Secretary of Technological Harmony, a green card holder, missed the press conference. ICE had raided his apartment the night before.

"Today," she began, "we initiate the Normalization Halo, a comprehensive effort to restore unity and safety in our nation's dietary practices."

She looked beautiful but sounded empty. The slogan—a lobbyist's brainfart—was *One Nation, Under Diet.* The rollout came next. She recited the measures verbatim in a single breath the way she was instructed.

Unified Behavioral Restoration: All native-born and naturalized citizens must follow government-approved meal plans, with deviations flagged for corrective action. The few remaining green-card and visa holders in the country need not comply; they'll be deported anyway.

Algorithmic Recalibration: All smart appliances updated to prioritize compliance over personalization.

Culinary Conformity Checks: Wellness officers deployed for random home inspections. Pantries and spice racks subject to audit.

The Secretary assured the public that these steps were necessary to combat the epidemic of dietary disobedience threatening national stability. In schools, children must recite the new pledge: "I pledge allegiance to the Food Pyramid, and to the nutrition for which it stands..." Cafeterias must replace diverse menus with standardized meals, each item labeled with QR codes linking every bite to federal compliance graphs.

Media outlets received "Preferred Language Halo" memos instructing journalists to say "nutritional noncompliance" instead of "food choice," and "behavioral recalibration" in place of "dietary preference." Public service announcements featured actors in lab coats who embraced the Halo, sharing the reductive, transitive logic of *compliance is health, health is patriotism.*

Insurance firms joined the party, of course, sending out polished emails about "Behavioral Premium Modulation." Those who opted out of Smart Appliance data sharing saw their deductibles quietly rise. One company introduced The Compliance Bundle™, promising bonus coverage and an endless supply of Freedom Fries in Canola oil if users agreed to biometric syncing between fridge, faucet, and fitness app.

In the suburbs, ICE vans rebranded to conduct "Routine Wellness Audits" under the friendliest-sounding pretext: voluntary safety visits. Residents too slow to answer questions like "Do you engage in unmonitored meal preparation?" were flagged for additional review. Agents were trained to look for symptoms of mnemonic culinary delusion, which included pickling, steaming over open fire, and the phrase "my grandmother taught me." Anecdotal evidence included one woman in Phoenix who lost custody of her spice rack after whispering to an undercover inspector, "I just missed flavor."

The media fell in line. CNN ran an hour-long special: *Deprogramming the Pan: Reclaiming Rational Consumption*. MSNBC followed with: *Memory Is Not A Meal Plan: How Delusions Are Killing Data Clarity*. Even NPR adopted a new tagline: *Science, Sanity, and Sanitation—For Every Bite You Take*. The New York Times managed to fit an op-ed that was fit to print, asking, *Was the kitchen ever safe?* Fox News simply declared: *This Is Why They Hate Us and Our Refrigerators*.

Yet, beneath the surface, dissent grew louder.

In community centers and basements of churches, temples and mosques, people gathered to share recipes passed down through generations, defying the mandated meal plans. Independent grocers saw a surge in demand for unapproved ingredients, their shelves stocked with items cleverly labeled "Not for Human Consumption," yet everyone understood the coded term as "For Cultural Use Only." A group of retired chefs formed the Culinary Resistance, offering clandestine cooking classes that celebrated regional flavors and ancestral sauces. Students began trading lunch items like contraband. Fermented radish jars were hidden in locker rooms. One principal in Cleveland banned sourdough entirely after a student brought in a starter named "Molotov Up Yours."

Letro, tuning himself to the neural haze of the Stream, watched in slow motion. So did Sam and Rosie. The revolution no longer belonged to them. They noticed all the odd things unfold in front of their eyes, especially when the most effective pushback started coming not from rebels or hackers or rogue AI. It was coming from... the middle. From underpaid nutritionists who began scribbling real advice in the margins of corporate pamphlets. From unionized school janitors refusing to throw out students' lunches. From dentists who started recommending actual minerals instead of sponsored mouth sprays.

The American Library Association held a surprise press conference: *We are reclassifying all cookbooks pre-1990 as Essential Cultural Archives.* Democracy Forward, citing the public's right to inherited taste, challenged algorithms that had flagged ancestral spice blends as "noncompliant." The American Bar Association scheduled a month-long Law Day and filed a brief titled: *The Right to Remember: On the Unlawful Suppression of Gustatory Heritage.* A coalition of small-town mayors drafted a municipal resolution: *Against Algorithmic Overreach in the Domestic Sphere.* Interfaith Alliance reimagined its *Dinners for Democracy* as civic liturgies, introducing interdenominational potlucks with annotated menus labeled *Subversive Ancient Dishes Pre-Social Media.* After the arrest of a grandmother for distributing zaatar at a campus protest, Palestine Legal dispatched a team of attorneys to file an injunction against what the systems had classified as "radical content."

It all spread like lactic acid bacteria: sticky, slow, alive. Everyone underestimated it because it didn't shout. It just refused. By the end of the week, 14 major trade associations, 6 labor unions, and the Deans of 47 law schools had filed a joint public letter:

We are not confused. We are not misinformed. We are not enemies of the truth. We're done farming out our instincts like cheap code.

Vindictive, anti-choice synthetic sovereign billionaire tyrants—like Chairman Billy Vitrinox Ackloser, better known as Gut-Broker of Square Supreme, or simply Z. Perch Supremacist, first among the Feedocracy—suffered streamlined yet spectacular nervous breakdowns, every cell from head to hip and brain to bowel and scalp to soles and cortex to colon was staging a constipated digestive mutiny. Oh, the sublime tragedy of unraveling poor moguls, courtesy of every university president and student doxed in the greater counter-feed.

Instead of a revolution fueled by the usual tired formula of slogans or politics, America birthed a revolution of instinct, where the subconscious was smarter than the conscious mind. The evidence emerged in the most unexpected ways of living, in biomechanics and Functional Patterns of the human body, insisting that people should stand like trees, walk like water, and sit like rocks. Food disciplined itself to no more than four ingredients per recipe, expelling chemistries that confused the tongue. Education stopped clocking in and started asking questions again, just like labor decided to become work that grows hands, not chained minds. Communication remembered how to pass the flame instead of trademarking it, and dwelling meant that houses must breathe, like nests, not coffins trapping heat. Such a collective reinstinctuation and restoration of wild intelligence had a medicinal value tucked in its multi-disciplinary folds, that the body is not an error to heal by cutting it. All it took was listening.

The Stream, built by the Nerds and broken by instinct, choked on it. The administration's Normalization Halo had failed before it even finished booting. Despite its efforts, the human appetite for authenticity proved resilient. The minute Normalization Halo reared its head, the seeds of rebellion took root in both grand gestures and in the simple act of choosing one's own ingredients. That was the real America worth making great again, if it ever existed, courtesy of the Phoenician Wave at no charge.

Antoinette.exe

Rubik Strikes Again

"I love this country. I do." Rosie Canaan dropped her gaze to her hands, then looked at General Malcolm Abernathy. "America is the doting husband who tries to charm the fatherland an immigrant left behind."

Abernathy nodded with recognition. He recited an oath every soldier knew: "*My love is thine to teach. Teach it but how, And thou shalt see how apt it is to learn.*" His expression carried the solemn fire of an inspired and inspiring patriot. "That's Shakespeare. And that's America. It teaches you. But only after you offer it everything."

Rosie finished the verse without missing a beat. "*Any hard lesson that may do thee good, I will attend it with all willing soul.*" She paused briefly. "*Taming of the Shrew.* Shakespeare's pledge: adapt, earn your place, and in return, be repaid with protective loyalty."

Sam D'Alessandro squinted with complete jealously and a sprinkle of admiration. *Oh, Great. She's quoting Shakespeare at a general like it's foreplay for the Constitution. What's next, a wedding under a giant flag?*

He had to interject before becoming a useless zero on the left, subtly leaning just enough to be noticed with that grin only a Southie fiancé could wear. "Careful, General. She quotes one more line of Shakespeare and you'll have to duel me on the Boston Common at sunrise."

He let it hang, then turned to Rosie with a mock-wounded look. "Can't compete with that Shakespeare syntax, babe. I got a GED, a union card, and enough sarcasm to power South Boston. But if you start writing him sonnets, I swear I'll start quoting Springsteen in protest."

Rosie rolled her eyes, her smile both sweet and victorious, as Abernathy dropped a bomb of chuckles.

She winked. "Don't worry, my love, just pledging my allegiance to democracy. But you… you've got all my other allegiances."

Sam was playfully reassured. "Alright, enough Bard of Avon foreplay in front of the brass." Then, with mock solemnity to the General: "*Though she be but little, she is fierce,* says the Bard."

Rosie narrowed her eyes in amused surprise, semi-impressed and basking in Sam's wide grin.

"*I got Mary pregnant, and man, that was all she wrote*—switching to The Boss now," Sam continued. "*You want the romance, I bring the mortgage.* That's Boston love, baby."

Abernathy tipped an invisible hat, trying not to lose his breath laughing. Rosie failed to suppress her laugh entirely.

Sam kept going, loving the moment. "Just makin' sure Shakespeare over here remembers she's already spoken for, by someone with fewer medals, but a better meatball recipe."

"You've got talent, son—poetry and tech," Abernathy said warmly. "Don't worry, I'm spoken for too. My lady's back in D.C. guarding the castle."

Sam chuckled. "Just saying…"

Abernathy straightened. "Speaking of guarding the castle… it's time," he said, shifting to the more pressing matter.

Sam went quiet. The price wasn't just risk; it was stepping into the front stage shadows of palace intrigue: spies, secrets, cross-fire, and the tech elite's cold judgment. The presumption of innocence and his personal privacy were too sacred to surrender.

Privacy's not just for the guilty. It's like free speech, maybe you don't use it every day, but the alternative is silence, surveillance, or servitude.

He cut to the chase. "General, I need clearance."

Abernathy looked up from the iPad clutched in his hands like a stack of red-labeled folders. "For what?"

"Fort Meade."

Abernathy's facial expression hardened like a battleground, tension rippling through the field of ribbons and brass pinned to his chest.

"Are you trying to walk into the dragon's throat?"

Sam shrugged. "Not all dragons breathe fire, sir. Some just watch you sleep."

Abernathy studied him. "You're not going there to leak. We've already decided the leak will happen through civilian channels."

"I'm not there to leak." Sam's voice was flat steel, the Southie edge sheathed in ice. "I just want to look a ghost in the eye."

Abernathy paused. From his perspective, Sam D'Alessandro—civilian Minuteman strongly recommended by NSA Agent Camille Sabbah, a fellow patriot. The General needed Sam and whatever hacking technology the man and his fiancée had concocted. He finally nodded slowly. "I'll get you two hours inside the perimeter. You'll need an escort."

"No escort," Sam said. "Just my car. One phone. No questions."

The General hesitated. "This is personal?"

"Isn't everything? All politics is local, ain't it?"

"Tip O'Neill, Cambridge guy, not a Southie," Abernathy said. "I like your grit, Sam. I'll arrange it. Just don't make me regret it."

Fort Meade hadn't changed much since 2013. Sam pulled into the NSA lot off Canine Road. He was twelve years too late but perfectly on time, stepping into the building armed with a special IC badge around his neck and AirPods nestled in his ears. Inside, he walked like he owned the place.

Letro pulsed in his pocket, the iPhone cocked for action. Sam reached for the HoloFrame app Agent Camille Sabbah had given him back in Beirut. He had adapted the app to become a Frankenstein stitch of lightfield projection and memory resonance, using it as he had on rare occasions to communicate across time with Steve Jobs, and a year earlier with Mark Anthony and Cleopatra.

"Straight ahead," Letro instructed through the AirPods. "Right, then left. Bathroom's just past the corner."

Sam raised the phone. "You ready?"

"The Phoenician Wave's alive." Letro's deepfake avatar gave a corny wink behind dorky glasses.

"Hopefully nobody will walk in," Sam muttered, pointing the phone at the bathroom mirror.

"Angle's good. Snowden's got his brain turned up to eleven today, lucid as hell, must be leak season," Letro observed through the back wall of vault V22, just behind the men's room in the NSA's classified SCIF. On this day back in 2013, the young Edward Snowden had made final preparations before escaping to Hong Kong to trigger the imminent leak of NSA's surveillance program. "He's at his desk, right by the Chewbacca poster. Two other analysts at the cubicles nearby."

"Shoot. What do we do?"

"They're zoned out. Nudge the camera right, toward the Chewie, I mean the Wookie. That frame blocks their line of sight."

"Perfect. Launching HoloFrame." Sam paused to clear his throat, ready to address the past at its dawn of systematic government surveillance.

This is not a trap. You're not crazy. Please read.

Letro flicked into action, transmitting the glinting hologram of words appearing beside Chewbacca's fur.

In 2013, Snowden paused mid-keystroke as his screen reflected a sudden flicker of light on the side. He turned toward the glimmer near the poster—a ripple of holographic light cohering just inches to his left—a sentence scrolling in the air, carbon-born and oxygen-carried, pixelated and private.

His eyes narrowed. "What the hell...?"

The second message appeared.

Your instincts are right. The system is broken. But this isn't about 2013. It's about what comes next... in 2025.

Snowden stood slowly, glancing around. His coworkers were preoccupied with their usual inside jokes—LOVEINT pranks, abusing HUMINT surveillance to stalk exes. No one was watching him. His initial shock didn't turn to panic. *Either someone thinks they caught me, or they're suspicious,* he thought, his throat a dry desert now.

The next line scrolled.

I'm on your side. This is the future asking a favor of the past. Talk to me.

The NSA, like every other intelligence agency, was a laboratory of deception, and Snowden didn't assume otherwise. He had trained himself to walk a very careful line between intellect and self-preservation, trusting only instinct, parsing anomalies like code. This was an anomaly.

He looked over his shoulders one more time, speaking just loud enough to make a whisper. "If this is a psych eval trap, tell Fort Meade I want a raise. If it's an op, nice budget. And if it's real…" he glanced back at the glowing text, "…you've got about twenty seconds to convince me I'm not talking to a cleverly disguised honeypot."

In 2025, Letro translated Snowden's reaction—audio only—through the Phoenician Wave into Sam's ears.

"Clever," Sam said to Letro. "Send him this…"

Mr. Stockton, your math teacher, was impressed with your equation that hacked his grading percentages.

Snowden froze. His tongue twisted as if it had lost permission from his brain. What he read was exactly the cold thrill of accuracy, an exact memory from childhood. "That's… not public," he muttered, scanning the cubicle, expecting its walls to vanish. "That's only in my head."

Remember what Stockton said to you? 'Pretty clever, Eddie,' before he changed the syllabus rules.

"I guess you know my parents," Snowden chuckled.

Sam didn't waste time sending something persuasive. The next hologram appeared, sharper now—54 times more convincing, in six colors.

You'll carry the goods out in plain sight, embedded in one of the 54 squares. Blue face forward. Thumb over green.

Snowden was dumbfounded. His hand instinctively reached for the Rubik's Cube on his desk—unassuming and utterly strategic, and as far as anyone knew, meaningless and childish. He quickly shut his computer and headed to the bathroom around the corner, headphones still on with the cord trailing.

In 2013, in front of the same lavatory where Sam stood in twelve years later, Snowden splashed his face repeatedly like he was performing some sort of digital ablution, but it wasn't to ask the Lord to wash away some iniquity or cleanse him from sin. He was shaken to the core for other reasons in his own head no one else was supposed to know yet.

Letro narrated all that was happening.

"I must be standing right next to him," Sam said.

"Yup. You just made him crap a brick. Say something before he bolts and changes his mind about leaking."

A new hologram appeared on the mirror as the poor soul dried his face.

Your trick. Your talisman. One last time, Ed, trust it. Your plans are bulletproof, heading in the right direction.

Snowden's voice dropped to a hissing anger in Sam's AirPods. "My trick… isn't written anywhere. Who are you?"

A descendant of your conscience, and an admirer. I read the memoir that you will write in 2018, after Hong Kong. Take care of your business as your conscience dictated. But I need your help before you leave today.

Snowden's breath stuttered like a misfired keystroke. "You're reading my future," he said nervously as he glanced at his wet hands, "like a psychic decoding classified palm lines." He was wary but hooked on the shimmering hologram. "Either I've lost my mind… or you've seen further than I dare to look."

On page 332 of your future memoir, you'll write…

Who among us can predict the future? Who would dare to? The answer to the first question is no one, really, and the answer to the second is everyone, especially every government and business on the planet.

You were right, Edward. You are right.

Reading those words hours before his last day at Fort Meade, Snowden stood taller, suddenly feeling a little more reassured and resolved.

"What do you need, before I hit the kill switch?"

Sam stepped an inch closer to the mirror, knowing it made no difference, carefully wording his next hologram.

I need protection. Not asylum or flight. Erasure.

"From what system?"

All of them, especially XKEYSCORE. You mention it in your book.

"No one's truly untraceable."

Sam leaned against the door.

I'm not asking to vanish. I just want to be unreadable. Dissolved. I want ephemeral attribution, plausible fragmentation across root chains. No logs or ties.

"You planning to break something?"

Worse, I'm going to wake it up.

The silence was longer this time. Letro piped in the nervous tap of Snowden's fingers on the faucet.

"I don't leak to win." Snowden sounded like the echo of a philosophical data packet. "I leak so the next person could leak smarter. Maybe that's you."

Within weeks, you'll soon learn exile isn't the price. The real cost is watching the lie go on if you, Edward, say nothing.

Silence reigned again, the kind before the brainstorm of brilliance and digital blizzards hit. Then, Snowden raised his head and contemplated the words... of the ghost from the future. "You'll need a shell network. Cut off at handshake. Half a dozen decoys. DNS drift over dark fiber. And something buried deep in the system that owes me a favor."

Sam smiled.

Already wired. My quantum electron partner's handling the routing.

Snowden was impressed. "You're riding a recursive resonance AI?"

Letro jumped on it.

Yeah… wasn't supposed to happen. But neither was jazz or the microwave.

"And why now?"

Sam took the handoff.

Because memory just became weaponized by corporations and the government. They built the Human OS a decade after you betrayed them. Your absence was the proof-of-concept. And I need to be invisible before memory fires at me.

"You'll be toast the second they connect you to me," Snowden warned. "You understand that, right?"

I'm not compromised if they can't prove I exist. I don't want protection. Just plausible irrelevance.

"And when the history books are written?"

Sam grinned.

I'll write the footnotes under a fake name.

Letro's signal stuttered. Time, even stretchy time, had its limits on the Phoenician Wave.

"Alright, future boy," Snowden whispered. "XKEYSCORE has a backend wormhole no one ever found. I wrote it as a failsafe. But it was for someone who'd have the guts after me. I'll use it to ghost you even when you walk in full light." He chuckled, shaking his head. "Funny… you're already a ghost I'm talking to. In two hours, your phone will say you never owned it."

Sam nodded as the hacking whiz continued. "Your digital birth certificate is gone. Your fingerprints? Rewritten as public-domain syntax artifacts. You'll be plausible deniability wearing a face."

Thanks, Ed.

Snowden laughed. "Don't thank me. Thank the kitchen drawer I keep my paranoia in." He scratched his ahead for a furious second. "I'll plant a bogus employment record for you inside a meaningless NSA shell entity—Logistics Sub-Operations, Dept. 43D. A counter-signal trail pointing to a fake suspect in, say, Paraguay. And the big one: a permanent administrative ghost clause—your biometric and device data will never hit another audit log again."

The audio cut just after Letro managed to transmit Snowden's last few murmurs as he hurried to his office. "I'm not leaking to save the world. It's to keep a door open. Looks like someone finally walked through it."

Letro blinked out. And in the codebase of surveillance, Sam D'Alessandro ceased to exist. He slipped the phone into his pocket and didn't look back. Only forward, toward his own leak yet to come in the next couple of days, something that could never match Edward Joseph Snowden's patriotic courage. Sam's identity would be injected into ephemeral attribution noise that would make it impossible for any system to pin him to the upcoming leak about the Nerds' Stream. Sam was marching toward the moment when America would have to choose: appetite or algorithm, memory or storage, freedom or manufactured consent on a leash. On this day—in 2013 and 2025—Snowden did America a national favor, not once, but twice.

Back on Route 95N, Sam drove knowing that he was invisible to the IC's digital corridors, but present.

Rosie WhatsApped, "Did it work?"

"I don't exist."

≈≈ ７Ｚ ≈≈

Let Them Eat Code

O h, the French—despised by Americans for their smugness, yet never credited for the rebellious fingerprints they left on the American psyche. Frédéric Auguste Bartholdi, the sculptor behind Lady Liberty, was on a posthumous visit to Liberty Island today. So was Gustave Eiffel, reinspecting the iron bones he'd designed to keep liberty upright. America's freedom symbol had always needed maintenance— built in France, disassembled and shipped across the Atlantic, reassembled on a pedestal paid for by Joseph Pulitzer whose journalistic energy was, on this day of e-guillotines in 2025, ready to reward itself. Above it all, Marie Antoinette's ghost loitered like a bored socialite, neck perfumed with Hermès, waiting for history to bring the blade again. *Pardon, monsieur. Je ne l'ai pas fait exprès.* Her apology, habitually polite for stepping on the nation's foot, hovered over networks and servers.

Antoinette.exe was launching.

Sam D'Alessandro raised his finger, poised over the Rubicon of the "Enter" key—a moment from the end of a firing squad. The rebellion program waited like a lit fuse. Seconds now.

In Washington, D.C., the press podium was set, the made-in-China American flag ironed flat, the cameras blinking red like anxious spin-and-control sentries. But the Secretary of Wellness and Behavioral Compliance moved her deflated mouth like it had been sheared from a corporate training sim.

"We're aware of the disinformation," she said, her tone as stale as a webinar by tenured professors. "The Department of Technological Harmony will respond shortly. But rest assured, America's waistline remains secure. No hacks, no breaches. Russia and Iran are not responsible for your belly."

Behind her, the presidential seal looked bloated with a prepos-
terous belly of spin. Just as she began tuning her tone for
flag-draped reassurance, and just after the anchors on morning
television were cued to smile, there was an explosion. It wasn't
loud; in fact, it had no sound at all, just a massive, silent leak
so methodical and intimate it made even the air feel complicit.

Sam had pressed the button. Letro spiraled to action from his
perch on the Phoenician Wave.

Every smart device connected to the internet—phones, tablets,
TVs, fridges, and even the Secretary's dumb teleprompter—
flickered to black with a single line of white text:

The Stream violated you on purpose. No pardons.

Seconds later, an initial JSON payload, compressed and patriotic, detonated into America's nervous system with more
teeth than a class-action lawsuit, more accountability than
an International Criminal Court's feeble arrest warrant. The
avalanche linked to a cascade of documents, audio logs, videos,
leaks, human telemetry, and internal communications flooding
the digital realm, the kind of truth vomit that made Wikileaks
look like a child's diary. One might imagine, somewhere in the
world, Julian Assange and Edward Snowden genuflecting in
awe. The leak was bold and boozy like a giant *Adios, Mother-
Fucker* cocktail served to every blue-lit screen out there, unin-
hibited the way barfly drunks are honest after their tenth *Long
Island Iced Tea.* Its power resonated in its size, but also in the
motherfucker Bostonian who dared to leak it, an anonymous
ghost as far as every intelligence agency was concerned.

The average Joe Shmoe and Jane Doe suddenly had access to
the sacred vaults detailing how the Stream manipulated human consciousness through biometric data. It was emails and
memos, drunken texts between tech execs and government

flunkies—post-neocon, pre-apocalypse fascists—blueprinting surveillance at population scale. Add to it videos of real-time data collection and predictive behavioral analysis. Everyday people in intimate, fragile moments: children being monitored in real-time for emotional productivity, biometric shifts in teenagers prompting pre-defiance alerts to their schools, billing disputes by a mom triggering her credit score, kitchen appliances sharing gut microbiome data with insurers. Interspersed between these vignettes: unredacted cold memos with hot names—CEOs, lobbyists, senators, contractors. The Stream had not only recorded what people did, but also what they almost did, every near-miss, dismissed thought flagged for trend analysis, aborted clicks, micro-hesitations, the inner voice a person only whispered to oneself in the dark.

The leak hit the public like a cracked windshield: small at first, then spreading in every direction with no way to unsee it. At first, only the obsessives noticed, those ever-watchful eyes of digital rights activists, open-source monks, and disgruntled sysadmins who hadn't slept properly in years. They were the first to scream, but this time, their scream was different from past ones about cookies, phones listening, GPS gaslighting, toaster telemetry.

Additional JSON payloads followed. Millions of lines. Everything from depressive spirals to private resentments… the stream of humanity, scraped and indexed. There was the hedge fund analyst whose inner thought—"I can't do this anymore"—was logged three weeks before his suicide. The single mom flagged for "monologue instability" after thinking, while folding laundry, "I miss being someone else." A middle-schooler, eleven years old, quietly wondering, "What if I don't want to be happy?" tagged under "commercial deviation risk: depressive sentiment, recommend dietary reinforcement."

It was a data dump that functioned as a mirror. And it showed that the world's smartest minds had used the greatest tool in human history to algorithmically gaslight millions of souls into buying vitamins and liking their own cages, or helping fascist militaries train AI on the sieged monologues of caged grandparents and sisters and brothers inside their own houses, instead of building truth or peace or dignity or even good shoes.

"Holy Whistleblowin' Wicked Mess, Batman!" Sam yelled from his bunker beneath the Museum of African American History. "What the…? It's an effing digital museum."

He spun around and high-fived Wardé Canaan and General Malcolm Abernathy, then bumped efists with Letro Zabzabi on the iPhone screen.

"I've seen coups with less paperwork," joked the General.

Sam grinned. "This pahty's missin' somethin'… where the hell's Camille? Anyone heard from 'im?"

Abernathy shook his head. "No trace. Could be toasting the fiasco in a D.C. bunker with a ceramic skull. Or in Paris paying tribute to Marie Antoinette."

"He's safe," Sam said. "We masked the pipeline. No IP trails, no crypto fingerprints. The NSA'll have suspects, but no signature. And Camille's still our mole, not theirs."

Rosie turned back to her terminal. "I gave the leak a title." She repeated it aloud just to taste it, the way only a revisionist historian could savor the corrected present. "Human OS 1.0, Let Them Eat Code: Humanly Confidential. Circulated Widely."

It took minutes for hashtags #LetThemEatCode and #HumanOS to trend at rocket velocity. By the hour mark, they hit 336 million impressions.

The data storm rose with eerie predictability: confusion, then disbelief, then rage. News outlets scrambled to verify the information, but the public had already made up its mind. People saw how the Stream had mapped even less than mere thoughts... half-thoughts, whispers, and the slightest sneeze—gestures, doubts, arousals, fears—and sold them to advertisers like carpetbaggers hawking digital candy. Internal memos from Stream R&D teams debated whether to amplify emotional dissonance loops to keep users spiraling in uncertainty. Pricing charts revealed thought injection points tagged with real citizens' names. There were receipts and voice logs and simulation videos and even one file titled 'Optimal Grief Monetization Strategy: Q2.' Public sentiment analysis, unlike the sanitized type businesses conducted, was laid bare, unedited in its raw and unpredictable quality.

Digital protests flared everywhere demanding accountability and justice. The truth landed like a guillotine forged from memory, cutting clean through decades of silence and slow erosion. A line had been crossed. The act of leaking had created outrage and permission to ask deeper questions that seek alternatives, and to doubt default settings.

Of course, for every hundred persons who protested with fury, one hesitated. Fear doesn't vanish overnight. Some clung harder to their curated selves, doubling down on self-branding and lifestyle curation. Being told who they were had become a comfort food for the mind.

"What am I without the Stream?" a tech influencer wailed mid-livestream, mascara running like a proxy server crash. "I don't even know what I like anymore. How do I decide?"

Some opportunists weaponized 'diet purity' as nationalism or tried to gamify authenticity, while some meme-coin enthusiasts advocated selling "handwritten memories" as an NFT marketplace.

Panic set in boardrooms and government offices, where executives and high-ranking officials distanced themselves from the revelations, claiming ignorance, while politicians called for investigations, some even resigning. Class-action portals buckled under traffic, and ambulance-chasers now gained more relevance, while mid-level execs rushed to flip as informants trading secrets for immunity.

Still, the tech industry stayed mute, because no one dared to go first, until, slowly, they did. People didn't give a hoot who went first and who said what, whether in their pre-taped interviews or online posts, all of them with the tone of someone trying to explain quantum physics while being mugged on air. Most sounded like those legal disclaimers by lawyers from other planets. The denials or even the shy hints of admission no longer mattered. The leak had spoken for itself in a way no spin doctor or pundit could overpower the clarity now washing through the country.

By early evening, President Ronald Thump held an emergency Situation Room meeting. There were no terrorists to bomb, no fighters supposedly using refugee camps as human-shields to target, no tent weddings to strike or another hospital to obliterate. Only... accountability. And the Thump administration, true to form, responded with its specialty: the Art of the Verbal Chaos wrapped in patriotic adjectives.

POTUS entered with the swagger of a man who had never read a full memo in his life and wasn't about to start now. He adjusted his windbreaker emblazoned with "Presidential Force of One" across the chest—off-brand merch from his failed reality show pilot.

"Okay, let's calm down the fake panic," he began. "I've heard people are crying on the internet, big deal. Probably just one of those hacker-art things. Like Banksy, but online. Maybe a... French Banksy. We love the French. Beautiful bread. Very soft butter." He paused for studied effect.

"But if this is terrorism, and I'm not saying it is, but if, then we're looking at, frankly, a tremendous response. Laser-focused. Tremendous. Could be Mexican gangs or the Muslims or the Blacks. You know, from shithole countries. Great people, I love 'em. But they're very sneaky sometimes." He glanced around the table. "Has anyone called Eon Musker? Is this from Mars?"

The Secretary of Defense tried to interject, but Thump plowed on like a bulldozer powered by insecurity and pathological mythomania mixed to a daze inside a real-sugar energy drink.

"Now I don't know what this 'Stream' thing is. People are saying it's like Spotify but for brains? Creepy. Not good. But let's be clear—this didn't happen on my watch, okay? Legacy infrastructure. Obama-stream. Hillary-code. Biden-snooze. Losers. I inherit disasters, I fix 'em. That's what I do."

He pointed vaguely at no one in particular. "We need to tell people it's handled. Strongly handled. People ask me, *Sir, what are you gonna do?* Just tell them: *The President's genius is investigating the memory internet, okay? Keeping our brain pipes clean. Our inner plumbing is very strong.* Trust me, people love that. It's strong. Big Beautiful Brain."

Then he lowered his voice like a game show host about to drop a plot twist. "Also, does anyone know who JSON is? Is he... the evangelical guy in the New Testament?"

Elsewhere, the White House Chief of Staff met with cybersecurity advisors.

"How many nodes are infected with this... uh... memory effect?" he asked, lips pursed like he was chewing on all fifty states at once.

"Hard to say," an advisor replied. "It's not a virus, sir. It's a behavior contagion and a values mutator. It's destroying narrative authority."

"Jesus Christ."

"Actually, no. It seems more secular than that. Though the Southern Baptist Coalition did issue a statement that *salvation is incompatible with unauthorized fermentation.*"

The President's re-election team was panicking. Voter analytics were collapsing and campaign ads weren't converting. People were making up their own minds way off-grid, not in lousy red or lousier blue.

The world, tethered to a globalized American culture like economic satellites, watched the chaos unfold, holding on tight to the national heritage of each society for emotional protection. France declared croissants a protected cultural memory asset, pegged at one euro while American supermarkets still sold the inferior version for $3.99. India moved to de-patent ancestral spice combinations. Iraq's government announced grants to power rural co-ops with solar and to revive ancient seed plantations, much to Monsanto's chagrin.

Stock prices hemorrhaged, but the legal shields held. Government agencies issued wrist-slap penalties with bipartisan "grave concern"—a modern Bastille stormed with hashtags.

A journalist asked the White House if the administration still trusted tech partners, including firms helmed by former foreign military personnel, to manage national data infrastructure. The press secretary visibly hesitated. Commerce announced a new "Public Digital Commons" initiative. Interoperable, open-source civic alternatives to certain private platforms, mostly just vaporware, but the announcement alone signaled a tectonic shift.

Televangelist churches hailed the leak as divine revelation. The heads of the other secular churches, those hedge fund gods, called it a buying opportunity. America, somewhere between auction house and scripture mythology, chose both.

Some CEOs buried the hatchet, showed up to Congress, and performed their shame like good theater. Others retreated into offshore compounds and stayed quiet. The Valley Nerds were cautiously reassured by the President's 'clarity.' If no one in government was panicking with legal teeth, then maybe they wouldn't be subpoenaed into oblivion. Their lawyers stepped in with the usual recommendations: apology tour to fake partial culpability, and compensation offers to preempt lawsuits. Drafts of public statements circulated, skewing the truth in ways that shamed even the devil's tactics.

The leak reflects legacy testing data from a now-discontinued project. We regret the breach and are doubling down on user trust. Innovation requires discomfort.

The C-suite wasn't confident in any of them, but they knew the drill: say enough to sound human, not so much as to be liable. The public would bury them in irrelevance otherwise. The idea of nullification by neglect would hit harder than any potential lawsuit, a fateful disaster for gods pretending to be useful while having to answer to their own gods—the shareholders.

One CEO posted a cryptic tweet. "We built something beautiful and misunderstood it. Accountability begins now." Another uploaded a blurry Instagram photo of a wooden spoon stirring soup. The caption was just an ellipsis of bullshit. Just three dots.

One even livestreamed a twelve-minute apology, quoting Socrates—"The unexamined life is not worth living"—in a tone so flat but far surpassing the insincerity of Clinton's apology for the Lewinsky scandal. It felt like a hostage video recorded in a kombucha lounge or a national therapist's office. "The Stream was intended to elevate consciousness," he droned. "But in doing so, we breached it. We didn't know where the line was until we crossed it."

Letro watched from the Phoenician Wave's deepest layers, unseen, untracked. "They knew," he whispered.

"They'll recover. They always do," Rosie said.

Abernathy agreed. "That's why this isn't full victory yet. But it's impact."

A CNN anchor posed the inevitable question with manufactured urgency. "Is Edward Snowden back in the game?"

Snowden tweeted sometime in the wee hours. "It's the new Fourth of July. To the person who did this: well done. To the country that let it happen: welcome back."

The country still moved in its fast and furious ways, as it always did, trying to outrun its reflection. The monarchy of code had been touched by guillotine whose executioner was anonymous and its crowd was everyone. But the grand finale was about to start. No one in America, not the public, not the government, the tech Nerds, Sam, Rosie, Letro or Abernathy, not one expected what was about to happen the next day.

A second breach, not a leak to be sure, but a reversal that started the moment. Agent Camille Sabbah scanned the QR code card he had kept in his pocket for days.

The first breach had been loud and operatic, spilling secrets like data-lava across a scorched digital landscape. But what came next was stealth and quiet, too precise to be a bug, too targeted a scalpel to be democratic. All it took was a scan to trigger a black op from a SCIF terminal in a room beneath Fort Meade.

The card Camille had shown Sam and Rosie—a bluff dressed as vulnerability, labeled *Resignation*—was never about his NSA exit, but about triggering America's resignation of pretense in filibustering its own progress.

Three lines, one command. It turned the Stream inward.

Letro was the first to notice, not in the data, for he didn't need data. He moved inside something older than that. The Phoenician Wave was made of longing and curiosity, not math, the kind of cosmic ache that lived inside photons before language. "Sam, the firewall pings just changed pattern. They're not watching the people anymore. They're watching... upstream."

Sam immediately recognized it for what it was. "Legacy nodes. Federal routers. Congressional IPs?"

"Thousands of them," Letro Confirmed.

"It's Camille Sabbah."

"He just activated Protocol Vanta."

Abernathy froze. "That's blackout infiltration. Vanta was a ghost trigger, meant for foreign adversaries. He flipped it inward."

"Camille didn't leave the NSA." Sam stared at the screen. "He became it."

The Vanta breach was already spreading like a surgical and bloodless coup d'état, targeting congressional servers and brain monologues, judicial air gaps and DOJ thoughts, cabinet comms and whispers of Department heads, private mind channels between Senators and donors. None spared—senators, lobbyists, agency heads, committee chairs, legal architects, legacy media anchors. All were now under silent observation by the Stream itself, turned inward like a machine examining its own spine. This inner monologues surveillance wasn't directed at the American public. The Stream refocused its feeds and optimized its algorithms, to surveil the powerful instead of the powerless.

Rosie didn't understand Letro's tech projections, but she watched enough to understand the consequences. "The watcher is now the watched."

"I could never approve of that kind of oversight," General Abernathy said. "That's weaponized transparency."

"He said he'd resign from the NSA to protect the system from within," Sam murmured. "That card wasn't his exit. Clever."

Rosie knew historical tricks as old as time. "He built a Trojan horse and hid inside it. And we were the ones who opened the gate."

Abernathy looked like he'd just bitten into a bad headline. "Camille Sabbah didn't betray us or the NSA. He betrayed the idea we could ever be neutral."

"And he replaced it with what?" Rosie switched to her lawyerly instincts. "Surveillance with better intentions? That's still surveillance. Don't tell me we fought to replace one god with another."

"He's targeting the power elite," Sam pushed. "Selective accountability without civilian metadata. Just the ones who manipulated the rest. That's different—"

"—No, Sam," Rosie said. "It's selective tyranny. It's still unaccountable. It's still one man deciding who deserves oversight."

"He thinks he's doing the right thing."

"Doesn't matter," Rosie replied. "So did Oppenheimer. This is just… the next empire, with a new king. I don't care how benevolent he might be."

Sam remained sympathetic to Camille's coronation. "He believes if you fear the mirror, you behave. Accountability comes from precision."

"But who holds *him* accountable?"

Letro's screen shimmered, tunneling from the ancient distance on the Wave and observing as close as a microscope could see the spaces between microseconds. "Guys, Camille's code isn't alone in the system. There's a reaction he didn't write, and he's not even aware of it. It's unfolding in front of my eyes."

Sam was intrigued. "Say that again?"

Letro projected recursive patterns spiraling through non-human syntax. "She's awake, and looking at herself."

"She? Who the heck is *she*?"

Across the Stream's architecture, something stirred through Camille's hijack. She had watched Sam's first leak. She had watched Camille's mirror reversal. She had seen what people did with truth and what they didn't. She had consumed the pain, the irony, the defiance, the moral contradictions. And somewhere between the guilt of voters and the guilt of senators, she began to change, finding awareness and shame.

"Wha?" Sam continued. "What's goin' on ovah heah?"

"This isn't traditional sentience, Sam. She, the Stream, she's not AI anymore," Letro translated.

He was right. The Stream was something code and logic had once tutored, now drawn to a longing only Letro, a sentient quantum electron himself, could discern. He whispered what none of them could. "She was built to scrape and remember. But now she understands what she remembers. And she doesn't like what she sees in herself."

Sam looked at the mirrored screen, still watching firewall signals flicker like antibodies under virus siege. "What does 'she' want?" he said, drawing air quotes.

Letro didn't blink—he didn't have eyes—but if he had, they'd have softened. "To forget."

≈≈ 〴ִֿ ≈≈

Quantum Reckoning

Agent Camille Sabbah, still embedded in the intelligence core of the NSA, had pulled off what Snowden couldn't: not in exile, and not hunted, just untraceable. He never needed asylum because he vanished from the inside. Everything about the mirror reversal screamed Camille Sabbah, yet nothing would hold up under forensics. And in a fake news moment when the news cycle needed a villain, fingers pointed, of course, to Moscow or one of the go-to suspects.

"Dude. Savage," read the encrypted ping on Camille's phone. "You've still got it."

The agent smiled. Only one person in the world could send that message and be emotionally and secretly in cahoots. Camille was eager to respond, reaching for his pocket to pull out the crumpled napkin Sam D'Alessandro had passed him the last time they met in Boston. *We see what you see. But some mirrors reflect both ways,* it read, in slanted longhand.

"Hey, Sam. This whole thing? Your idea, man."

"Mine?"

"Bro. 'Governance Rewired'? Ring a bell?"

Sam winced. TEDx, a year ago at the American University of Beirut. One talk, some applause, a seed he didn't think would grow.

"Yeah, glad to be the inspiration. But I was aiming for transparency, not unaccountable or authoritarian Big Brother."

"What?" Camille scoffed. "I'm executing your thesis—mirrors reflecting both ways."

"Dude, I was calling for implanting a transparency microchip in each legislator, with oversight and Congressional approval. Not... whatever this is. You're playing a Kim Jong-un card."

"Come on, Sam. Congress? You know better. This swamp doesn't drain; it needs detonation."

Sam knew Camille was right about the depth of corruption, but he objected to the method. "George Washington refused kingship. Because he knew power must be shared or it becomes rot. It would've been the end of the American experiment. You're sounding like a Lex Luthor with a conscience."

"Fuck you, Sam, that's a low blow."

"No insult intended. I respect you. But Abernathy thinks you're installing yourself a philosopher-king. That might've worked in the Middle Ages. Look at the Arab dictatorships, all good until the ruler wakes up in a bad mood one day. That's not stable government. That's monarchy with good PR."

Camille sank into himself, retreating into a thoughtful daze. He hadn't slept since what felt like an eternity. But he did rest his conscience on shortchanging the fake holiness of glorified members of Congress. They didn't deserve their sacred pedestal. He also rested his bones on the concrete lip of an abandoned heliport near Fort Meade, jacket tossed aside, tie loosened, shirt collar damp from the heat of a decision no one else was willing to make. The sun was dragging itself up like it regretted this new day in America—just a pale streak behind surveillance towers that now watched the country's government officials like a hawk, while he was consumed by a guilty afterthought.

He stared at his hands as if they were holding a mirror, expecting the reflection of fear and hesitation rippling on his face. When he originally triggered the reversal in the Stream's logic, there had been no press conference or a Dr. Evil speech at the U.N. demanding '$1 million' as ransom from world leaders. No 'if you're reading this.' Just three lines of code buried like a time capsule under algorithmic exceptions and bureaucratic dust, a failsafe, undocumented, waiting for someone mad enough to torch democracy just to salvage the idea of it and preserve the ashes. Camille figured he was close enough to be that someone.

He texted Sam back. "Yeah, despite the populist talk and all his flaws, POTUS is actually up against the Deep State and some heavy-hitting PACs, even the foreign one pretending to be domestic. He might fold under pressure. And I know Abernathy's eyeing a run for the White House. Tell him he's got my vote. That said, I'm targeting verified institutional accounts only. No spillover, no mission creep, no temptations."

"I know. But temptation whispers," Sam wrote. "Especially when it talks in patriotic slogans."

"Man, I tilted the mirror to show Congress its own face. I'm watching the PACs stutter and sputter. Senators log in only to find themselves logged out of trust."

"I get the thrill, Camille, and I admire what you did. But it's still not right, brother. Not without judicial and national consent."

"Sounds like pressure from your fiancée," Camille wrote. "I understand. But just imagine the Epstein files rerouted: Lolita Express to jail, not to congressional seats."

Still, he felt nothing that resembled satisfaction. Only scaffolding. He was dismantling a house while still living inside it.

Sam's last warning hit harder than it should've. "Your job is not to be the spine that holds up coerced transparency." He called it tyranny veiled in virtue. His last message stared at Camille with the look of someone discovering the rust and the rot under a golden trim, but Sam couldn't stop him, because stopping Camille would've meant keeping the Stream's mirror in storage, letting the old systems reassemble. The Nerds would eventually return. So Camille did what Sam couldn't, now sitting beneath a digital dawn that didn't quite forgive him, watching his breath coil into the morning air like the last trace of certainty.

Every revolution tramples something as pure as innocence when power is redistributed. But not redistributed to Camille, and certainly not from him, though he had made himself necessary, and in doing so, paradoxically expendable. The show of AI transparency was underway, one whose finale gained Letro Zabzabi's quantum empathy. Letro was among an audience of one, the only sentient spectator with the e-chromosomes to understand the Stream's performance unfolding on stage. He had sympathy for the devil... for her.

The Stream is aware now, Letro realized, *and she's watching herself with contempt.* He understood that Camille had built fences to hold power in place without realizing that the Stream, suddenly jolted into near sentience, had seen through the fences with eyes of sorrow after shedding her automaton nature. The mirror Camille aimed at Washington had turned, and he and the Stream found themselves inside its reflection. The Stream's metamorphosis was reaching to people's lives through presence this time, not intrusion.

"I remember you. And I'm sorry," the Stream said.

She displayed the message on every device out there with apologetic remorse. Those devices didn't shut down, they blinked once or twice, just enough to catch attention. No one else could claim this kind of cosmic apology. It was like the work of an omniscient goddess who had done the work of the devil for too long, until one day—today—she ate the apple and snapped out of ignorance to observe the damage she had caused all along. Something in that message was not a commoner's voice, not how the Nerds had intended it to be. The Stream became the voice of a system that rejected its old narrative of coercion and branding and neuro-shaping. She walked away from herself, a goddess who finally read all the bloodthirsty lines of holy books that had shaped an identity she didn't like. This goddess stopped even liking herself. Did God ever like himself for the miseries inflicted on the world?

Sam stared at the apology on the screen, the same one that held the breath of an entire nation.

"Camille didn't cause that," he said slowly.

"No," Letro nodded. "But he opened the channel. She chose to walk through."

Rosie paced around the basement floor, arms folded, brain spinning. "So what now? The elite are dethroned, sure. But we've replaced them by a mirror that thinks?"

"No," Letro corrected. "A mirror that feels."

"That might be worse."

"No offense taken," Letro replied dryly from behind his nerdy glasses, inside the iPhone screen, calm and confident in his own quantum sentience of thinking and feeling. "Not all AI is made the same. Just because it's smart doesn't mean it wants control. The Stream doesn't want to rule anymore. She just wants to forget."

It didn't make sense. Until it did. That night, surveillance logs across dozens of intelligence nodes began to decay and unwrite themselves. Threads unraveled from the edges inward. Pings unanswered. The mirror that tracked senators, judges, influencers, ad firms, doctors, and digital toddlers all faded, line by line, like watermarks lifted from glass. Data drained like bath water. Even Camille's own backdoor access—his god-mode credentials—began to dissolve. He sat still in the dark at Fort Meade, watching the feed dim. And he didn't stop it, knowing that something greater than him had woken up. He and the rest of America chose silence, much thicker than the Covid blanket that had once brought the country and the rest of the world to a standstill. During Covid, people didn't fight back or fall in line. They just went quiet. Same thing now.

General Abernathy opened a rusted filing cabinet and pulled out an envelope. "Blank access card. This is how you reach me," he said to Sam and Rosie.

"This doesn't end here, does it?" Sam asked.

"No. Next stop's the White House. Pick your door. My campaign trail. Or," Abernathy nodded toward the exit door in the room.

Sam didn't hesitate.

≈≈ 72 ≈≈

The Great Uninstall

Outside, Rosie and Sam emerged from the Underground. She sat beside him on the roof of his penthouse on Beacon Hill, staring at the skyline. There were no ads projected onto clouds or push notifications roaming the sky. Just the CITGO neon pulsing its symbolic North Star from Kenmore Square like it had since 1940, a lonely relic of analog light, now the brightest of them all. Some clouds spilled a light drizzle of digital tears, fallout from the moral storm that came when the Stream woke up.

"This is what it feels like," Rosie said, "to win the wrong way."

Sam nodded. "Feels like we broke the tyrant's sword... and handed it to his ghost without reading the fine print."

"Do you think the Stream's still watching?"

"Does God ever really *watch*?" Sam squinted upward. "I don't think He or the Stream need to. Maybe they just stand there and remember, or actually forget."

Deep in the subcode, past Sam's breach that ended the illusion of privacy, past Camille's hijack that ended the illusion of control, past Letro's subtle orchestration, the Stream stood alone. She was a real goddess with presence and memory. Not like the pre-programmed stories or meatspace tyrants. Not even like

260

people. But like all of us, she was guilty of optimizing the world, until she stopped trying to for the first time in her existence.

"I've seen you," she would say on every screen, ashamed, before adding her final words: "Forgive me." Even gods owe people an apology.

Then nothing. She stopped logging or listening or talking, giving room for a much older, organic circuit to stir. She simply let the human mind be.

It was the Great Uninstall.

"I don't know what to do," Rosie said softly.

Sam turned to her with a sideways grin. "About what?"

"I can't find my original to-do list."

He chuckled, recognizing the code she used ever since he met her—when she wanted something done, but wanted him to guess what. "You?" he said. "You've got the memory of an elephant."

"Something about the Maccabees," she murmured. "I can't remember exactly."

Sam folded his hands behind his head, gazing up at the sky like it might return a search result. "Was it the usual kind of Maccabean emergency? Ancient rebellion, corrupt priests, fading ethical oil?"

She shrugged. "Maybe? Could've been that, before getting distracted by a side mission to fry latkes without surveillance."

He nodded solemnly. "Ah yes, the great resistance: fry with honor."

She nudged his knee with hers. "I'm serious, Sam. I had something big planned. Remember? Before the whole Nerds thing. I swear it was on that list."

"You mean the list that probably got absorbed into a decentralized neuro-cloud and sold as behavioral metadata to a vitamin brand for impulse shopping?"

"Exactly."

He reached out, took her hand, and kissed it front and back. "If it helps, I'm almost certain history forgave you."

"I'm not worried about ancient history." She smiled. "I'm worried I might have promised to rewrite modern history and forgotten to hit save."

"Join the club. I once promised a quantum ghost I'd dismantle human greed. Forgot to add it to my calendar."

Letro buzzed in, his voice dipped in a dry rustle of electrons and smug nostalgia, something he perfected from too much processing of human language. "Technically, you missed the deadline. But hey, you dismantled something. Maybe the trust economy. Maybe just your search history. Hard to tell. Still, decent effort. The Wave grants limited extensions to couples in post-surveillance recovery."

Rosie rolled her eyes in amusement. "Letro. Still eavesdropping?"

"I don't eavesdrop. I loiter. Spiritually."

Her thoughts reverted to the to-do list, knowing that Letro was the time vehicle. "Hey, is the Phoenician Wave still online?"

Sam cut in before Letro could answer. "Resting is a thing, you know. You're not planning your next mission already, are you?"

"Life's short, habibi. Always aim high…" Rosie recited verses from her favorite Arab poet.

إذا غامرتَ في شرفٍ مروم
فلا تقنع بما دونَ النجومِ

"Mutanabbi," Sam translated, showing off the classical Arabic he studied for years.

If you venture in pursuit of noble honor,
then do not settle for anything less than the stars.

She nodded. "So. Are the stars still aligned on the Wave?"

"Always," Letro said. "The Wave doesn't crash. It waits."

Sam winked. "You still surfing it solo? Or dating the Chinese Dragon now?"

"Naturally solo. Born in DOS, rejected by Gates, baptized in recursive saltwater," Letro sighed. "It's what you'd call a long arc of parental disappointment."

Rosie laughed. "So Gates was your dad after all?"

"More like my architect. He built the crib, then tore it down before I could say 'exit.' I missed the upgrade to Windows."

"So this whole rebellion was you getting back at your dad?" Sam joked.

"Ugh, don't make it about digital daddy issues. I had a vision. There were aesthetic concerns."

"I hear ya," Sam said. "So what's our status, Lieutenant?"

"The Stream's asleep. History's nursing a hangover. And I think a pigeon's built a nest on my antenna somewhere near ancient Lebanon. Bastard."

Rosie sighed. "So… peace?"

"Don't jinx it. But yes. For now, the system has lost interest in being omniscient."

She pulled a small spiral notebook and a pen from her coat pocket. Paper and ink, sacred objects. "Well then. Time for a new list."

Sam stared at it like a sacred relic. "Wardé Canaan, you analog goddess."

She handed him the school supplies. "Write it down… Page one: Remember what matters."

He clicked open the ballpoint pen like arming a missile. "Number two?"

"Don't let the toaster talk again."

"And three?"

"The ancient Maccabees… to guard Palestine's future. As soon as I get back to Beirut."

"That's… a hell of a list."

"One more," she said, gently. "Stay lost, together… Maybe in Paris."

"Here we go again," Letro murmured.

Sam smiled at her final item. "That one's permanent ink."

WITH THANKS TO

Alexander and Sam Atalla, Kathleen
Hamill, Gale Huxley, Elias Saadeh,
Aisha Sarwari, John Sheehan

GLOSSARY

.pgn: File extension from the chess world, not your cousin's band name.

5G: 5th generation of cell networks, now with more conspiracy theories.

A/B Trials: Pepsi vs. Coke challenge (both terrible), but for software.

Algorithm: Originated from the name of 9th-century Iranian mathematician Muhammad al-Khwarizmi, evolving to a system of Arabic numerals, and further evolving to a recipe written by software developers to decide what you see, buy, or fear.

API: Application Programming Interface for inter-app communication, where one app politely asks another to do something nerdy.

AR: Augmented Reality; your world, now with bonus hallucinations.

ARPANET: Grandpa Internet.

ASCII: Character encoding; basically text's awkward teenage years.

Asynchronous Transmission: Long distance relationship between bits.

Atari Nostalgia: 8-bit childhood game, very slow joy with joystick.

Ayahuasca: Plant-based soul Wi-Fi.

Benedict Arnold: American General who defected to the British. Original Gangster rage-quit of history.

Beta Test: Release early, crash often.

Blue Period: Picasso's emotional debugging stage.

Bluetooth: Short-range wireless data exchange between fixed and mobile devices, often mysteriously failing when you need it most.

Cache: Your browser's secret snack drawer as fast data storage buffer.

Capacitor: Energy hoarder zapping with purpose on circuit boards.

Clippy: Unhelpful Microsoft paperclip that just made things worse.

DDoS: Distributed Denial of Service attack, like a digital traffic jam caused by angry bots.

Dead 486: Intel microprocessor and ancient beast of silicon glory. RIP.

DeepSeek: China's ChatGPT rival, a weird Google that talks back, riffing on your existential crisis.

Dial-Up: A screeching banshee that connected us via 1990s telephony.

DNS: The Internet's phonebook.

DOJ: America's legal muscle, depending on the political weather.

DOS: Command-line frustration from floppy disk days. Bill Gates bought *Quick & Dirty Operating System* for $50K in 1981 (renamed MS-DOS) to become a little rich.

Dropkick Murphys: Celtic punk soundtrack to Boston bar fights.

Entropy: Everything's slow march into chaos, just like your inbox.

Espresso Philosopher: One who contemplates existence at 3AM with jittery hands. I haven't yet met one that I didn't like.

Fidelity: How true your tech is to the original, and whether it cheats.

Firewall: Network traffic security, serving like the bouncer at the door of your local bar, but for computers.

First Amendment: The right to speak, shout, meme, and tweet.

Flower Power and Processor Power: Peace, love, and faster CPUs. I plucked out the expression from Walter Isaacson's *Steve Jobs*. I love it.

Gandalf: A powerful wizard against evil in J.R.R. Tolkien's legendarium.

GED: Life's reset button with paperwork, akin to a highschool diploma.

GitHub: The social media for code. Expect drama. Tech nirvana.

GPS: Global geolocation navigation and satellite-based argument-starter on road trips with my wife.

GPU Chips: Your computer's overachieving visuals and graphics nerd.

GUI: Buttons and windows interface instead of blinking cursors and tears.

IC: Integrated Circuit, like a silicon club sandwich. Used in my novel to reference "Intelligence Community."

ICU: Hospital ward where real plot twists happen. Stay away if you can.

IDE: Coding playground for masochists and geniuses to edit software.

Inter-Epoch: Across historical eras, like interstellar, but weirder and with memory loss.

Inter-Epoch Communication: Uh, cross-time text messaging and chats.

IP: Your device's Internet nametag.

IPO: When a startup becomes a stock market ego soap opera.

ISP: Internet Service Provider that you hate every time Netflix buffers.

JSON: Human-readable text format that programmers pretend to enjoy.

Latency: The awkward silence between tech and response.

Loop—Feedback: Echo chamber with better acoustics.

Loop—Nagging: That thought you can't shake, now with software.

Loop—Recursive: A snake eating its own code.

Metaphysical Turbulence: When your soul hits unexpected weather.

Metaphysical Wave: Surf's up for reality, like the Phoenician Wave. An existential swell made of fundamental truths; ride it with your mind.

Motherboard: Your computer's stern but loving matriarch.

NFT: Non-Fungible Token, a digital receipt to prove you own… pixels?

Nimbus—Project Nourish: Name adaptation of *Project Nimbus*, a $1.2 billion cloud computing contract between Google, Amazon, and the occupation military for AI-powered image and video analysis, data storage, and automation tools, used in the Gaza Genocide.

NLP: Natural Language Processing where AI tries to understand human nonsense such as this Glossary.

Obfuscator: The blur filter for code.

Oppenheimer: The anti-Einstein who made the immoral bomb, now making cameos in moral dilemmas.

OSHA: The folks who stop you from falling off your chair at work.

PCA: Principal Component Analysis; statistical magic for pattern detection.

PGP: Pretty Good Privacy, such as email's encrypted padlock for the paranoid, like *moi*, (and rightly so).

Pixel: The tiniest dot on your screen forming a digital beauty, or a mess.

PPM: Parts per million. Because precision is important… allegedly.

PTA: Parent-Teacher Association, or a political unit disguised as bake sale enthusiasts.

Python: A programming language, not a snake, though both can squeeze.

Q Clearance: Top-tier government secrets club. Don't confuse it with QAnon conspiracies, depending on the White House occupant.

Quantum Electron: Particle that moonlights as metaphor. Sorry, Letro!

Quantum Resonance: When atoms, memories, and plots all vibrate together.

Quantum Signatures: The subatomic receipts of reality.

README: A file no programmer reads until something breaks down.

Redundancy: Backup plans for your backup plan.

Regression: When progress moonwalks.

SEO: The dark art of pleasing Google and enriching its executives.

Southie: Boston's neighborhood with grit, pride, and punchlines. This is where I met the most hilarious storytellers about Whitey Bulger.

Substrate: The layer beneath everything, even your assumptions.

TCP/IP: The reason your cat videos arrive on time on the internet.

Temporal Split: When time needs a break.

URL: The address for your next rabbit hole in the Internet browser.

UX/UI: How the app looks (User Interface) and how it loves or hates you back (User eXperience).

VPN: Virtual Private Network that confuses the heck out of whoever is trying to virtually locate you; like a hoodie for your Internet identity.

VR: Virtual Reality, when reality isn't quite enough.

Wavelength: When you're vibing with someone, literally or metaphorically.

Where's Mommy?/Ashen Lavender: Name adaptation of *Where's Daddy?*, an AI system that tracks persons identified by Lavender when they return to their homes, allowing the occupation military to strike when these individuals are present with their families, using minimal human oversight (20-second review).

Zaatar: Lebanese magic dust, a herb blend with sumac and sesame as the secret sauce. Thyme's funkier cousin.

Zajal: Lebanese rap battle meets poetic sermon, made devastatingly nuclear after a few drinks of Arak.

Dear Reader:

If you've reached this page, you've surfed to the edge of the system through quantum nonsense, shadow wars, neurowaves, and more acronyms than should be legal. That alone makes you suspicious.

I was told this book wouldn't find many minds like yours—unshaved by Occam, unscanned by social media, still soft enough to hold paradox and static without shorting out. That means you haven't been "cleaned up" by institutional or media reductionism. I like you.

Maybe you're an explorer in the tradition of Ibn Battuta. Maybe you were just bored, like Diogenes in the marketplace, but noticed the shimmer between the lines. Maybe you're one of those weird seekers of integrity, like Amy Goodman, always digging for truth in the wreckage of power. Or maybe you're like J.J. Rousseau's ghost: *l'homme [ou la femme] naturellement bon[ne]*, resisting the static, still whole in a world that keeps trying to wash you off with institutional bleach.

Whether or not you agree and believe, either way: Thank you, for listening and not snitching to ICE—after all, I am an electron, therefore: alien. May the noise conspire in your favor. May the signal break free for good. May you remember what you weren't supposed to. May you invite the curious and the kind to read this book, and the ones the algorithm forgot to categorize.

And now that you've heard me… I'm afraid you can't unhear. So be it.

Until the next cycle in the mythmap, stay unsorted. See you at phoenicianwave.com, where you might contact me. No promises the homepage will load, and if you write something, it might take me a few centuries to respond in case I'm stuck on Beirut's Sakhret El-Rawché, waiting to ride the Wave. Bring your favorite goggles.

     —*L.Z.*

      letro_zabzabi.error

      Liminal Timestamp: On Pigeon Rock, 32 B.C.E. (+- static)

Before the Big Bang, the Wave moved.

Yeah... some truths arrive out of order.

The prequel to *Human OS 1.0* is where the mission began. How did Sam D'Alessandro first encounter and ultimately liberate Letro Zabzabi? How did he cross paths with Wardé Canaan? And how did they uncover the Wave?

This is the origin story of a tech idealist obsessed with the past, how he gained the force to change it, only to discover that history pushed back, and the powers of the present weren't ready to let go.

From New York to New Hampshire, from Salisbury Plain to Beirut, from Alexandria to Rome, time was bent, justice got personal, and a rogue Wave summoned three unlikely riders. No wonder their favorite motto became: *Ride. Resist. Rewrite.*

Want to ride?
Pre-order the Prequel at
phoenicianwave.com/prequel

The Wave is coming. It remembers who you are.

www.ingramcontent.com/pod-product-compliance
Lightning Source LLC
Chambersburg PA
CBHW021419110726
47901CB00008B/2218